Contents

THE FIRES OF AUTUMN

It was unthinkable: the great autumn herring fishing failing. For a seatown like Brenston, built on herringbones, the end was nigh.

On his moonlit voyage home Johnny Hallows, a deckhand on the *Bounteous*, receives the call as a fisher of men. Johnny Halo, as he becomes known, has the fisherfolk of north-eastern Scotland repenting in shoals. Then one day, as mysteriously as the herring itself, he disappears. Forty years later he returns as a high-powered professional evangelist with a skeleton in his locker. Even more radiant than the homage to the herring that opens this book is its hymn to a humble sinner who aspires to a saintliness that is not of this world, only to lose it in a strange country – America, that jungle garden of evangelism – and whose second coming is as different from his first as a whisper from a rushing mighty wind.

By the same author

The Last Fisherman

THE FIRES OF AUTUMN

DOUGLAS RAE

ROBERT HALE · LONDON

© Douglas Rae 1990
First published in Great Britain 1990

ISBN 0 7090 3965 4

Robert Hale Limited
Clerkenwell House
Clerkenwell Green
London EC1R 0HT

Photoset in North Wales by
Derek Doyle & Associates, Mold, Clwyd.
Printed in Great Britain by
St Edmundsbury Press Ltd, Bury St Edmunds, Suffolk.
Bound by WBC Bookbinders Limited.

PART ONE

Burning Waters

They had set sail under a banner of hope, south to where the moon was silver. Southward the sea was on fire, shimmering as if the stars of heaven were tripping the light fantastic upon it, and the fire of the hunted had entered the souls of the hunters. Autumn. The high-water mark of the northern year. The herring fleet steaming south with the commotion of leaves scudding before the wind.

It was the season of the oyster and the morning glory, of the falling apple and the rising, soaraway swallow. It was the time of the gathering in of crops, when mother earth put a bloom on the cheeks of her children as they laboured on the land to replenish their bread-baskets. Glorious as was the festival of bringing in the sheaves, it was but a straw in the wind blowing before the most momentous event in the lives of men over whose eyes there slid a wild and mysterious silver scale. The world of the herring drifter had turned full circle. The great annual exodus of driftermen, with flocks of petticoated birds of passage streaming in their wake, was under way. That miracle whose course no fire nor flood nor raging pestilence could check had come round again. Harvest time on the sea.

While the wheat farmer warmed his heart at the sight of the fields of gold that rolled across his land, the fisherman's eyes were lighting up at the prospect of the fields of silver that rippled over the sea. Those fields of silver herring that in his memory's eye he could see waving in the wind, ripe as a roasted ear for the reaping. The sea had changed like a tree into its autumn weeds. More subtle than the tints of the tree were those of the sea. From tree-green to burnished silver the sea changed. And a dry twig of a man it would have been, a boneless wonder with no sap in his veins, who would have said that a litter of maple leaves in sugary sunlight was a bonnier sight than a scatter of herring in slippery moonlight.

With the fall of the leaves and the rise of the herring, the working year, like the sun and the moon themselves, had reached maturity. Hopes were at their most radiant, boughs at their most fruitful, harvests at their most silver-golden. Britain was an island surrounded by herring. There were more herring swimming in the southern sea than there were leaves twisting to earth in the northern land. Whereas the Hindu, looking up with wondering eyes at the full moon, saw a hare, his brother seeker of another clime saw a herring.

That the moon had been more of a hare than a herring of late was just a passing phase. When the moon was in one of those moods, mad as a hare in heat, the herringer would have been better geared for the hunt had he carried a gun or a greyhound instead of inch-mesh nets. For when the moon was a hare the herring was uncatchable. There was, after all, a bit of the witch in the hare. No man walking down to his boat would have dared to board her if his path had been crossed by a hare. The long-eared rodent and the nosy parson being birds of the same ill-omened feather: signals to turn back.

It was with a curl of the hare-lip that the moon was looking down on them now as the fleet set sail under a banner high with hope. Since late spring – a spring that had sprung early, the hawthorn out in the hedgerows and the birds nesting in February – the crews had worked their way from west to north to east, clockwise round the coast, all the while winding themselves up for the full-scale assault on the south in the autumn. The trip to western waters had barely paid the fuel bill; nor, as the fleet headed north, had things picked up; with the upshot that, as they ventured their way down the eastern seaboard, the fear surfaced that they had been chasing their own tails.

It was getting to be a common fret, this catching a cold in the summer. Even their fathers had complained of it; even they had known trips when the west and the north and the east had been none too generous, yielding precious more than a sharpening of the knives for the banquet to come. Yet while the chill they caught had made them crab and snuffle, it had not given anybody cold feet. They had learnt to wrap themselves up against such draughts, to slide into the protective shell of time-honoured ways, almost cosy in the knowledge that the south was waiting to bail them out, that the months of the full-moon tides would keep them afloat, saving both their face and their faith.

Since the first moon rose over the North Sea it had been so. Same time, same place, same fish. Sure as fish eggs is fish eggs, natural as the melting of the ice-floes, regular as the swallow's bolt into the southern blue. Autumn. East Anglia. The herring. You could have set your calendar by it, your compass, maybe even your clock. Like some celebrated rite of the church, it was an immovably movable feast.

The herring had spawned a way of life and everybody was caught in its net. It had made the most home-loving, family-centred breadwinner a migrant. It had turned him into a dauntless hunter who pursued his quarry as the Eskimo pursued the reindeer. Fishers long since turned to fossils had travelled the sea road south before there was a land road. The herring spoke to man like a whale, and like the whale it obeyed God's voice. It spoke to man's mate, too. As the fleet followed the shoals, so the shawls followed the fleet. The cream of a town's manhood and womanhood was milked for the chase, the lasses choppy with excitement, like liberty belles going off on an extended splore, the lads putting on an air of devotional calm, like pilgrims to some distant shrine or knights in cloth caps tilting out in quest of the Holy Grail.

Lining the quays, the crowds. They perch on the edge of the piers and on top of the pier walls, on barrels, ropes and carts, the little ones on the rock-steady shoulders of their elders. Some set themselves up as lookouts and hover on the green hill overlooking the town. They have flocked to see the passage of the migrants on the swallow-tail of September. The departure of the fishermen preceding by a breathless week or so that of the last wave of women (the first wave already being halfway there as they work their passage down the English coast). If the staid old railway station is turned into a place as bustling as a sales ring when the women entrain, it will surely not be so bustling as the piers are now.

The air is charged with an expectancy that plunges and soars. There is a flutter of wives and sweethearts and an exultation of children. There are grandmothers swaddled in shawls and grandfathers that lean on rheumaticky walking-sticks and swollen, fevered memories. Toddlers who have been bundled into wheelbarrows and pushed down to the harbour are dumped where their fathers' boats lie moored, champing at their ropes. Every pier is awash with a wave of leave-taking. Wives hug their husbands, fathers kiss their children, mothers hug and kiss their sons; and all the while the twofold shawls and the rheumaticky sticks stand by, an arm's length or two adrift from the swirls and eddies of excitement. High and dry as laid-up boats are those old voyagers, and the old gutting girls are their sailcloths. They hang their heads, drear old dears, as if weighed down by the ponderables of the past, on top of which lie the imponderables of the future.

Copper coins rain down on to the decks for good luck as the last man boards his vessel. A few ha'pennies, aimed and skimmed by the more larky children rather than just dropped, bounce off the decks and plop into the water. Spanking as new pennies are the boats with their fresh coats of paint. Every mast is as bright as a stick of lettered rock.

Inside as well as out everything is beaming. Below deck every bunk has been scrubbed clean as a washboard by the same fair hands that have filled the mattresses, the donkeys' breakfasts, with chaff gathered from the threshing mills on the local farms; the same farms in whose fields the freshly tanned nets were spread out to dry. Thus the land, whose only use for a herring net is to throw it over the roof of a cottar house to keep down the thatch, is roped in to lend a hand with the harvest of the sea.

Leaving on the same tide, outward bound for the treasure-chest known as the Knoll, are scores of boats bearing the names of people and places and flowers, and at least four of the seven virtues and one of the seven deadly sins. The *Moana* and the *Fulmar*, the *Fortitude* and the *Morning Glory*, the *Girl Eve* and the *Sea Fire*, the *Autumn Bough* and the *Brenston Belle*, the *Fragrant Rose* and the *Bounteous*, the *Radiant Hope* and the *Boundless Faith*, the *Charity Queen* and the *Northern Pride*. All with horseshoes nailed to their masts so that their luck may hold in the fair wind that has been called down from heaven by the men of the manse at the Blessing of the Nets.

'The sea of life is stormy,' a voice like a singing rafter had rung out from the pulpit to the congregation of dark-blue suits and boiled shirts with their starched white collars, 'and the storm has to be weathered if we are to reach port. No waters can swallow the ship that has the Master of oceans at the helm.'

With which storm-stilling words the nets, and every skipper who thought that the master of oceans could only have meant himself, were blessed, so that faith as well as hope sails with them.

One by one they cast off and slide away. Steam drifters with smoking stacks. The old hands on deck spitting over the port side for luck, the older hands on the quays shaking their heads as if to say 'I've seen the day.' They have seen the great days, these same older hands whose backsides warm the bollards, the great days when the boats were made of wood and their crews of iron. They have seen the lugsailed Fifies lurching and leaning in the wind, huge brown-black birds floating on the water, and the Zulus rearing up like dark pyramids on the horizon. They have spent half their lives in boats that had no decks, or at best half a deck, so that if they were not up to their knees in herring they were up to their ankles in water; boats whose sea-legs were none too steady unless they were pinned down by a few tons of stones. They have sailed in luggers whose foremasts would have reached to the kirk steeple and beyond, whose mizzens were as long as the belfry is high, whose spread of sail you could have wrapped like a shroud over a few score graves in the kirkyard – the canvas black as the grave itself. The Zulu was more than a dusky warrior among the English redcoats: she was one of the nobility. Aye, they have seen the day and many a night as well. Their marks left even now on the rocks where they had tarred their ropes before embarking south all those tides, all those moons ago. Threescore years or more it must be since they broke their teeth on Yarmouth rock.

No sooner has the great armada slipped away than a sense of abandonment, like some cruel tide, sweeps in from the sea, encircling the hearts of those that are left behind. Into the creaky old bones there creeps a sudden moony urge to throw away the walking-stick and jump aboard the last drifter; but between the spirit and the flesh there yawns a gulf as wide as the North Sea is long. Not that the old flesh, after a lifetime used to the feel of oak and larch and elm, would be so easily fired by the promise of rubbing against those steel hulls; nor is the spirit without its second thoughts about going to sea in a steam kettle, with a cigarette, a wild and reeky Woodbine, for a funnel. Steam drove nothing so much as the bonny, billowy black sail from the sea. How can you drive a boat with your hand on a wheel instead of a tiller? Seamanship will get rusty even before the salt begins to corrode those steel shells. And the noise of those propellers threshing through the water ... it must frighten away the herring.

'Ta-taaaa ...'

The crowds shuffle and hop and get up on to their tip-toes to wave their handkerchiefs; spring-heeled children blow kisses out to sea. The old men mumble into their steel-wool beards tinged with rust, and not a few of them find their minds drifting back to the war that has just been and to the boats that are missing – missing, presumed dead, they said of the young men who had manned them. Game old craft they had been, too, setting off to fight the Kaiser with a three-pounder gun on their foc'sles and a pennant number on their bows; requisitioned, as the Admiralty put it, called up to do their bit as tenders and colliers and liberty boats, some of them drafted into patrol and escort duties and boom defence. It was a one-way ticket to Crockanition. Boom – the watery grave. Blown to smithereens by mines or sunk by submarines. Lost at the end of the war, too, a few of them. Watch out there, boys. Kaiser Bill is still bobbing about out there, showing his horns.

Where's your Grand Fleet now? There they go, sailing for the Battle of the Herrings. And what a grand head of steam they are getting up as they cross the bar, smoke belching from the funnels and their hooters and klaxons sounding. Wives and sweethearts, having hastened to the outermost points of the piers, are waving in wider, slower arcs now. Up the hill the children have frisked to catch a last, lingering glimpse of their fathers' boats. While into their shawls the older women mutter a wish, if not a prayer, on behalf of their sons; they pray, not for miracles, not for water to be turned into wine, just for the sea to be changed into bluish-green silver scales. Crab-like and crabbed the old men sidle away as the rheumatics play up again, adding to the pain of the incurable conviction that, a sight to swell the heart though the exodus is, it is not a patch on the blue-blooded Zulus making a regatta of it as they braved south in the days of sail.

All eyes now are on the sea. The gentleness of heaven is upon the sea, so plain that they remark on it to each other, the old bodies who will never see autumn again. As the boats smoke and steam into the silvery distance, the crowds, drained of everything but hope, drift away from a harbour which has suddenly become sad; a harbour at half-mast, bereft of its very life and soul; a harbour at such low water that it mists the eyes of the abandoned old fogies just to look back at it (and clouds, albeit with a silver lining, the eyes of the young as they look down on it from their perch on the hill). There hangs over the town a fearful emptiness that nothing can fill until the men return, when the arms that have waved them off will reach out and welcome them home again.

2

Jutting out as it did like a dislocated bone from the cold, rheumaticky shoulder of north-eastern Scotland, Brenston had all the appearance of a town built on herringbones. Had the jaws or ribs of the herring been as big as the jaws or ribs of the whale, every gateway in town would have sported an arch to the glory of *Clupea harengus*. Since the decline of the whaling, the health and wealth of the place had hinged on the more delicate structure of the more insular fishery. An undying memorial to this was the kirkyard, its lofty obelisks, lordly crosses and monumental vaults having been paid for by the humble herring. The kirks themselves had every cause to bless the nets, to bow their high-borne heads to the low-born fish that sustained them. And if the choir of kirks owed their proud architectural grace to the herring, so to the same faithful fish did the promenade of villas along the southern approach to the town owe their existence. Herring Row, as this douce front of villas was called by the humbler denizens at the other, business end of the town, was where the curers and the boatowners and the hot-shot skippers lived with their grand pianos if they were temporal men and pipe organs if they were spiritual. Thus did a stranger to the port, coming upon it by the south road, perceive at first glance an air of solid prosperity.

A town of curing yards and cooperages, carriers and coaling sheds, timber yards and net stores, boatbuilders

and fish merchants, Brenston lived for two-thirds of the
year in a barrel and for the hollow months of winter in a
white-fish basket. So pickled in the brine was it that to
the stranger it was something of a mystery to find not
the slightest shimmer of a herring worked into its civic
coat of arms. The shimmer was all in the soul, if not
worked genetically into the bones, of its citizens. As a
sea-fashioned community it was not only close-knit, it
was as close-knit as a herring net. All the sights and
smells of the place proclaimed to the world that
Brenston without its herring would be like Samson
without his hair.

Out of sight, if not entirely out of mind, of the villas,
within smelling distance of the sea, in a street which
would have overlooked the harbour had not a
sailmaker's loft intervened, in a house at the bottom of
the barrel that was Brenston lived a fisher lad whom the
old-timers looked upon as a pocket Samson and the
young as a sawn-off Jack Dempsey. Johnny Hallows had
the prow of a prize-fighter and the hull of a performing
strong man. He might not have succeeded, with a
last-gasp prayer and an almighty puff, in bringing down
the pillars of the local prison-house with his bare hands,
or yet hit upon a way of dumping Jess Willard on the
deck with a right to the jaw, but he was a lion when it
came to hauling in the nets and a champion at seeing off
an ugly customer in the public house.

Standing five feet nine and a bit in his hose and
tipping the fish-market scales at around one hundred
and eighty pounds, Johnny looked, from his square
stance as he advanced on man or boat, with his
fisherman's crouch and weave that were almost like
street versions of a boxer's body language in the ring –
he looked, from his surprisingly fleet flat feet to the
point of his jaw that came within a whisker of being
taken for over-pugnacious, a mean and hunky lad; one
who was, as the papers were saying of Dempsey after the

massacre at Toledo, 'engined to his beam'. His face, too, was strikingly like the one that had been built for Jack: dark and rubbery, but with a skinful of Scotch blood in the pedigree where the other man's was Irish and Cherokee. Johnny Hallows did not mind being mentioned in the same breath as Jack Dempsey; if anything, his vanity was tickled when he read that there was a measure of Scottish blood pumping through the veins of the slugger who could lick any man in Brenston, aye, and with his right hand tangled up in the warp during a big haul, or even caught in the winch.

Where a tiller of the soil would have described Johnny's build as one made for the plough, to a tiller of the sea it was the perfect frame for hoisting the forelug of a Fifie or handling the huge dipping black lugsail of a Zulu in a squall. Every Hallows had been built like that – chunky as the barrels that were mustered in ranks along the quays like soldiers waiting to embark. From as far back at least as his grandfather on his father's side (the one who wore the ear-ring and looked like a pirate), every one of the breed had not only been coopered from the same block of wood but chipped out by the same adze. And like barrels, too, they mustered in their cottages down by the harbour: five generations of them under one roof, one generation living on top of the other, the youngest feeding off the backs of the four that were there before it. And when one of their number branched out in marriage, the others rolled up their sleeves and built a place next door for the newly weds. Four houses it took to contain these branches of the family, so that the numbers seven to ten inclusive in the street known as Sailmaker's Close might, with a skimmering of wisdom as well as wit, have been nicknamed All Hallows.

Hallows were saints in ancient times, though nobody in Brenston would have had the guts to claim such a pure and rarefied bloodline in his ancestry; rather would he have preferred it that he was descended from a reiver who had swung from a roadside gibbet. If saintliness had ever shown its face in Brenston, it must have been in the fearful dark when a body would have been spared the pickle of wondering who or what it was; but even a stealthy visitation like that was doubtful among the communion of latter-day Hallows living in Sailmaker's Close. (Which was not to say that Johnny had ever been without a reason to hold up a contrite face from his pillow in the conscience-stricken moments before slumber).

Johnny had been an artful dodger of a kid. Such a fly one that if he had been born with wings he would have been a gull. And not just a common gull foraging for scraps, but a herring gull plundering the herring. As a beast of prey he had made up for his lack of wings by the beadiness of his eye and the keenness of his appetite as he went about his imitation of a herring gull swooping upon the fish that spilled from the baskets while they were hoisted ashore in the hotfoot months of summer. There had been no humbler baptism than his in the herring-catching business. Johnny had started, a kid from the Close with a running beak and plumage sticky with tar, as a scavenger of the quays.

The herring that tumbled out of the baskets and into the water were the herring gull's, and the ones that fell on to the quay were Johnny's; except that the herring gull, being no great champion of fishing rights and always one who was way above the law even of thieves, would constantly poach on Johnny's territory. Nor was it only flocks of gulls fouling his pitch that he had to beat off: there were flocks of boys as well, beady-eyed and brazen as you like, swooping and scooping up everything from under his very mandibles. Johnny and his featherless friends, in spite of their territorial scraps and squabbles, were links in the same chain, artful dodgers all of them, hired hands whose light fingers did the dirty work for The Scranner, the ringleader plying between the boys and the back-street merchants who made a killing off the fish that walked. If Charley Bates was a picker of pockets, Johnny Hallows was a picker of baskets; if Fagin wore his black heart on his greasy sleeve, The Scranner wore his measliness like a rash on the skin.

Johnny, his scran-bag swelling with herring, would slither off to the thieves' den, fast as his legs could carry him (when evasion demanded it they would carry him under the belly of a carrier's horse), and hand over his haul for a beggarly bawbee that would just as quickly be spent on a sherbet dab, a pink mouse and some candy mixture out of the glass jar in Maiky's wee shop at the corner of the Close. The merchants had more than their pink mice out of it; if the scavengers, winged or wingless, were sharp, the merchants were cut-throat; many a merchant, if the truth were to sneak out, had started off in the fishy business of buying (if that was not too fine a word for it) the spoils in Johnny's scran-bag, the sweepings of the pier, and maybe that was why they never lost their eye for the quick chance or their nerve for a shrewd bargain. Merchants were more like the herring gull than Johnny was in that they were born with their eyes open.

Which was what his mother was tempted to think of Johnny as he sat in the family pew in kirk, his boots a match for his father's shiny black bible, his fingers twisting into tiny shapes meant to be steam capstans the papers off the sweets that he had bought with the money his mother had given him for the collection plate, and gawked up at the minister while he was delivering the prayer. To spend your collection-plate penny on sweets, on what his mother, in a tone that was like a clout in the lug, called 'smacherie', was a sin of a deeper dye than filching fish for The Scranner; while to remain wide-eyed and wandering when everybody else was blind in prayer was a crime for which you might be damned to transportation for life.

He had been banished once before, if only from the house, for sniggering when his grandfather began to read from the Good Book one Sunday evening. 'Hebrews, chapter twelve and one', his grandpa had announced, and before he could get as far as the opening words, *Let brotherly love continue*, Johnny sniggered. Chapter twelve and one. It was not that his grandpa could not count beyond twelve: the old dotterel was yielding to superstition in avoiding saying thirteen. Johnny had to stand outside for a good twelve and one minutes until he took aboard some respect and apologised. When he got back indoors he may not have been as reformed as Charley Bates was when he went from picking pockets to picking potatoes on his own farm, but he had learnt to be more forbearing with superstition.

And more forbearing, too, with the life that had fertilised it. It was surely a sprinkling of respect for his father's honest toil that made a nipper want to earn, by hook rather than by crook, his own regular copper or two. The very shipshape and true-blue fashion of his father's life worked, if not like a charm, then like a watchword on the boy; a watchword that he could have sworn he had heard whispered in his ear by some unknown voice after his tarry fingers had helped themselves to a lucky-bag as Maiky's back was turned one evening when he had been sent round to the shop for a hank of twine for his father, who was up in the loft mending a net before setting out for Yarmouth. He would gladly have swapped that gut feeling of guilt for the warm and secret glow that filtered through him in the covert act of buying from one of the bigger boys — for Maiky would have ignited like a match at such a request – his own five of Woodbines with his own clean-gotten gains.

There was something manly about that kind of guilt. Which was more than could be said for the glow that crept over him when he smuggled his grandfather's pipe out of the house and stole round to the back of Connacher's curing sheds to puff himself sick as a cloud. Greener than a Zulu's bottom were his gills by the time he had smoked himself out from the back of the sheds, a fagged-out stub of a thing, changed in a puff of bogie roll into a creature as green with age and as blue with melancholy as the dottled old stump of a grandfather whose pipe it was. Johnny was never to put a pipe to his lips again. He would sooner have smoked an old boot. Or a herring.

And well might he have been doing just that, judging by the amount of herring that was swimming in his head as he puffed around town on the five-of-Woodbines errand known as Running the Billy. Every day of the autumn fishing he would high-tail it out of school and scoot to the fish merchant's office to read the bill in the window: the bill which gave the day's catches at Yarmouth and which the fish merchant posted in his window for the boys to see so that they could skip round to the houses of the skippers and their crews and pass on the figures to their families. The world and his gird would be there, swarming in front of the window to see who had landed what.

Johnny might have to elbow his way through them, and if he saw that the *Moonbeam* had netted a good shot, two hundred crans or thereby, he would be off like a good shot himself, more than a quarter of a million herring swimming in his head as he cut every corner in his haste to tell the skipper's wife, who would be so far over the moon when she heard him gasp 'twa hunner cran' that she would cross his fevered palm with a silver threepenny bit. His pocket thus lined, and with a whoop that might have been heard on the blind side of the moon if only that body had not been so hard of hearing, he would scurry off to the homes of the *Moonbeam*'s crew to pick up a penny here and a penny there until at the end of the Billy-run he would be feeling as loaded as the skipper and his boat.

Ten houses he might take in on one mad skelter of a round. But if he got a good run for his money on the Billy, he also got good money for his run: some weeks he could afford to go wild on the Woodbines. The legs which had scampered up the hill the day the boats sailed away to the south fishing, and which had carried the news of their catches to all points of the town six days a week for around ten weeks, with a well-earned rest on Sundays, would scamper back up the hill the day the boats sailed home again; and as soon as Johnny the lookout had identified a vessel making for the harbour (sometimes he could tell, Red Indian-like, by the smoke from the funnel), he would glide down the hill on the wings of the wind and descend like a sigh on the houses of the crew, earning a last honest copper, and maybe a slice of bread and treacle, for being first with the news of a homecoming that offered, after the boatloads of expectation that had attended the leave-taking, barrels of fulfilment for one and all.

Johnny had set out on his life's voyage when the tide was high and the moon full and his father in the south bringing in the harvest. The herring were gathering round the Knoll more thickly than leaves on a forest floor when his wet head poked to the surface. The same heaven-hung harvest lamp that was lighting the way for his father was shining on the son's face through the cottage window in the Close as though the planets were trying to make up for the boy-child's drawback in not being born with a silver spoon by coating him in the mysterious silver-plate of the moon goblins. Inasmuch as they were begotten by the moon, Johnny and Buddha were one.

Granny Hallows was the first and, not being one given to bowing before Buddha or his begetter, the last to see the moon-child lying in the scull basket that served as a wickerwork cradle on the floor at the foot of its mother's bed. When she slunk into the room and saw the moon gazing down with a lunatic eye on to the face of the child she was so discountenanced, as though a peeping Tom had caught her in her birthday suit, that for a mad, impatient second she stared up at the po-faced object in the sky and, before drawing another breath, drew down the blinds. Superstition exerted as strong a pull on Granny Hallows as did the moon on the tides. What else could that stark, staring-mad chinless wonder of a moon be after but mischief, beaming with sheep's eyes into the milk-white face of an innocent lamb like that? To glower through the window was a liberty enough without crooning over the cradle, pinching the bairn's cheeks almost, wooing him with the open arms of a child-stealer.

It was, too, a liberty verging on the diabolical that such a fair, decent old woman should allow such dark, indecent thoughts to steal through her mind at the very moment when that same heavenly light was guiding the child's father on the southern sea. For the moon had no need to bear away the new-born babe that night. If the stars exerted a particle of the influence they were said to exert on the destinies of men, then the boy's fate was as cut and dried as a cod in the sun. Had he not been born under the seventh sign of the zodiac; the sign that pointed south, the sign of the scales, the sign that brought forth autumn fruits? The moon had kidnapped Johnny without his grandmother knowing it, before she had even entered the room. The stars had lit a path for him, and that path pointed south. South to another kind of scales; south to the herring. No fisher lad, even if he could have arranged it with the Great Skipper in the sky himself, could have been put in a finer rapture for the shoals of autumn.

And as sure as the moon pulled the autumn tides, so the autumn tides pulled Johnny. He had been born with scales over his eyes all right: herring scales. When he thought of the herring, even as a boy picking bones with the one on his plate, he saw a cataract of silver fishes. Or rather he saw herring where his teacher in school saw herrings. In Brenston only Miss Macarran saw herrings: everybody else saw herring, singular. And singular, too, in the eyes of the small fry was the day their fathers set out for the hunt. (It was a day off school for the whole town.)

At first Johnny saw it in the outlandish light of grown-ups going on a picnic. Until one day it came to him, with a grey dawning, that these grown-ups were going on their picnic with work baskets. Then, when he was about knee-high to one of these baskets, he began to see in the fleet's departure the solemn earnestness of a voyage into the unknown. They were not picnickers now so much as pilgrims; and the more he looked at them the more it struck him that their hearts seemed no lighter than those of the Puritans that Miss Macarran talked about in school.

This feeling about his father and the rest of them – the feeling that Jondy Hallows, if only for a season and of his own persuasion, was a pilgrim father – might have belonged to the day-dreaming world of the classroom, might have rung as false to Brenston ears as the word herrings itself, but it was a feeling that Johnny carried beyond the school gates when, with a clang of overwrought iron and a rattle of rusty chains, they closed on him for the last time. Looking into his father's face before the *Sea Thrift* turned about on her pilgrimage south, south to what his fancy took to be some sort of trading post built inside a palisade of barrels, he saw the same gleam of steel that belonged in the pages of his school history book, that might have come straight out of that picture of the wanderers westward of three centuries ago, setting their stern puritan faces to the blear-eyed gamble of sailing out of an English autumn and into a New English fall, in pursuit, as his teacher put it, of a new life and an old liberty. If the voyage of the *Mayflower* was an ocean apart in spirit from that of the *Sea Thrift*, or of any other flower of the herring fleet, there was not so much as a spit of water separating them as voyages of soaring necessity.

Out of this necessity, if nothing else, did Johnny, once he had won his water-wings, become a pilgrim himself. There had been no fear of his getting his lines snagged as he fished around for a job after leaving school; not with the sea knocking on his door. There had been no need to choose the sea when the sea had chosen him. Nor had there been even a choice of boat on which to launch his fishing career. Father knew best, and so it was that the *Deep Pastures* was preferred to the *Sea Thrift* in the paternal belief that serving under an uncle rather than the old man would be the making of the lad. Besides, Uncle Buck was a deacon at his craft. And so, donning blue gansey, moleskin breeks, flat cap and kerchief, and with a clean new knife in its sheath by his hip, Johnny steamed rather than drifted towards a berth on one of the knackiest steam drifters in the Brenston fleet. He was as happy as a willie-gow in a glut.

His buoyancy was to prove as perishable as the fish that had inspired it – a fleeting thing that was barely to survive the moment his knife drew first blood. Johnny, his hair tacky with tar, would coil endless rope as thick as his wrist while the nets were being hauled; with his knife he would gut a fry for the crew's breakfast, a fry straight out of the net and into the pan, so fresh that the herring sizzled in their own fat, ten for every man bar Uncle Buck, who was a man and a half with fifteen. As a cook Johnny took as much buffeting as the dumplings he boiled in the broth and about which his uncle said they were so wicked that if one of them ever landed overboard it would foul the propeller before it sank to the bottom. Johnny boiled a brisk and sometimes angry kettle for the deckies' tea; and it was with a teasing relish, which on not a few occasions he feigned, that he ate his meat from the same plate as he had supped his soup from and then licked it clean for his pudding. If there had been a long hauling, the nets filled to overflowing, he might not get as far as the pudding, or even the meat; his head would fall into his soup, heavy as one of his own dumplings with fatigue.

Johnny was a galley-slave who at times felt that he was treated no better than a rat in the rope locker. Not that a rat in the rope locker was treated too badly. To Johnny's raw and timorous eye it seemed that the boat was run, if not overrun, by rats. This bane he learnt to live with after his father had explained to him that rats were lucky. A boat without a rat would be like a farm without a cat, his father had argued. So Johnny, instead of putting down poison, made the rats feel at home. Should they ever leave the boat he, too, would have to leave her; for a boat that a rat abandoned was doomed; such a boat was sure to sink.

His Uncle Buck was as hard as rat's tack; and for downright coarseness, too, he took the ship's biscuit. Johnny learnt what shit off a shovel was. His uncle would go down into the engine-room and squat over a shovelful of coal and do his motions on top of it, afterwards consigning the lot to the furnace. He said it was more comfortable than going up on deck in a howling gale and turning his stern to the fishes, a spectacle that he had inflicted on fish and goggle-eyed crew once or twice in the past when the sea was not too much of an inconvenience. If his uncle took suddenly bad with the piles he would apply tar to his beam-end for relief. There was nothing, he said, like a lick of tar for the buff. (Or, he might have added, for the inside walls of his cottage, for these also had he tarred to keep out the damp.)

If the nets were pulled in empty Uncle Buck would go into a slow-burning rage, hauling the sea over the coals for treating him like a lump of dirt and then punching holes in the sky as his fist laid it squarely at the door of the One Above. Once when the catch was small he threw it back in the sea, spitting out an oath and an invitation to God to breakfast on it. 'He'll do more than breakfast on it,' one of the black squad growled, his bones rattling with some fearful apprehension. 'He'll have us all for dinner before this trip's over.' And raising a fist that might have punched a hole in the skipper, he vowed that next time he was in the Shetlands he would fix the old demon up with a pair of ram's horns.

While Uncle Buck had the devil of a job trying to read a book – one of Johnny's chores was to read bits of the almanac to him – he was a classical scholar when it came to reading wind and wave. The sea was an open book to him and the sky was his daily newspaper; and so well had he scanned both of them down the years that a lot of what he had read he knew by heart.

Not always was it a sea of serene shot silk; more often was the silk shot through with ruffles. It was all swish and swirl the day a wave hit Johnny and washed him like a fish down into the hold. When he got up he was so groggy his uncle gave him a drop of something out of a bottle, and not until a couple of hours later, when Johnny was seen in the engine-room shovelling coal into the furnace, did his uncle tumble to the fact that he had given the lad cascara. The mixture was better the time Johnny was caught by a rope as by the tentacle of an octopus and pulled into the sea, his oilskin trying to keep him afloat while his sea-boots kept dragging him down. After he was hauled back in his uncle offered him a tot of hot rum. If the cascara tasted like arsenic, the rum was as smooth as the lace on a bride's gown.

What with his head dropping into his soup and his body dropping into the sea, Johnny was earning his salt as an apprentice fisherman. At fifteen years of age he was a man. And things began to look up when one day his uncle went below for a bowl of pea soup and handed over the wheel to Johnny until he got back. No more boiling the kettle for the deckies' tea. No more coiling rope until his head was going round in circles. No more lighting the skipper's pipe – and singeing his moustache in the rolling of the boat – while the skipper held the wheel. No more was he at the beck of Uncle Buck and at the call of the men down below. Johnny was king over all the rats in the rope locker, he was lord of the bounding, boundless sea. The *Deep Pastures* was butting along and Johnny's was the hand that was leading her. For the time it takes a skipper with the hunger of a hunter to spoon down a bowl of pea soup, Johnny's destiny was in his own hands. There was more inebriation in having your hand on the wheel than there was in a tot of hot rum after a ducking in the sea.

That inebriation was to intensify when he joined the crew of a boat in which, as a nipper at school, he had been privileged to sail on her trials. On that trial trip the whole town seemed to have been extended the same privilege, so awash was her decks with people, and although there was not a lifebelt between them she looked, from the way she cut through the water – the builders said they had given her the head of a cod and the tail of a mackerel – as if she could have taken on board the lifeboat as well before capsizing. And when her passengers stepped ashore at the end of it all, they were treated to lemonade and biscuits.

A fisherman now, a big lad whose lemonade had to be

laced with something stronger, Johnny joined that same
bonny boat that he looked upon as not so much one of a
thousand steamers from the land of the carvel-built
Zulu as one in a thousand. Skipper Croll, taking him up
on a tip-off about the young Hallows's artistic flair at
school, asked him if he would paint her name and
registration number on her bow before he set out on his
first trip south in his new boat. Johnny painted her
name with pride in gold. And there on the pier waving
off the *Bounteous (BN 160)* that autumn, and throwing a
kiss in letters of gold at Johnny, was a young lady who,
as a nip of a girl at school, had been sick on the boat
during her trials. In a week or so Hannah Gale, too,
would be on her way south, with a procession of lasses in
her train. With attendants of such fairness in tow, it was
little wonder that in the autumn a young herring
fisherman's fancy lightly turned to thoughts of love.
Southward ho! the sea was burning bright.

3

A freckle of a lass hopping barefoot as a gull on a hot tarry roof was Hannah Gale when first she drifted into Johnny's life; or rather when first he felt the presence of her as you might a quickening breeze on the cheek. She would have been about ten at the time, with a tear-stained face and a tar-stained frock and a tangle of hair which, when she ran squalling into the wind, would have scared the feathers off a brooding sea-hen. An untamed creature among the wild life of the shore, she seemed to float on air. Over rock and wreck she would clamber with the best of them and, whereas other lasses would sit down and cry over spilt blood, this child of nature would lick her wounds like a cat, sucking the blood from a gash in her knee as if it were jam on the fingers, and yet with the sticky-eyed intent of someone observing some crude rite arising out of a belief in the preciousness of every drop, a belief that ran in the very blood that was being spilt.

To the same rock-pool on the windward side of the North Breakwater close to where she lived she would go to wash her doll's clothes. Spotless as the driven spume was that doll; the east winds were not allowed to snap and howl in its face. Whereas other lasses played at being mothers who were as waxy as their dolls, Hannah had to be the real thing, the kind of mother whose maternal instinct showed itself in the sacrificing of her own appearance for that of her offspring.

There was something thoroughgoing about the Gales. Hannah's father was as even-keel as any wife could wish her husband to be, according to Johnny's father who sailed with him in the same boat; and Hannah's mother was not only as well-ordered as apple-pie, according to Johnny's mother who worked with her in the same yard, but as a packer of barrels she had no peer. The tightest barrels that ever came out of Brenston were packed by Winnie Gale; so tight did she pack them that once the heads were on you would have to burst open the barrels to get at the herring; and even without the support of the staves the herring would still stay tight. Herring and salt, time about in layers, each layer of fish arranged at if it were flowers, until there was nigh on a thousand herring in her barrel, the last layer a sight so glittering that the buyer, if not the sniffy-nebbed inspector, would clamp such eyes on it as a commoner might reserve for the King's crown, and so mouth-watering was it for some that they could have made a beast of themselves there and then, like old Mr Gorbelov, the Russian, who was himself a sight to make anybody slaver, picking up a herring and popping it in his mouth and shuffling on to the next barrel with the bree running down his chin.

All that salt rubbed Winnie Gale up the wrong way until one winter she was laid low by an eruption of the skin that made her body come out in scales, as though she were turning into a herring. That was to put the lid on her life as a packer. Hannah was allowed to leave school before her time to lend a much-needed hand at home. Then, still fresh from school, still a freckle of a thing of thirteen autumns, she stuck her first knife into her first herring.

Before her classmates could turn their soft, chalk-white hands to their first job of work, Hannah had already worked her fingers near to the bone as the family's supplementary breadwinner. Not that she had jumped into her mother's boots in the yard: to have become a packer after seeing what it had done for her mother would have been to rub salt in an unhealable wound. Hannah had become the only other thing that the female spawn of a one-fish seatown could have become: a gutter. And as a manipulator of the two-inch blade she let neither town nor family down. She was as thoroughgoing as any Gale.

Wherever the herring abounded Hannah would be there; wherever the governor listeth she would be there plying her trade. For she, too, had become a migrant. Big, dry herrings in the north; small, oily, rich ones in the south. To the far north she followed the fish trail, travelling on the deck of a steamer with a couple of hundred others, feeling like one of a drove of heifers in a cattle-boat and sounding like one as, lying flat on her back with a tarpaulin over her, she began to low pitifully to herself through a sea that was a towering babble of five tides – so many points did the wheel in the skipper's hand move in this turbulence known as the Five Ways that it was as if he were writing the names of his crew in the water – and if she threw up once she threw up five times over the side. Twice was once too often for those voyages north; for twice had she arrived there spent as a spawned herring, and twice had she arrived home feeling as though she herself had been gutted.

Hannah found the south more magnetic. There were no tides to stem, far less the Five Ways to cross, when she headed south; there was no upthrowing over the rail as she pitched and rolled overland under the steam of a locomotive.

If, to the far north or to the magnetic south of Brenston, there was a mountain to be moved, Hannah would be there, gutting twenty thousand herring or more in her twelve-hour day; a rag bandage made from a flour bag bound round each finger to protect it from the blade of a knife that flashed like greased lightning, her hands a blur of bandages as each herring was slit from throat to tail and disembowelled with the precision of a surgeon, the whole operation lasting little longer than a second, all the while talking and joking and singing and sometimes not even looking at what she was doing. Hannah could gut as she could knit, with her eyes shut. She was one of a team of three, two gutters and a packer. On one of her best days she might gut thirty thousand herring. And yet she made as much impression on that scaly mountain as the little bird made upon the rock a hundred miles high and a hundred miles wide, to which, once every thousand years, it came to sharpen its beak, and only when the rock had thus been worn away had a single day of eternity gone by.

In the living mountain of herring to which, once every year, a herring girl came to blunt her knife, Hannah had her own working scale model of the rock of eternity.

If not for so much as a blink of time everlasting, it was going on for the guts of half a lifetime that Johnny had known Hannah (although it would have been for a season or two less, on account of the attention she had lavished on her doll, that Hannah had known Johnny). Nothing misty, either, had there been about the moment they became mutually aware of each other, when Johnny knew that he was hooked on Hannah, and Hannah had set her heart on Johnny. Three words passed between them, and without ever having been spoken. A conversation lozenge said it all.

They were at a wedding reception in the Seamen's Mission. One of the bride's sisters came round with a bowl of lettered sweets and told Johnny to close his eyes and pick out one for his partner sitting next to him. The idea, according to the bride's sister – and she winked at the guests looking on with first-night mischief in their eyes – was to see if it was Hannah's turn to be the next bride. Johnny, his hand shaky, almost sticky, with excitement, did as he was bid and, in handing the lozenge to his partner (after having sneaked the discreetest of glances at its motto), he flirted with the feeling that he was offering her not just a sweet but a piece of his heart. Hannah, cradling it in her hand as a card-player might cradle an ace – which in Johnny's eyes it was, the ace of hearts – and slyly devouring its message while the rest of the lads and lasses ribbed and elbowed her, popped it in her mouth, the blush on her cheeks giving away something of the secret that she and Johnny shared and were confirming to each other for the first time.

I love you, the lozenge said, straight as an arrow from Cupid's bow. Three words that encapsulated Johnny's inmost thoughts. And as they melted in Hannah's mouth, so her life began to melt into Johnny's. Of all the sweetmeats that had lured boy into meeting girl, of all the lozenges that had opened up a conversation leading to courtship if not to the altar, surely, as the town of Brenston soon had cause to avow, there was none among all the bottled jewels in Maiky's shop that had spread more sweetness and tenderness around two young and innocent lives; such sweetness as no imagined knife-twist of fate could turn sour.

Their romance, launched in the matrimonial month of June, was on the crest of a deep-sea wave in the months of the herring moon. For the pair of them the autumn fishing loomed and passed and loomed again in a bright new light. If there was no fear of Hannah being seasick on the way south, it was a pound to a pickle of salt – such was the time between Johnny's departure by boat and hers by train and their linking up on the quayside at Yarmouth – that she would be lovesick. It was a happy day when she signed her name over a penny stamp and was paid her arles, her earnest money, by the curer, binding her bargain for the season. And happier still was she when she packed her kist, her sturdy wooden chest, packed it as tight with her possessions as her mother had once packed her barrels with herring, and gave Gurdie a hand to heave it on to his four-wheeled cart that carried, as Queenie the Clydesdale worked up a nose of steam, the women's kists to the railway station. If the bosomless Belle Duffus, who was always trying to be prim and proper, could drop a line to her landlady saying *Arriving Sunday, chest to follow*, then surely the buoyant-breasted Hannah could have been forgiven for dropping a line to her landlady saying *Body on its way*. For the breath of her life, the guts of her being, not to mention a large piece of her mind, had sailed on the *Bounteous*. Her heart was already in Yarmouth.

In that sandpit by the sea, in that bloatered town at the mouth of the Yare, as the summer recumbents moved out and the workers moved in, the landladies would be gutting their rooms, stripping the furniture, leaving only the beds. Two beds to a room, three women to a bed. More than once had it occurred to Hannah that these landladies could have packed a barrel or two, judging by the way they packed fisher lasses into a room. The wooden kists that the lasses had travelled down with – Hannah's so heavy that the landlord asked if she had a body in it, with maybe the trunkless head in the oval tin that she said was her Sunday hat-box – would be the only sticks of furniture in these unaccommodating digs on the south side of the town; and they had to double up as chairs, too, since the landladies would not have their chairs contaminated by the smell of herring. Though the lodgers themselves were held in good enough odour, their clothes smelt to high sea; and it was a smell that clung to things, clung to the washing on the line, got into your hair, wormed its way into the woodwork.

Feeling at best a gypsy and at worst a carrier of the

plague, Hannah yet looked upon her lodgings in the south as a luxury after the hut on the quay in the far north with its stove in the middle and its corner curtained off to form a glory hole that at the odd weekend saw some strange goings-on in the day and some stranger ongoings in the night. No landlady would have entertained the fishermen that smuggled themselves into that hut for a swallow of the moonshine and a lark with the girls and a squeeze of the melodeon until the bare rafter-beams were dancing in their sleep. Hannah saw there, felt with raw green eyes held up to the light of nature, the naked underbelly of life.

Rough as she lived care of a landlady with an oak chip on her shoulder, it was a luxury compared with the way she worked. It left so little time for living, rough or smooth, a day at the farlans: the long, shallow wooden troughs marshalled along the sea front into which the herring were dumped for gutting and to which at first gleam of day she was conveyed by horse and cart driven by Yarmouth's answer to Gurdie back home, a man who was every bit as willin' as Barkis in the story-book and, on mornings as sharp as her gutting knife, a bit too willin' for Hannah's liking.

It was a day that might begin with her fainting in the cold of the grassy wasteland known as the Denes, and end with her collapsing exhausted on a pile of rope on the wharf. In the yards the mountain of herring might be as high as last night's moon when she put on her leather boots and oilskin apron, and the same moon would be high again and silvery and wooing yet another mountain out of the sea by the time she took them off. The old girls, after a lifetime of standing over trough or tub or half-filled barrel, of humping barrels while the cooper stood and swore at them, would lift up their heads for the first time, only to let them fall again, bowing to the fact that they could no longer unbend their backs at the day's end. Hannah's hands would be

cut by her own erring knife or by the bones of the
herring itself; cut and ulcered, chapped and chilblained;
and stung by the brine as she stood at her station for
hours on end in all weathers, her long oilskin apron stiff
as a board with ice and spattered from neck to ankle
with the blood and scales of more than thirty crans of
herring, a stomach-turning sight that was enough to
give her landlady not so much an oak chip on her
shoulder as a whole solid old English oak. (And
Hannah, who had been roused at five sharp every
morning with the words 'Get up and tie your fingers',
would be roused by her mother, the morning after her
arrival home from the fishing, with the words 'Get up,
quine, your holiday's over').

Belle Duffus, a sergeant-major in skirts even if she
did not have the chest of one (or rather the hairs on the
chest of one), was not far wide of the mark when one
day she stood up to her queets in glaur – up to her
ankles, as the starched apron herself was not unliable to
put it, in mud – and said that she could imagine what it
was like to be one of the boys in the trenches.

It was a remark that triggered off yet again that
terrible vision that had been haunting Hannah every
night now for a couple of years, the vision of her dear
brother Watty, in which he was a braw sodger-lad in the
kilt one moment, and the next part of the dust-cloud of
a shell; bits of him she clearly saw being picked up by an
orderly and thrown in a bag, with no more ceremony
than a body would show picking up the offal in a
herring yard, and buried where he had fallen at the
Somme. (A fate that might have befallen Johnny, too,
but for the fact that, hard though he tried to enlist, for
he and Watty were of the same age, he was rejected on
account of his flat feet.) Even if Belle Duffus was wading
in blood and mud in the no man's land of the Denes;
even if she, in the cut-and-thrust of hand-to-hand battle
with the herring, was going up to the dressing-station to

have her wounds attended to like a tommy at the front;
and even if the North Sea did from time to time send in
its white horses as though to claim back its silver
creatures, neither Belle Duffus nor Hannah herself was
exposed, as Watty had been, to an enemy that blew you
to smithereens, scattered your guts to the gulls or to the
four corners of a foreign field, the flower of youth
ground to flesh-and-bone meal, yesterday's blooms
becoming tomorrow's poppies. From where Hannah
stood the glaur of the Denes was not so poppy-red as the
mud of Flanders.

The moon that wooed the mountain of herring out of
the sea also wooed Hannah Gale; when the moon was
full, so was her heart with love. An unbonny sight she
might have been amid all that slime and stink, a wader
in blood with a face blackened by the smoke from the
paraffin flares and the bubbly lamps, a shambles of an
object that might have crawled right out of that
mountain of herring, and yet she knew that she was
loved, blood-spattered apron or no, loved all the more
in herring scales because herring scales – if only her
landlady knew it – were the diamonds, the unsung
fish-paste diamonds, of the sea. Losing her heart made
more sufferable the long, hard hours spent at the
farlans; the rapture of it soothed the wounds of knife
and bone and salt and cold; it so loosened her tongue
that she would unfold for the women who were gutting
by her side the tale from the book that she happened to
be reading, or from the motion picture that she had
seen with Johnny. If she had not been up to her bows in
love she would not have burst out singing the way she
did, singing to the scaly mountain, singing like a lark
that has been serenading a nightingale, until the other
women, too, were echoing the song that was in her
breast.

Hannah's and Johnny's was a love that by mutual conviction not only sustained but, in its least worldly moments, conquered; a love so magical that it could have gone to sea in a sieve and come back safely. All around it there seemed to be cast a light in which everything took on a new vitality, and even the herring a fresh lustre.

In the transforming light of Johnny's eyes the herring scales which adorned Hannah were neither fish-paste jewels nor sea spangles whose resplendence matched the glitter on the dress of King Geordie's sovereign lady: they were reflections of the stars. She illumined his life's course as radiantly as the stars in the black yonder illumined his boat's. She was his harvest queen, so ripe did she look standing there like Ruth, breast-high amid the alien corn – the overspilling acres of English herring – a flush on her cheeks such as graced the women of the fields in those rosy bible pictures that were held up for him and his classmates to see in Sunday school.

Hannah could have stepped right into one of these pictures, it occurred to him in an inexplicable moment when the innocence of childhood returned to fire his vain adult mind, the only difference being that she was gutting herring instead of grinding grain, balancing an empty barrel on the crown of her head instead of a water-pot. Given a sickle instead of a knife, his Hannah might just as easily have answered to the name of Ruth. Nowhere in the land was there a rosier picture than that of her hoisting the barrel above her head and smiling, so braw and bonny-like, into the camera, as if to say that if you had put half a cran of herring in it for good measure, not only would the smile still be there, it would be as wide as the harbour mouth at Brenston.

Hannah would knit when she was not gutting, so that the fingers that had been a blur with the blade continued to be a blur with the needles. Her hands were never still;

they were busier, more tireless than the jaws of those men – her Johnny, of course, not being one of them – who chewed baccy. The needles, never fewer than four of them at a time, were extensions of her hands, extra fingers, and they flashed like knives wherever she sat or stood cooling her heels, which was mostly on the wharf, drinking in the scenery while waiting for the boats to land, or as she strolled along the streets with the rest of her crew, the purl of her tongue keeping pace with the clack of her hands. To Hannah knitting and gutting were similar acts in so far as they required no more concentration than half her mind was prepared to give to them. While one half was giving its undivided attention to the task in hand, the other half was weaving tales to its neighbour, or roaming the starry seas with Johnny.

Only once maybe did she concentrate her whole mind on the task, and that was when she knitted her lover a jersey, a true-blue gansey of five-ply worsted wool of a strength known as seaman's iron. So tightly did she knit it that it would have cheated water as well as wind. The pattern, diamond shapes with crosses inside them in vertical formation, was peculiar to Brenston. In the polonecked town of Yarmouth, Hannah could tell where a man came from by running her eye over the pattern he was wearing. If a man was washed up headless and tattooless on the beach she would know who he was by the pattern on his gansey. Some ganseys had ridges and furrows like a ploughed field; others had zigzags – marriage lines, depicting, so her mother put it, the ups and downs of life. (A notion that Hannah much preferred to her own, plainer one that the zigzags stood for the up-and-down roads leading to some of the fishing havens.) The tree of life branched out all over some ganseys. There were ropes and cables, diamonds within diamonds, ladders and trellises, flags and anchors, nets and chevrons, waves and starfish, sand

and shingle, hearts and love-knots and moss and lightning flashes and even herringbones.

Where the unseasoned townswoman in the polyjerseyed town of Yarmouth saw the same garment on every man's back — saw, as it were, a visiting army rigged out in the same uniform, in what Hannah's mother called 'penny fitting' — Hannah saw on these same backs as many configurations as she had seen among the rocks on the shore at home. When Johnny's mother wove a gansey for her son it was in the pattern known as Waves of the Sea; wherein she saw, in the play of light and dark, shades of the sea. When Hannah wove her second gansey for her lover it was not meant for the waves of the sea, it was meant for the promenade, for those happy times when the two of them walked out arm in arm, hers interknit with her own handiwork, and the pattern she chose was Links of Love.

In his Links of Love gansey Johnny serenaded Hannah on the Jew's harp. It was an instrument that he played like an angel, plucking her heart-strings as assuredly as he plucked the steel tongue of the harp. In his hands that trump could speak in tongues; he could make it sound like a lyre, even like a trumpet. Knowing how Hannah liked the bagpipes, he had learnt to play a bagpipe tune on it. She called it his horseshoe and, as luck would have it, one year, at the end of the fishing, she bought him a shiny new mouth-organ in a sleek padded box. It was the last she was to hear of the trump.

Johnny was no virtuoso of the harmonica, unlike Watty Gale, who had taken his one with him to the trenches; where, amid the clart and stour of Flanders, and in the words of Sandy Shunners, who was with him right up till the end, it was a concert listening to him play. Johnny's was a Hohner and he took to it like a boy to a new toy. He would vamp away until, blowing like a bellows, he would be so carried away that he reminded Hannah of the old skipper her father used to go on

about who tried to blow wind into his sails when his boat
was becalmed on the sea.

Hannah would sing to his playing as they strode along
the Parade in the slack of a Saturday afternoon,
eventually dawdling round the shops, where they might
lay down a deposit on their Christmas present for each
other, or send home a box of fruit and sweets for the
kids, or buy, for some relative who was never too distant
when the season of giving was near, a falderal upon
which were stamped the words *A Present From Yarmouth*.
(Hannah had put away for her providing a cup and
saucer Johnny had given her with the words *A Present
From Yarmouth To Hannah Gale* painted on the cup in
such flowery letters of gold as would have graced the
bow of the proudest ship.) For a whole week he had
been coffined in his bunk, just as she had been confined
to those digs of hers which were no less spartan than the
cabin of the *Bounteous*, so that only at weekends did they
meet.

Yarmouth was a one-eyed town until the weekend
arrived when it opened its other eye – and winked.
Come hither, it said, and Johnny and Hannah went.
They went to the picture house, a temple of a place that
might have been built by Solomon. (The very same
shrine to which Molly Mull, one of Belle Duffus's crew,
rushed straight from her pickling plot one night,
glumph-glumph-glumphing in her muckle boots, and
sat herself down, emptying two-three rows in front of
her as well as behind before she had time to gather her
gutting skirts around her.) They went up the Nelson
monument, a pillar that Solomon would have been
proud of, with its figures of women, Britannia abune
them a', waving their arms to the herring lasses on the
Denes far below. They went roving around a huddle of
lanes, each one no wider than the gangway of a boat, up
the row called Split Gutter and down its neighbour
called Snatchbody (where once the bodysnatchers

lived), clopping in single file over cobbles shaped less like the stones that might have dropped out of the kidneys of the snatched bodies than the kidneys themselves. (With the narrow lanes forming the bars, Yarmouth took after the grid-irons over which the bloaters were cooked.) And to The Three Bloaters they went, he for a jug and a jaw with the boys, she to hang about outside and commune with her sister spirits until their men reappeared, most of them, though not Johnny, at closing time.

On Sundays there was one unmistakable way of telling an English boat from a Scottish one: the former put to sea as usual while the latter stayed reverently in port. Johnny would not have needed much of a push to have fallen in with the English; especially when Hannah, in her Sunday hat and two-piece suit, hauled him, in his best blue gansey and Sabbath bonnet (a pair of walking mothballs, both of them), off to church, where he fidgeted like a fish out of water, his eyes crossing and criss-crossing the ceiling, drawing lines as if he were tracing the rigging of a windjammer, the sermon inspiring him to no more than an endless mental doodle. When he lowered his eyes it was to think of down-to-earth things like the mast they had lost last week, or the wheelhouse last month, or the little boat last year, or the cook a couple of fishings ago. His gaze would fall farther and linger upon his hands. They were still smarting from the stings of jellyfish, the wrists chafed by oilskins, the fingers calloused by ropes, the space between the thumbs and forefingers breaking out in salt-water boils. His eyes would stray to Hannah's hands, the right one red and swollen, the left bandaged where the knife had slipped. Those tight-fitting little cotton gloves that she held in her left hand – she must have carried them around in the hope that one day she might get her hands into them. Sunday was a day of rest for restless hands; even as the minister's went to work.

They had never handled a gutting knife nor hauled in a rope, these hands that the minister waved in their faces. White and spotless as his dog-collar.

Just the hands for conducting a white wedding in the kirk. The thought made Johnny shift in his seat. For surely Hannah, too, at some stage in the service if not before it – maybe as they walked together up the aisle to their seats – had caught the tinkle, coming from not so far off, of wedding bells. It would have been a popular match, the fleet-fingered Hannah and the flat-footed Johnny: the thoroughness of a Gale hitched to the four-squareness of a Hallows. Such a home-woven lass, as knacky at the fancy stitch as she was at the plain, and either with the needle or the hook, would have woven a cosy hearthrug for any man. No bottom drawer would have been better stocked, no home better decked out. The flags would be flying from the boats in Brenston harbour the day Hannah and Johnny took the plunge.

For three years did their romance fatten on the Great Yarmouth herring, ripening with each autumn as other, less salty loves blossomed anew in the spring. The three moons of Yarmouth were as sweet as honeymoons. Hannah was as happy as a sandgirl working in that sandpit of a town while Johnny was as joyful as a sand-hopper on a moonlit beach. Once during the northern fishing he had cleaned out her hut for her and she had not forgotten it; for more than once in the south had she gone down on her knees and scrubbed out his cabin. Theirs was a first love which was true and constant. Not a light, high-stepping, whirlwind affair with fiery nostrils and flying mane; but as steady, as workaday, as hearty and as pleased with itself as a Suffolk punch.

4

True love never did run smooth. No more for the humble servant at the court of King Herring than for the pale-cheeked daughter of the court of Athens condemned, so long as her heart was overruled by her father's head, to a life of chanting faint hymns to the cold, fruitless moon. Hannah had been close to the chanting stage herself on more than one occasion in the past while waiting for her heart's desire to drag himself out of a public house; but never had the moon been so cold and fruitless as it was one night outside The Anchorage in Brenston. If their love-boat had been rocked in the past, that night she ran into heavy seas.

That Johnny had made The Anchorage his regular port of call at weekends, and his haven in a storm in between times, did not vex Hannah unduly, chronic drinker of Adam's ale though she was. What embittered her was the waiting, the abandoning of her as if she were a doormat, outside the tavern door. The more Johnny dipped his jib into a jug of ale, the less he knew how to get it out again. The jug became a barrel whose contents he poured down his belly until he was as pickled as a herring bound for the Emerald Isle. And a pickled herringer it was that staggered out of The Anchorage that night to find his Hannah gone.

Still hopping mad when next she saw him, Hannah made it plain that she was not going to be anybody's doormat. No more would she wait for him outside a

public house while he drowned the sorrows of a week at
sea inside. From now on he could come home under his
own steam, or what was left of it after blowing off in the
bar. With Hannah no longer in tow, Johnny was as free
as his fancy to drink for as long as the spirit was willing,
a course fraught with the danger that this might
increasingly tend to be long after the flesh was weak.
With such licence he could weigh anchor at The
Anchorage and steer himself slowly and singlemindedly
towards the sea of drowned sorrows. Left to his own
vices, he could blow off enough steam as might afford
him a sickening, sacrificial glimpse of the deep,
blue-devilled waters of the dipsomaniac.

And that was how it went for Johnny, temporarily cut
adrift from Hannah, on his weekend blowouts with the
boys. So well oiled did he get once with Iley the engineer
(the pair of them, in the words of their skipper, as
pickled in rum as Nelson's mortal remains) that the
whole town got a whiff of it, not so much because they
were as blind to the world as the dead Nelson for
two-three days on end, but because Iley was so
sightlessly stoned that he fell into the harbour, Johnny
having to fish him out by the hair of his head, and Iley's
own son making the escapade all the more difficult to
live down by rescuing his father's bank book as it floated
in on the tide the next day.

No sooner had those ripples cleared from the
harbour waters than Johnny was plumbing the depths
of notoriety again. He could not wait until the end of
the voyage before making merry with the rest of the
crew, so when he boarded the *Bounteous* one Monday
morning he was in such a befuddled state that he had to
lie down, and not until the first shot was being hauled
did he sober up. When Johnny was as drunk as that he
would fight with the wind. Yet it was not entirely his
fault, according to Sauty the cook, who had enticed him
into the Quayside Inn in the first place, when he drew

his knife on a customer and got himself barred from darkening the portals of that good-for-nothing, god-forsaken butt of bad-taste jokes, the most disorderly den in town. Johnny's fellow regulars in The Anchorage found that one so hard to swallow that the mere thought of it lodged like an impediment in their speech. Johnny with Hannah was a ship with a sheet anchor; Johnny without Hannah was a ship ashore with a sheet or three in the wind.

It was the sheet in the wind rather than the sheet anchor that Brenston saw as Johnny strayed into the arms of The Anchorage instead of those of his dearest catch. The more he thirsted for his second love, the less he hungered after his first. And what he did at home he did with extended licence away from home: The Three Bloaters was, in all but name, The Anchorage on holiday. Hannah was the one who was more like a ship ashore; she was the one who was high and dry. Frustrating as it was to be dumped like a doormat outside a public-house door, a bass that every man who went in wiped his eyes on, it was nothing to the bereavement of being a glass-widow sitting by the fireside knitting and waiting for a pair of groggy legs to call in by or, more likely, not to call at all. There was no shortage of chimney-corner advice as Hannah sat there wearing her broken heart on her sleeve. She would be throwing her life away on a man like that, her mother said. Show him the door, her father said. She could count herself lucky, Aunt Emmy said, for had she not found out the wastrel before it was too late? If only, Aunt Emmy sighed, she herself had been blessed with the same chance …

All this affliction and advice did not have the effect on Hannah that her afflicter or her advisers expected. She did not round on Johnny like a woman scorned, sailing into him with that rage or fury of which not even a raging heaven or a furious hell was capable. When she made her move it was one of which neither her lover nor her mother would have thought her remotely capable; and, being who she was, she moved with the thoroughness of a Gale.

Gradually she cast off the deadweight that had lodged in her heart, that had been weighing her down like a sinker, so that come next autumn fishing she felt free to break out herself. Where better than Yarmouth in which to turn the tide; where else than the port of dreams, where every year fortunes changed for the better? The old Hannah went out with the tide as irreversibly as did the soul of Barkis, and on the lips of the new one that came in was a smile of disquieting willingness.

It was not a change that came over Hannah so much as a transformation. And if the town out of which Lord Nelson had sailed was prepared to turn a blind eye to what it saw, the lasses from Brenston were not. Hannah had been spotted going aboard an English boat. She was the talk of the yard and soon of the fleet. Putting two and two together and, by adding one for the unknown quantity, making five, they reckoned that it was not all filling needles or mending nets on board that boat; nor all nautical story or even naughty song. Where there had been about Hannah an air of quiet ardour before, and a lightish air at that, there was now a freshening breeze of restiveness; there seemed to run through her, and to her very fingertips as she gutted her fish, a tingle of unlived life which was at once feverish and cold-blooded.

Before her crew could put three and three together and make seven she met a local lad, a redneck from Yarmouth, or maybe he was a pea-belly from Lowestoft (Hannah had gone all clammy, or at best as slippery as a conger, with everyone), and the unconscionable hours she kept suggested that they were not all spent choking back duff or gathering wild sea peas on the shore. She began to live for the weekend; wishing her life away for those few fleeting hours of random pleasure at which she threw herself with the abandon of one who did not care if she died living it up.

Her defiance showed in a dishevelment that extended beyond the physical: her tongue could be as tousled as her hair. She called Johnny a pig. A *pig*. That unmentionable abomination. Not even the Hebrews called a pig a pig: it was 'that beast' or 'that thing'. The lasses in the digs would rather she had called Johnny a beast than a pig. For did not the devils depart from the man and enter the swine, who then ran violently down a steep place into the water and were choked? Did not pigs have the Devil's mark on their forefeet? Pigs could see the wind. To come out with such a word just showed how much the lass was cut up in love, because any Gale worth a drawn breath would have gone to the last straw so as not to mention 'that thing' by name. What about her own father when he ran out of salt at sea and hailed a passing skipper with the words 'Have you got some of that stuff we can't speak about?'; and the English skipper pretended to be baffled, and Matty Gale, swallowing hard on a tightening knot of frustration, shouted 'Some of that ... that white stuff ... not the stuff you put in your tea'; and by the time he got his salt he was grumphing like that other great unmentionable, a pig, a pig with a frog in its throat.

Hannah was fast becoming one of the great unmentionables herself as her wilful wantonness got more and more perverse. Letting off a squib at the feet of the Government inspector while his head was in a barrel sampling the herring did not endear her to the curer's man or to the more strait-laced of her clan. And no sooner had they all jumped back into their skins than she dropped another, altogether more explosive, device, a political squib that, if it was all that the more inflammable scaly aprons needed to set their ever-shortening fuse alight, endeared her a lot less to the bowler hats in the yard.

Hannah whipped herself up into such a foam about conditions of work that she fizzed around the place brandishing a red banner made from a flannel for keeping the cold out of her chest and calling on the workers to come out on strike for a better wage from the curers. Hell had no fury like Hannah with a gale in her tail. Not until she had the whole regiment of women grunting and snorting like pigs at the trough and trotting out of the yard in sympathy, one firebrand pelting with herring a protesting cooper on her way out, did she lower her fiery voice and matching flag. Benjie Firkin, the bowler-hatted boss of the Brenston Fishing Company, a man who knew as much about life on board a drifter as he did about the dog-star, and who was only barely more conversant than a bone was with the processing end of it, stepped in as peacemaker, only to be told to his face by Hannah, as she went at him (in the words of old Kirsty Rothick) like a day's work, what she and her family had often bitterly been told by their father: that when his time came he would have a curer and a merchant to port and starboard of his death-bed so that he could cross the bar like the Lord with a thief on either side of him. (Matty Gale, being of the sheet-and-halyard school, could not forgive Firkin for converting a noble vessel like a Skaffie – noble because the Skaffie leant heavily upon a heavenly wind to blow her on course to a righteous living – into a yacht for his own unrighteous pleasure.)

For the rest of that day the women stayed out, wandering back only when Benjie Firkin promised to look into their grievances. Maybe if he looked into the agitator who was behind it all, if he were to make an example of her to show others the errors of their wreckers' ways, he might cure not only all of their grievances with one crack of the whip, but some of the world's as well. She was turning into a proper firebrand, that Gale girl; getting a shade too pink round the gills, if you were to ask the yard manager. She had caught that foreign bug, that vile murrain from the ungodly East, and caught it bad. If he, Benjie Firkin, did not keep an ear to the ground-swell, the bug could spread to the other yards, maybe to the fleet itself.

While the bosses saw Hannah in this new light, the prickly light of a red dawn, the flaming light of a crusader's torch, the lasses closest to her merely shook their heads, unable to see her in any other light but the shady old twilight of a reckless liver whose tub-thumping and flag-waving, far from signifying a burgeoning political conscience, were just another calculated caprice of a shipwrecked heart. Why, they asked themselves with a sigh, should a broken heart be set upon leading a broken life?

Not even when Hannah told them that she was putting things past for her providing, handselling her bottom drawer just as she had done when she was going steady with Johnny, were her room-mates won over to the prospect of her seriously mending her tumbledown ways. How could she be serious when she had known the fellow for ten short, tearaway weeks? To which present-iment she replied that they would have known each other for a year by the time she came down south next fishing, which was when they would be wed. A year with a long absence, even if that absence made the two hearts grow fonder, was still not long enough to allay the apprehension of her room-mates; and knowing as they did the new Hannah, hungry as she was to flesh out the unlicked bone of life, gutsier than any gutter-lass for life packed to the barrel-head, they feared that the way she was going, a red peril at work and a rough diamond at play, the bottom could fall out of that barrel long before her silver darling wedding next autumn fishing.

*

That there was to be no next autumn fishing for Hannah became clear to the whole of Brenston by the middle of the following summer. Some people said that it was the doing of Benjie Firkin, branding her a troublemaker and poisoning her name over land and sea. Hannah herself blamed it on the salt stinging her skin, and while it would have been no surprise if the odd finger had started to go the way of her mother's hands, it had to be taken with a pinch that Hannah was suffering more than many another fair hand at the farlans, not to mention the packers with their festering sores. While there were people who saw a grain or two of truth in both accounts, those closest to her knew that Yarmouth was where she had not so much burnt her fingers as seared her heart. You could sheathe your fingers in cloths, but no medicine chest known to man contained a dressing that could be applied round the heart to protect it from the knife wounds of life.

These wounds she could to some extent soothe in Yarmouth with the balm of fresh friendships; whereas in Brenston they were open and rendering and the only medication to hand was that mixture which was as traditional as sin, as old as the dew on the mountain: the mixture of barley grains, peat-reek, burn water and yeast that the gutters from the land of the simmer dim called *uisge beatha*. The lass who once had rebuked her younger brother for whistling on a Sunday, who once had accused her elder sister of the height of recklessness for cutting her nails on a Tuesday, could be seen every day bar the Sabbath (and then only because the bar was closed) gulping back her proprietary medicine in her favourite drug-shop. She who had been burning the torch at both ends – a flambeau at work and a flame at play – became a torch herself, burning her guts out in that cross between a glorified soakaway and a civic spittoon, that hole in the wall that Johnny had been barred from crawling back into, the Quayside Inn.

Hannah of the Five Tides was dead, drowned by Hannah of the Sea of Sorrows.

Where they had talked in loud whispers about her before, they now went plunging in with sharpened knives. She was shorn of all standing or common decency as they stripped her naked, so naked that they left her with barely a blush on her cheeks. She had mortally wounded the honour of the Gales; she had sunk so low that she had to look up to see the dregs. She would have shoed the Devil's hoof, they said, for the price of a dram. She was a skate – the skate being a slithery jade that lived on the bed of the sea and had its mouth where other, more respectable creatures had their belly and was nicknamed the bedroom fish. Country folk come to town heaped upon her their own spadefuls of dirt, according to which every haystack for miles around bore the imprint of her body; just as every Quaysider, as a patron of that holey bar was called, was rumoured to have tried her out as a ground-sheet. Such a name was she making for herself that even her old gutting cronies began to see her as no longer a witeless soul caught in a tangled net of love, but as a denizen of the lower depths, and as such a poor catch for any man. And it was with a pain that all but put out of its misery a pining memory that they shook their heads when they heard the pious proclaim that she had caught the 'godless disease'.

She might well have caught the heartless or soulless disease as well, the way she traipsed and trolloped through the town, all tricked up like a dyed kipper with nowhere to go but the Quayside Inn. The Painted Lady, the more polite called her. And because there was not another hymn out of her, because never again, not in a month of Sundays, would she go to church (though it had become, so leprous in its morbidity was the split between her and it, more a question of could than would), the kirk busybodies rechristened her Jezebel.

Jezebel of the painted face and the bones fit only to be fed to the dogs. Jezebel whom the eunuchs threw out of the window for the horses to trample underfoot. No curer in town would fix Hannah up to gut or pack his herring and, had there been one glaikit enough to do so, no clean-minded lassie would have had her in her crew. Who could trust the likes of *that*? Not even her mother any more; not even to go to the baker's for broken biscuits or to the butcher's for a threepenny bone.

As cold-bloodedly as Hannah had turned her back on the herring, the herring had turned its back on Hannah. Publicly and privately Brenston had disowned her. She had become a taboo, shut out of decent, wholesome lives as if she had four trotters, bristles, a curly tail and grunted. Such a beast of bad presage that a man meeting her on his way to his boat began to take it as a sign only a shade less unfavourable than that presented by a reverend casting a shadow over one's path on one's way to the fishing. Brenston's cold shoulder shivered in the presence of Hannah's colder heart.

And yet possessed though she was by some kind of demon, if not a whole crew of demons, and with a wildness in her eyes and ways that was not of their world, there were still a hoary few who were willing to forget her trespasses in the light of her grandfather's transgressions as a cooper. For no mortal man or woman could have strayed more from the straight and narrow than he who made barrels, every one of which had a side as swollen as a sail in a bellyful of wind. Old Tubby Gale – now there was a no-good bad 'un, there was a soul as warped as the timbers of the Devil's coalshed. What man worth his pickle of salt would have turned his poor, trachled wife into a one-woman bairn factory because that was how he liked his women – pregnant as his barrels?

5

Johnny drank to the herring.

To the silver darling, the world's sweetheart.

He had sued and pursued her, she had lured and caught him. One entangled indivisibly in the other. An unbroken romance. Nothing intoxicated Johnny more than the herring. For all too brief a spell every year his heart beat as one with hers. She was the light of his life; the answer to a fisherman's prayer.

Love-affairs flowered and faded. Towns peaked and troughed. Nations fell in and out with nations. And yet did the darling herring hold high her head above it all.

Bigger than any boy, bigger than any girl, bigger than any boy's love for any girl was the herring. If there remained only one more fish in the sea for the boy who had split up with his girl, that fish would have to be the herring. The silver minion from whom there could be no estrangement. The loyal, royal herring. The first and last prize for any lad worth the salt in his porridge, a man's living treasure, the light of his eyes, his burning passion when all other passions were long since spent.

Ingratiating herself to him, a siren with a song of hope fulfilled, she had swept Johnny off his sea-legs. He ate, slept and drank her. He lived for her. She had enslaved him. And such was his veneration for this spoiled darling that he humbled himself before her.

Wooed by the world and his girl friend, the herring as she appeared to Johnny was such a winsome creature that if a man could have been dispassionate about it he would have seen the relationship as more than a blind date, more than a love-affair that never soured, more than an engagement, more than an arranged match; rather was it a contract demanding of him the consecrated allegiance of matrimonial bondage. The herring was of Johnny's bone, flesh of his flesh. He had taken a vow that was for better rather than for worse, since generation after generation had signed over their lives to the selfsame partner, and the marriage that had been passed down the line and the troubled centuries had lost none of its fascination and less of its flavour.

That such a marriage was indissoluble was a conviction of Johnny's born of the miraculous survival of the most hunted animal in the sea, one whose powers of regeneration would have put the phoenix to burning shame. If to every thing there was a season, to every autumn there was a tint of herring. Twelve million hundredweights landed the year before the *pickelhaube* put all Europe in a pickle – one hundredweight for every family in Britain. More than a thousand million of them caught last harvest and now, glutting the same incorruptible green sea a year later, another thousand million. And every one as welcome as the rain after a drought. Truly, in Johnny's eyes, could the world have touched its cap to such a high and mighty throne. And acknowledged, as the old patriarchs did, that the herring was there by divine appointment. Every one a silver penny from heaven. For God so loved the poor that He gave the herring to feed them.

Gave with such overflowing charity that it was their breakfast, dinner and tea. Summer and autumn they would live off the fresh herring; come winter and spring, their heads would never be out of the barrel in which they had put by fish salted the previous autumn. Dished up as the Highlander's two-eyed steak, the herring was more nutritious than meat, eggs or milk and three times as good for you as cod. Miss Macarran taught him that. Having gorged the sun-soaked plankton, the herring abounded, she said, in the vitamin that gave growing children sound bones. Such wholesomeness tantalised the stinking rich; so that that which stopped the hungry cries of the anonymous poor provided His Grace the Duke of Argyll with breakfast. In the bluest of blue-blooded circles the classless herring moved, gracing the most polished of tables. As a life-sustaining diet, the salted herring was as much at home in the impoverished cottage as it was in the besieged castle.

She fair exulted in the herring, did Miss Macarran.

Lent, she announced to the class one spring day. The time of the beholding of the lilies of the field. The time of penitence. When the sinners of Europe, remembering their Saviour's fast in the wilderness, eschewed meat and held body and soul together by eating salt fish instead. The springtide of the herring. Those forty days of lenten fast were feast days of the herring. The Festival of Saint Clupea Harengus, beginning on Ash Wednesday and ending on Easter Day. Well might the herringfolk have commemorated it, the thought later occurred to Johnny, by moving their Protestant lips to prayer for the Pope and all his orders. Well might they have prayed on Fridays, too; for every Friday was a day of fast, when Catholic Europe opened its great gullet to receive the two-eyed steak.

Lo, was not that which was good for the soul said also to minister to the sinful flesh? Miss Macarran had not felt obliged to tell him that. Sex-starved sailors who ate their herring raw were supposed to be haunted by visions of beautiful girls. And how did they eat her? In penitential sorrow or in anticipation of sexual ecstasy, there was only one way to eat the herring: from tail to head. Eat her the other way round, as the buyers did when they were sampling the catch, and shoals yet uncaught were liable to turn tail, forsake their hallowed haunts and stay uncaught for the rest of the season.

Show me, Johnny would often ask himself the rhetorical question, show me the fish that has made a bigger ripple across the face of Europe. Inspirer of wars and not a few rumours of wars. Feeder of invading armies. A greater influence on the health and wealth of nations than the coffee-bean or the tea-leaf or the spices of the Orient. *He who draws a fish out of the sea draws a piece of silver*. Johnny liked that. And yet the wise man who said it would have been no less wise had he said: 'He who draws a silver fish out of the sea draws a piece of gold.' Humble, the herring? Maker and unmaker of nations. Creator of piers and villages and fleets and companies and bodies local and national and busybodies governmental and inter-governmental. Mobiliser of more ships at Yarmouth than assembled at Troy to fetch back Helen. Exported to Riga and Königsberg and Stettin and Danzig and Hamburg and Rotterdam. Pickled for Ireland, salted for the Baltic, smoked for the Levant. Her guts sold to farmers for manure. The little fish that carried towns on her back. Towns like Brenston, whose every kirk was a landmark, if not a seamark, to the glory of the herring and of God.

She was worthy of a man's worship. Every inch, every mesh-inch, of the way. And in his way Johnny worshipped her as other men worshipped the sun or the stars. He honoured and obeyed her. His belief in her was absolute. How he sighed for her at the start of every season. His devotion was such that he could have decked with flowers the sea in which she swam. And yet he had cause to fear her as some folk had cause to fear their Maker.

For on that shimmering, star-shot sea to the south the entire human firmament of the north had, since the first glint of the commercial fishery, pinned its hopes.

Young men rocked themselves to sleep counting the crans. Older hands, dyed fast in the colours of autumn as the most fruitful time, slept secure in their vision of the killing to be made. Yarmouth, for one skipper at least, would be a grand piano lashed down in the hold of his boat, like the lamb he had bought at a market during the northern fishing and brought home last spring. Barrel-chested lasses, when they were not gutting or packing the catch, would be keeping one eye skinned for new knitting patterns and the other for gewgaws and Hogmanay handsel. Anxious mothers, scarting around for the means to clothe their families in the winter, leant heavily upon the autumn windfall. Stay-at-home daughters, already love-knotted, would be hitched and spliced when their golden darlings returned on the crest of the fruitful wave. Children, no sooner having waved their sugar-candy daddies off to the Sea of the Silver Hoard, were driven to the edge of the pier with impatience for a doll (the kind that went to sleep when you laid it down); or maybe it was the year of the roller-skates, or the tricycle, or the model ship. While in their dreams their mothers would hold out their hands for their handbag; or maybe it was walldogs, or a harmonium, or, if the moon was blue, the wind to raise a bonny new house with all the mod cons. And for all except grandmother, who had little stomach for it and no teeth, there would be rock candy with the legend *Yarmouth* running through its core like a code, a watchword, a shibboleth in letters of sweetest, deepest red.

That was the herring Johnny drank to. And loved. And to which he had dedicated his life with a deep, undying faith.

There she sails, strong as a mackerel in a herring sky. A moon the size of an arle-penny. A moon ahead of her orbit. A moon too soon, a moon as unripe as green cheese.

A sudden qualm holds Johnny back from looking at her full in the eye. She's bonny the nicht, he mutters to himself, content with basking in her reflected glory in the mirror of the sea. That reflection is enough to turn a man's head, to make even a drouth like him love the moon more than moonshine. She's a silver darling herself, that one, he thinks with a rare tenderness in his heart. Hunting the clouds while the herring hunts her. The sea creature's land of dreams.

She's a mad, mad moon tonight; mad as a bat in a moth-eaten sky. Her pull on the waters the pull of a flame to a moth; her hold on the herring that of a lodestone on iron filings. Just as the mackerel is carried away by the wind, so is the herring seduced by the merry moonlight. Mix a full moon with a high tide and the result is firewater. It goes to the herring's head, makes her as high as the wind's eye; lit up to her gills she is like a soak on a Saturday night.

If Johnny were one for tattoos he would have the herring on his left arm and the moon on his right. Miss Macarran never ever mentioned the moon. Mysterious, he thinks to himself this night, after all her fine spiel about the herring. Would she have mentioned Punch without Judy? Johnny was long left school before he began to learn about it as a man whose life was influenced by it should. And he was still learning.

Never point your finger at the new moon, he remembers his mother telling him, and she was pointing a finger at him when she said it. Never let me see you looking at the new moon over your left shoulder, he remembers her chiding him on another occasion when in his moon-eyed innocence he had done just that. And there was yet another time when, a penniless limb of Satan though he was, she told him to remember to turn the silver coins in his pocket when he saw the new moon, because by so doing his wealth would increase as the moon went from silver to gold. It was to be many new moons before Johnny was rich enough to have a silver coin in his pocket to turn. Meanwhile his mother would not cut her nails or her corns under a waxing moon for fear that, as the moon grew, so would her nails or her corns.

Sometimes his mother was given to weaving spells of words. He would be toddling home with her from a visit to his deydie, as he called his maternal grandfather who lived at the wind-scrubbed, wave-washed northern end of the town, when all of a sudden she would give the jumpy little hand that she held in hers a tug, and look up and give mouth to 'I see the moon and the moon sees me, God bless the fishermen on the sea'. Johnny was to hear many another litany, and hear of many a stranger cantrip, as the shepherds of the sea made their ritual observances to the moon to protect their stocks.

Around that ball of herring-light he for one had placed a girdle of glory so that he might feed the fire in his soul as he prayed for a deluge of herring.

Beckoned by that beacon to these waters on this braw, bright, moonlight night, the *Lunar Venture* and the *Lunar Rainbow*, the *Lunar Bow* and the *Starbright*, the *Moonbeam* and the *Argentine* and the *Diana's Dawn* are names shining forth as they dip a solemn bow to her that begat them and watches over them now with an eye made more mysterious by its being ahead of its orbit, the green eye of a yellow goddess.

Johnny is struck by that moon. To the farmer she may be no more than a round disc the size of a cheese, but to the fisherman, startled out of his wits though he may be when that cheese is green with prematurity, as she is this mad and magical night on the southern sea, she is never less than a host crying 'herring, herring, herring'.

6

'Hair'n!'

It is as though the sky has fallen in and the stars are swimming for it. In the twinkling of an eye the sea has been transmuted from deadest lead into quickest silver. Johnny, one minute in his bunk reading a wild Western, and the next on deck gazing at what looks like gunsmoke on the water, draws a fast breath.

'Hair'n!'

There is such an eerie beauty before a silver strike that for a blinding moment all that the fisherman can do is catch his breath. Johnny's skin bristles; his heart leaps. His eyes scaled with herring-light, he rakes the moon-charmed waters.

This night the sea is burning. It is sprinkled with radium salts as well as spangled with stars. It is strewn with sequins and sapphires and emeralds, all dancing in a frenzy on the deck of the sea. This night a vapour is rising: air bubbles form a haze as if Neptune himself were heaving great fiery breaths into the frosty air. Phosphorescence may be the glow-word for this phenomenon, but in the breast of every man who is privileged to behold it there glows another, unuttered response to such unutterable beauty. If Johnny has a word for the glow, it is that it is one of the wonders of the deep.

Even as it warms the soul, this fire in the water, it chills the flesh. Johnny can feel the goosepimples rising

under his oilskin. It is a queer kind of tryst when the
moon is wooing the tide; and queerer still when the king
of the sea (as the pilot herring's pursuers commonly
address him) is courting the queen of the night, and the
waters are crowned with glory.

A scatter. A blue flash. They are coming up for the
swim, they that dive by day and rise by night. Swim up,
my darlings. Swim up, my dearies. There is enough
herring to fill one of the craters, if not one of the seas, of
the moon.

It could not be more unearthly, the sight of these
ghostly hosts tormenting the waters until a level-headed
man is driven near to lunacy with the indescribable
magic, the unfathomable mystery, the providential
miracle of it all – it could not be more unearthly if it
were the vapour of a mind made delirious by the high
fever of the chase.

For half the night they had been groping in the dark.
Well might Skipper Croll of the *Bounteous* have hailed
the *Ocean Roller* with the cry that Captain Ahab
trumpeted from his ship of fate: 'Ahoy, have ye seen the
white whale?' With the same solicitation might he have
hailed the *Princess Mona*. And the *Silver Sovereign*. And
the *Cynthia III*. And any other boat that happened to be
passing in the course of a long and lengthening voyage
during which not so much vapour as might fill a wraith's
pipe had been seen on the surface of the sea. 'Hast seen
the white whale?' For to see the white whale is to see the
unforgettable: the leviathan shoals of herring.

If Skipper Croll were to nail to the mast a sovereign as
a prize for the first man that spots the herring, or even
the white whale that leads to the herring, the one who
would win it would be Skipper Croll. In Johnny's eyes
the skipper is like a bat at owl-light: the blind can see.
He is as moon-eyed as any Red Indian, as any bushman

of Southern Africa to whom hunting by night means hunting by sight. Skipper Croll has more than an eye for the herring, he has a nose and an ear for them as well. He can smell them out when he is asleep and, cupping his ear with his hand, he can hear them in the water when he is up and about, as an owl hears a mouse rustling among the leaves on the forest floor. Skipper Croll sleeps slit-eyed and with ears half-cocked; and when fishing by echo-location he will reel and roll and waver in his flight across the deck, a soundless shadow, not a tu-whit or a tu-whoo out of him, an owl on the prowl, up to his ear-tufts in nocturnal death-watch.

Johnny has herring-light in his eyes while Skipper Croll has it in his soul. A tame rooster by day, the skipper of the *Bounteous* becomes a game predator at night. Never has his singlemindedness been so singular. He has the haunted look of a hunter whose prey is preying on his mind. It is as if the king of the shoals has become for him what the white whale was to the avenging Ahab. All season he has been shaping as if to chase the elusive shoals round the globe, round perdition's flames if necessary, and, as testimony to his desire to catch them, part with a leg or an arm in the process. Not that Skipper Croll wants to behead the king herring: he seeks no more than to behold that mystical one who always gets away. He seeks no more than to find, and restore his faith in, that creature who is so strange that he could be the figment of a mind tethered to the man in the moon, that spook-fish with the tail of a rat and the snout of a rabbit, that kingfish with no bones or scales or teeth to call his own, in whom a bit of the shark and the fox dwells, and whose kinship with the water is such that once he is drawn from it he quickly dies. King Herring is a figurehead that an old loyalist will go out of his way to tip his cap to, a mysterious luminary whom he is impelled by legend to track down at all costs and, once he has found him, chuck him back into the sea for luck.

So desperate is the chase that the *Bounteous* is prepared to take up arms in order to capture the king, to take the lives of others in her quest for the silver hoard. A crack shot with a gun, the skipper shoots a gannet and opens it up to see if it has been dining at the king's table. Not a scrap of herring in its gizzard. In case the gannet is off its food or, plunging deeper into improbability, is a poor fisherman, he hooks up a cod and disembowels it. A dozen herring. Avast! Shedding the last vestige of the sheep's apparel that he wears ashore, Skipper Croll dons the clothing of a wolf. 'Call all hands!' It is as if Ahab has spotted the snow-white hump in the equatorial sea. Here is the cod to catch the whale to catch the leviathan shoals of herring. Open up the whale, the skipper wagers, and you will find a barrel of herring inside him. And so the *Bounteous* becomes a poor man's *Pequod*, and the hunt for the herring becomes a hunt for the whale with a barrel of silver salted away in a corner of that processing factory to which the human minnow gives the name of stomach.

On the look-out for what he calls appearances, Skipper Croll puts Johnny in mind of a whaler who has lost his way following the herring. A floating oil spot. A phossy look on the face of the deep. Sperm whales. Porpoises. Dogfish. Silvery gulls. Gannets. Gannets circling and then plunging. Gannets spewing up herring to lighten their load before take-off. With eyes that are harpoons the skipper scours the sea for the signs that say the herring has come up to play. No artist has a truer eye for the colour changes of the sea. No eye is more sensitive to those nuances that indicate a swim of herring. Not the kichie shade of brown which is the spit-image of baccy juice: no herring there. Not the reddish-brown of the feeding months: the herring is not yet in her prime. What the eye thirsts for and drinks in until it is glazed is the milky green of the oil spot that is given off when the throng is ripe for the kill.

Skipper Croll sniffs the wind. Nor-west. Not such a maker of catches as a blow from the south-west, but better than an easterly. How she loves to butt her head into the wind on her drift south, the great little sprat-whale of the North Sea. A wind on her tail, a northerly, just as surely holds her back as an easterly draws her away from the coast. Whithersoever the governor listeth, be the wind prevailing or unavailing, the herring swims into it. Into the wind, and the night, and the south she swims.

Swims in a shoal whose playground is miles long and miles wide and whose play transforms the face of the ocean. Two hundred herring for every cod that breathes. Johnny reckons that if every egg that the female lays on the stones of the sea's bottom hatched and matured, all the seas of the world, three-quarters of the globe, would be solid with herring in ten years. Partly because the haddock loves these sticky eggs, and partly because the cod takes to the spawn like a hungry child to tapioca pudding, it does not happen.

For from the time that she is but a seed on a stone the herring spends her short span running for her life. Disturbed by every fish that swims. Picked on by every sea-bird that flies. Guzzled by cod and whiting. Ravaged by seal, shark and dogfish. And hounded by the same mass killer that brought the buffalo to his knees. What man catches is but a morsel to the mammoth meal laid on for fish and fowl. Johnny has seen the green eyes of the dogs in the dark, the heads and skeletons of the herring after the dogfish have savaged them. Such is the appetite of man and beast, or rather such is the beast in man, that he will not be satisfied until he reverses nature and there are two hundred codfish to every herring.

Skipper Croll sniffs the water. He rejoices at an appearance that is no less tangible for being invisible: the wind has dropped and it is milder and warmer now. It is more than he can do to stop himself baying as he strains to pick up the scent.

Open-mouthed over the rolling underwater meadows, a combine harvester bigger even than the whale shark, the *Bounteous* moves. The fleet a thousand strong from the north, and a thousand strong from the south, with a fair-sized armada from ports in between. All combining and converging at the Knoll. Masts and rigging in such profusion that it is as if a pine forest has taken root in the sea; a forest that has caught fire, for the fleet is more lit up than Brenston on bonfire night. If every boat were to lay her nets end to end they would be hauling up fish from the Paps of Jura to the Cape of Good Hope; if all the nets were stretched out in a line there would be enough to go round the moon, and what was left over might just about span the almighty Herring Pond itself.

For a couple of moons now at every dusk the pine forest has taken to the sea, and at every dawn it has returned. Every trip a race against the tide and the clock and the boat alongside; a race to the shoals, to the market, to survival. Skipper Croll and his crew, like every man afloat, have not been asking for the moon; just for the Sea of Fertility.

There. On the lee beam. Thar she blows. The great little sprat-whale of the North Sea. With the porpoise as your pilot, there can be no mistake. 'When you see him 'poise,' as the cannibal Queequeg might have said if he had sailed out of Yarmouth instead of Nantucket, 'then you quick see him 'erring.' Quick as a flash they see her. Beyond the milky sea to which the *Bounteous* has been drawn by the living torpedo that is already exploding on the target ahead – the porpoise, like Skipper Croll, likes his sea milky – the surface is like a furnace, the water burning, the herring-glare almost blinding the eyes of the crew. A shimmer. A swarm. A swim. Johnny can scarcely see the sea for herring. Floating, swimming islands of herring. A great ball of herring, God alone knows how many, maybe five hundred million in a square-mile dance; and with six square miles or so to a shoal, and a shoal three fathoms deep, the ballroom is crowded.

Johnny has seen nothing like it since he watched, in a rising gooseflesh of awe, a whale beating the water into a foam and spouting a cran of herring into the air, the silver fountain of fish glittering, before it tumbled down over the whale's back, in the last rays of a winter sunset, and the birds catching the glint and, while still on the wing, the herring. That day it seemed that the waves were made of birds and fishes. Stencilled upon the memory though that phenomenon is, the very sight of the herring at night is enough to make a man break out in gooseskin; for then is the common run phantasmical, the herring loving the dark as the vampire loves it, even if she hates the sight of blood as the other the garlic.

His eyes harpoons that have left the gun, Skipper Croll orders the *Bounteous* to shut off her engine. He orders the first net to be shot. 'Over for the Lord,' the crew chant, doffing their caps as though in prayer. They shoot their nets on the starboard side, according to The Book, according to John twenty-one, verse six. For a mile and a half their nets drift. It will be an hour or two before they pull them back in. Meanwhile, as the *Bounteous* drifts along on the tide, the crew wait. Looking over the side, Johnny can see the herring, clear as a brand-new shilling. He and his mates have cast into a sea of such solid silver that ordinary men like them would have been performing no miracle by walking upon it. As the *Bounteous* rides at her nets, Johnny fishes with hook and line for predatory cod.

His eyes drift to where, more moonish than the moon, the herring play. They spray one another with water, like a school of children gone potty with water pistols. They swim up to the nets and dart away like blobs of mercury. They flip out of the water and fly, high as a whale's eye, over the floating buoys. (Cod loup into the air after them like dogs begging for a bone.) Pieces of silver, pieces of silver, as Long John Silver's green parrot might have said if she had sailed on the *Bounteous* instead of the *Hispaniola*. Like children in a playground, the school make a noise while they play. Aye, she's bonny, richt bonny, the nicht, Johnny mutters to himself, his eyes aglitter, the moon a lantern hanging from the mast. King Solomon in all his glory was never arrayed like this sea. No crown or sceptre could hold a candle to it.

Catching the glint, the other boats dive in like birds with their tails on fire. Their rudders can hardly move for fish. Out here on this enchanted sandbank this mild and warmish autumn night you can pick the darlings up as easy as wink. Tomorrow they will be burying their light in the sand again at the bottom of a sea that by some strange alchemy whose formula eludes the net of man will have been transmuted back into basest lead.

Becalmed in a moon-glade, the *Bounteous* rides before a cloud steals up, a killer in the night smoring the moon's face with a pillow. How the bat-mad, fly-by-night herring loves it, Johnny reflects as he looks over the side. How he himself loves it. For a timeless moment he is full of the wonder and of the mystery of it all: the wonder of nature righting herself, obeying one of her own laws, so that a fruitless summer shall inherit the windfall of autumn and the season shall yet be crowned with glory; and the mystery of a fishery, the very apprehension of which brings on a shiver that might have come up from the depths of the briny kingdom itself, leading a man with a doubting cast of mind such as his into the temptation of half-believing that the migration of shoals, like the migration of souls, is guided by none other than the hand of the Supreme Fisherman Himself.

*

Wave after silvery wave. Engulfing the boat. Leaping, rushing waves of herring. Flooding the hold. Washing over the deck. Herring by the hundred, by the thousand, by the hundred thousand. Over the gunnels they come like white horses with the galloping fever. As if they have been driven into the nets by some supernatural beast of the deep and are now swimming to the safety of the boat. Swimming up in a solid silver tide. Nets so laden that the floating buoys have sunk out of sight under the weight of fish. Every net a killer. Every mesh of every net a diamond. Everything, everywhere, glistening.

Under the arc lamps and the moon Johnny hauls. Spits in his hands and hauls. Hauls and shakes the nets so that the herring scud through the air and down into the hold. Sneezing, one of them. Sneezing as she is pulled out of the water. As if she were catching a cold. Skipper Croll seizes with his gutsy talons the first fish that hits the deck. Male or female? Female. Good. Good season ahead, boys. And reaching for his bag-net, he catches the ones that try to get away. Improving the shining hour with that pole, he is. Trapped in his own thoughts like a man netting butterflies.

Bonnier than any butterflies, these herring glistening like diamonds in the killer nets. Golden and blue. Becoming dark blue and green. Then silver. Bluey and silvery, and fluorescent with it, like the sea. Changing colour, just like the sea. Golden tints when fresh out of the water, sides and back giving off a lustre, a kind of moon-glaze. Then silvery. On these same sides, and round their bellies, a silvery tinge. No Red Admiral ever sailed up like one of these silver-washed, swallow-tailed, scale-winged monarchs of the sea. Sail up, my dearies. My bonny, bonny dearies.

Just like a town out here at the Knoll. Lights as far as the eye can see. Lights and smoking chimneys. No room to swing a storm lantern. Look out there, *Starbright*, you'll foul your propeller on them there nets. Still they come. Leaping, crashing, spilling over the bulwarks. Ten hours. Fourteen hours. Still hauling. Johnny's arms ache. Drowned herring make the nets heavier. One net breaks away, sinks under the weight of the catch. Out of another net the belly falls, leaving only the ropes and floats. A third net has to be cut adrift lest the weight of it hauls the boat down with it. Stricken with conscience rather than stung into a largeness of heart, the *Bounteous* hails the *Laurel Bough*. Would ye like a net? Under the strain of her own burden the *Laurel Bough* creaks. Aye, well, all right, then, we'll make room for it. A third of a million herring she must have in her hold already. Just like us. Fifty tons deadweight.

They'll talk about this. This jackpot. Giving them away. In pub and pew they'll talk about it. Heaven-sent, they'll say with a pitch of the head and a roll of the eyes. Heaven-sent at the eleventh hour. East Anglia shaking like Lebanon with the fruit of righteousness. At the eleventh hour of the season. They'll drink to it in The Three Bloaters. Drink to the year that the sun came up and the sun went down and they were still hauling. Johnny will drink to it himself. Here's to that braw, moonbright night at the tether-end of as gutless a season as you ever did see: when one acre of sea was worth a hundred acres of land: when we hauled for more than fourteen hours without stopping to blow our noses, and we could no more find the will to wipe the scales from the mug of tea that we pressed to our lips afterwards than we could find the power to wash our hands before falling over into our bunks for a dose of sleep.

Them nets. See to them nets, Johnny. There's no room to stow them nets, skipper, they've done their job too well for their own comfort – there's no space for passengers, skipper. Then they'll have to cadge a lift back to port, Skipper Croll says, his eyes gorging three hundred or so crans. It's so hot amid all that herring oil, these nets will catch fire. Raise some steam, Iley. Benjie Firkin and his lasses are waiting for us on the quay. Home, James Iley, and don't spare the white horses.

7

All night they had toiled, and taken nothing. Moonshine, all of it. They had swum up, the shoals, but only in men's dreams. All season the dreamers had let down their nets to catch a draught of fishes, and all they had caught was a draught. From the straits of the south to the firths of the north and beyond to the sounds of the west they had known nothing like it: the year the herring sought a change of scenery: the year the imperial, immeasurable, imperishable herring, the unerring herring, went on a grand mystery tour: the year Yarmouth caught a cold and the north-eastern lung of Scotland went down with pneumonia.

All night, all season the *Bounteous* had rolled, her timbers had shuddered, Johnny had stood erect hauling, hauling for hours on end in the dead riggings of the night, and never a gleaming scale, never the sniff of a herring, just the endless hauling of black yarn (as Johnny called empty nets), wet and empty nets that piled up in the hold waiting to be sorted out on the way home.

Not a single porpoise had louped to the surface, not a solitary solan goose had dived beneath it. Where had all the whales and the dogfish, the gulls and the gannets gone? Not even the eagle, who was said to see a fish two miles up, could have spotted a flash of silver. Man and mammal, sea-bird and science – all had been groping in the dark. They might just as soon have looked for strawberries in the Dead Sea, or moonbeams in a coal-mine, or little red herring in the wood. Every month the moon had been reborn with a wooden spoon in her mouth. Every week the tears of men whom the herring had made spoiled darlings silvered the sea. Every day the boats, having done no more than wet their nets, returned like the tatterdemalion remnants of a beaten army.

It was as if the locusts had taken to the sea, swarming so that they obscured the moon and devoured the crop for miles around, turning the watery plains of East Anglia into a dust-bowl. Dry and clean as a husk was the *Bounteous*. No scales formed a silver skin on her timbers, no blood was there for Johnny to wash away from her deck. There was barely enough herring to fill his kerchief, scarcely a fry for the pan in the galley; and those that he did catch were so small he could have packed them in a matchbox. Seventy nets went over for the Lord one night; but were there three score and ten fishes landed? One herring. One mackerel. One garfish. Johnny could not say which was the longer – the gar's snout or Skipper Croll's face. Looking at the black yarn that he had just hauled out of the water, Johnny suddenly saw it in the nightmare light of a child, as just a lot of holes tied together with string.

Nowhere did the rumble of dawn resemble more the rumble of doom than along the Denes. Where had all the women, the women that sang as they toiled, gone? Along the wharves they gathered, hung around like half-shut knives, knitting their brows as though fashioning a face for doomsday. Two days' gutting out of thirty, one said, pulling her shawl about her face. More herring cured in one day in the north, a curer growled, than he had cured all season in the south. He would have to walk the four hundred or so miles home, or else float back in one of the tens of thousands of empty barrels.

A fair first week had ended with the weather taking a turn for the foul. It happened just when there was a prospect of middling catches, just as Skipper Croll was spoiling for a south-west wind, a bit of motion to stir up the grounds. High seas and higher winds kept the fleet in port. Over the whole of East Anglia there was not so much blue sky as would patch a pair of trousers for a tinker's bairn. In what the older skippers called Armistice Week the weather was more fitting to the mud of Flanders.

Autumn had turned over a new leaf: the year had shed a season, a law of nature had been abolished. Something had upset the regular rhythm of the shoals. What that something was, or rather what Skipper Croll was told it was, would have filled a cran basket. A woman had stepped over his nets; a change was working on the currents of the North Sea; hiding in the sand, that's where he would find the herring; God's judgement on the English for fishing on the Sabbath; gone back to the Baltic, where they belonged; and the doom-laden voice of the drunken deckie stretching a point as it held forth that a town built on sand could not stand.

Nearer to the drift, if not the trawl, of Skipper Croll's thinking was the school that argued that three times as many herring were caught by steam as by sail, which meant three times less herring in the sea, and that the trawlers, those spoilers of the sea, were sweeping up everything from the floor of it as if they were vacuum cleaners doing their spring cleaning, their sweepings fit for no more than pig or pet or trawl skipper. If a sea-bed is made for spawners, he argued, and that sea-bed is beginning to look unmade, for how much longer are your spawners likely to lie on it? Give the herring no rest during the day, and how can you expect her to come out and have a ball at night? Kill the babies, and how are you going to raise the grown-ups? It was infanticide, if not genocide. Rotten farmers these trawlermen would have made, slaughtering their cows when they were calving. And yet the rottenest farmer, when Skipper Croll came to think of it, had the horse-sense to put his cow back in the field if he did not like the price being offered for it, an escape hatch denied the fisherman, who could not throw his fish back in the sea and whistle them up again when the price was right.

Out of the sadness of the sea the land extracted a gladness as perverse as it was peculiar. Ever since man ploughed his first furrow upon earth and water it had been so. Never having sown, the fisherman had no right to reap. Thus spake the farmer like a true stepchild of the Lord. Maybe the fisherjocks would think again before beating their breasts about their fertile pastures and record harvests. Sink them, damned herringfolk. Eating all that salt fish was enough to make a body break out in leprosy. So much for their great fishery. Guided by the hand of God, my boot. Well, their God's failed them this time. He's dumped them like a load of dung on my doorstep. Mooching around the farm for a job, damned holy willies, on Monday. Like cats to the churn. Let them muck out the byre, Geordie.

Maybe the damned unholy country geordie had a point, Skipper Croll conceded. That there was a divine hand in it, as though God cared if there were five crans or five thousand, was a belief as blind as the assumption that the rest would do the stocks a power of good and that the landings would be all the bigger next season. There was as much divine hand guiding the herring as there was divine command in a monkey picking its nose. And yet the conviction was growing in Skipper Croll, growing out of a fear that he knew was not totally irrational, that these were the last days, that now was the winter of the autumn herring.

It was a winter that had set in a few world-shaking years ago when, just as the herring was coming up for the swim, the Bolsheviks seized the helm in the great October Revolution. It was a winter that had continued into the following autumn when the doves of peace exploded over the trenches on the Western Front. A world that had been up to its gunwales in war, civil and uncivil, was in no shape to haul back on board the herring that for the duration of hostilities it had abandoned. Mother Russia, whose tsarina-sized maw had opened up a bottomless market, had turned deepest red; while Germany, groaning with the hunger of tummies on the march, and paying for her consignments in currency so devalued that she sent it over in bales (cleaning out the curers, one of whom papered his house with Deutschmarks), was as good as dead. Flatter than Flanders or the steppes of Russia was the world of the herring in the wake of the war. And now, after everyone had pinned their faith on her surviving it, and had gathered to greet her as a conquering hero returned, she had gone missing, presumed dead. Or as those who began to see her as a judas-fish preferred it, shot as a deserter.

So clear was the bell that tolled the knell of the Knoll, and so muffled the roll of the name off the tongue, that Yarmouth unequivocally and undyingly engraved itself on the slab of remembrance, the town virtually becoming a place of the fallen, a resting place to be uttered in the muted tones of those stations of the little white wooden cross, Ypres and Arras and Mons and Verdun, a one-word epitaph running through the core of a nation's being.

How to scrape the barrel when the bottom has fallen out of it? How to face the winter if autumn never comes? For the herringfolk who knew what a wintry autumn was, there never had been one so wintry as this. Brenston was more than bumbazed: it was disembowelled. Just as the strong man shorn of his locks lamented his lost strength, so Brenston deprived of its herring wept for its departed glory. The decline of the whaling was as a glacier to the thunderbolt that was the fall of the herring. Greater than the slaughter of the whale had been the slaughter of the herring, who had been hunted in the wild and woolly east as the buffalo had been hunted in the wild and woolly west — until that which had seemed indestructible appeared wellnigh extinct.

One by one the boats crawled back from the south. Heading in despair for home, the more inconsolable crews were nagged by a feeling, almost a tugging, at the back of their minds that maybe the shoals would show up once the fleet was too far away to turn back. No such Devil's luck. Not even that could be offered in mitigation of a fishing whose only scrap of comfort for its prosecutors lay in their being reunited, albeit in the embrace of empty hands and full hearts, with their loved ones. Hoping against hope, a few boats stayed on in the south, scouring an empty sea; their crews could not afford to come home, those who returned said. And if those who returned had more tears in their eyes than tar in their hair, that simply told of the sorrow that had been on the sea.

Everybody was weighed down as by some unbearable cross. Not only had they failed to make enough sustenance to ride the storms of winter: they came home with less money than when they had left, the paying out of expenses plunging the share men deep in the red, so deep that the whole coast was up to its cliff-tops in debt, all credit having been exhausted save from the piggy bank, a raid on which in the hours of slumber looked as likely as did a petition in the morning to the Government to bail them out.

One by one the trains, too, slunk back. Could these be the same chuffers that were packed with the same women who had been over the moon with themselves as they larked and lilted their way south ten interminable

weeks or so ago? These ghost trains? What kind of ill
had got into them that they returned with no presents,
no fairings, no 'Yarmouth' for the kids? You would have
to be a schoolteacher or a dentist to see any good in such
contrariety, to appreciate the blessing that was disguised
in the promise of a lot less toothache about, a lot less
peppermint breath, thanks to all those boatloads of rock
candy that were not to be, that would not now be doled
out to the kids.

Ghost ship and ghost train steamed home to what in
their absence had been, and would continue to be long
after their return, a ghost town. Everybody was
suddenly living under a shadow as of some great
disaster at sea. Not only had the autumn fishing become
sad: it seemed that man no longer held dominion over
the creatures of the deep. Brenston had lost more than
its living. It had lost also its soul.

Famine rose out of the sea and stalked the land. Its
gaunt shadow fell over the town. Under a sky as inky as
the vasty, empty deep people mooned around, helpless
as herring out of water. It was the end, the old men said,
the same old men who had seen the decline of the
whaling, their backs as bent now as the blade of a
cooper's adze, and their tongues as blunt as the hammer
end of it. It was the end of the world as the herringfolk
knew it.

Young men bowed their backs, too, as though laid low
by some crippling shame upon which had been served a
crucifying judgement. Young men who had set off as
tanned as the lugsail of a Zulu, only to return as pale as
the moon; who had come back cleaned out save for a
few shifts of underwear for their mothers or their wives
to wash: a kistful of dirty linen where their mothers and
wives had expected a kistful of silver. All of them had
fallen in the midden glowering at the moon.

To return home without having earned enough salt for your porridge; destitute of the means to pay for the knitting wool got on tick from the shop; when you could not find a herring to eat even as an act of penance on a Friday: it was enough to drive the sons of those Highlanders whom the Clearances had driven to the coast and thus to the herring back to the land of their fleeced fathers; it was enough to drive a body to the poorhouse.

Damned herringfolk, the farmer muttered, as always, the farmer who did not know what it was like to wake up one morning to find his land turned to barren waste. Let them live, damned holy willies, on bread-sops. Bread-sops being a distinct spectre as they waited for God to send down food, borne on the beaks of ravens.

Had Brenston not prided itself on its being able to hold out indefinitely in a siege on the strength of the herring salted away in the barrel at the back of every house? Well, Brenston was under siege now.

And what then, when the siege barrels were scraped hollow? They would eat the mussels and the limpets gathered as bait for the winter haddock lines. Hunger being a sharp hook, they would swallow their superstition and poach for rabbits, the farmer's foe becoming the fisherman's friend. They would eat seagulls, if only they could catch them. Half an egg once a week on Sundays from now on if they were lucky. They might even stoop so low as to drink the cat's milk. Or eat a bread poultice that in less stricken times they would have served up as dressing for a wounded hand.

Not that there would be bread for poultices. Soon the last loaf would be under the knife; and the kids like sparrows with a tapeworm as they pecked at the crumbs that fell from it; the kids so thin that before long they would be able to slip through the mesh of a herring net. Flour bags would become dresses and old coats would be turned into trousers. Weddings arranged for the end of the season would be rearranged for another, better time. Whenever, if ever, there was a better time.

What could they have meant, the canny folk of Brenston, by throwing all those coins on to the decks before the boats started out for the south? Luck? Pitching and tossing away on an old wives' tale all that hard-gotten siller. If they had saved their luck-pennies for the arrival back of the fleet rather than the departure, every boat in the town would have been that less worse off. Maybe folk thought that they could buy the herring. If the herring could be bought the skippers would be richer men than they were now; they would not have to go grovelling after the money-box under the bed, a misfortune that for some was as painful as losing an eye-tooth. Blessed were the skippers that had a few bawbees in brine, a bit laid by against the day when the seas dried up.

No matter how long it would last, this particular rainy day, no matter that the mothball money would not stretch to the next pot of broth, the old men would rather see themelves hanging from a yardarm than go on the parish relief. Not for them the workhouse. What if they could no longer chew the quid and spit baccy-bree in the world's face, as a fulmar spits food into an intruder's? They would light up a bit of broken old herring basket and smoke that. And as they sucked and puffed they would look out to sea and let their famished eyes feast on the memory of the Zulus making flat out for home, racing one another, breaking records as if they were tea clippers on the China run. They had something to race home to, the Zulus. Then up at the great canvas that was the sky the old men would look, as if waiting for a light to break through. And when no light broke they would retire indoors to their bread-sops, or rabbit stew, or boiling of mussels, or seagull pie. And round off their day with a prayer. If only He would send a wreck ...

Young men could not wait for old men's prayers to be answered; they would be wrecks themselves before the wreck came. They could not allow themselves to rust and rot like their gear; they could not eat the bread of idleness; they could not live on the slate for ever. And so to the land they would look, to the farmer who was as willing as the good earth itself to dish up their bread-sops in return for a fair darg. There was aye the odd orra job around the farm. Well might the extra-orra men of Brenston be glad, as the prodigal son was glad, to go into the fields to feed that abomination, that unmentionable, the curly-tailed creature of which, given the prevailing luck of the fishing, they were in no fit state to speak. Glad might they be to fill their bellies with the husks that these sinful old grumphies, these unclean spirits of the farmyard, ate.

However grieved to the guts they were, young men could not afford to mole about at home, visionless as a threepenny bit in a clootie dumpling; there was nothing else for it but to jump to it like a flea in an army blanket. They would gather whelks. They would dig ditches. They would mend holes in the road. They would take up pick and shovel and help to build a promenade in the town. And those among them with a half-blind belief in such things would set a barrel alight and roll it along the quay to bring back their luck. For when all else had failed, when all that science and its lights, all that the natural world could do was to stand and shake its bamboozled head at the herring, it was time to renew an old nodding acquaintance with the rum ways of one's forefathers.

PART TWO

Tongue of Flame

One of the last of the armada to set sail from Brenston for the open sesame that was Yarmouth, and one of the first to point her crestfallen bow for home, the *Bounteous*, her name as empty now as her hold, was butting through lumbering, lambent seas when Johnny Hallows went up on deck to try to catch a glimpse of the morrow before turning in for the night.

And he saw the moon.

Never had he seen her so braw, so bonny. She was brawer than the fieriest ball of herring-light; bonnier than all the herring, the ghostly galaxies of herring, that he had been reaching out for and never finding all season. Surely this was not the same lure that had failed to raise a fish at the Knoll? How could such a lantern have no magic in it; how could such a moon look down on less than a bumper harvest? Johnny stared at her in benumbed and benighted dumbfounderment.

Restless in his perplexity, he tried to look away from her, only he could not. He who had wooed her and lost – was he about to be wooed by her and won? Hare-brain that she was, she was trying to snare him. Not content with ravishing the senses, she had to snatch a body's soul. And so she pulled him towards her, drew him to her in a stark, staring-mad frenzy of possession.

He began to feel unsafe, unsteady, as though he were astride a floating log. He was lost. He was at sea in a

sieve. They were all lost. They were all at sea in a sieve.
Only the thickness of a plank lay between him and
eternity. He shivered like a plucked goose.

Astride his log or aboard his sieve, he seemed to be
drifting out into some unknown sea, its waves pulling
him towards them. His head swam. With eyes as full as a
cat's in midnight heat he stared at the moon. Gooseflesh
was rising all over his body. The sun by day, the moon
by night. Behold the moon walking in brightness. He
appointed the moon for the seasons. The heavens
declaring the glory, the moon the handiwork. One day
the moon would cease to shine, the stars would fall to
earth, the earth would quake and the heavens tremble,
the sea and the waves would roar, the sky would roll up
like a scroll and darkness would fall upon the whole
wide wicked world.

Lord, help us.

How small the herring was. How small was man. If
the herring could vanish off the face of the sea like that,
could not man and his world disappear at the flick of a
magic wand? With a sudden jerk Johnny's eyes were off
the moon and drifting over the heavens, the glorious
heavens, until they came to rest restlessly upon the
water. Whereupon, for the first time in his life, the
scales fell from his eyes. And he saw, as it were, a sea of
glass mingled with fire.

In a flash in the night, in the twinkling of an eyeless
sea it came. The light. Not the stuff that blinds; not a
liquid whiteness, not an earthly light; but an illumi-
nation of which the physical was a wishy-washy
reflection. In the deeps of the night and on the surface
of the sea it came, an inward thing that made the soul
luminous, burning with more fire than a shoal of
herring in a Brenston skipper's sweetest dream. For a
moment that surely was for ever Johnny and the
Bounteous were encircled in that light. There descended
a great calm in which, instead of rolling about in

moon-infested waters, man and boat seemed to have found a haven between the waves, a rapturous shore somewhere beyond the seas.

If he had caught the moon in his net, or somehow had landed on deck her reflection in the water, it would not have been a more exquisite moment. He was like a flower that opens at night. Everywhere he looked his eyes were full of a serene radiance. Gazing into the distance, he lifted his eyes up as though to some delectable mountains of the sea. If his legs were feeling slightly watery, it was not because he was afraid so much as filled with awe. For he knew that it was not the moon that was turning his head, it was not the moon that he was bending like a moonflower towards – giver of new life, mother of twice-born children though she was. It was not the light of the sky nor of the sea that was breaking for him. It was that light which is the shadow of the infinite.

Such was the tingle of awakening in him that the moon seemed to wax ever brighter and the stars to burst out singing. Johnny thought he could hear trumpets. An unsung chord in him had been struck. He was seeing the moon, the stars, the sea, the boat, life, himself – he was seeing all things in a purer, lighter light than ever before. If the moon was in his eyes, the sun was in his soul. His whole being glowed.

Was this the light that Paul had seen, that had appeared unto Constantine, the great emperor of his schooldays, as a cross in the sky? Was this the light that had shone for many a heavily laden traveller stumbling his stone-blind way from darkness to deliverance? In a flash he knew that he, too, was being lit as a candle, if not as a flare, for the cause of light and life and joy and peace. He called on his Maker, cried aloud the name that for the first time he was not using as an oath, and was comforted. He wanted to bear witness to this light, to this night, even unto the great day of wrath when there would be no need for the sun and the moon – the one doomed to turn black as a tar-barrel, the other red as the blood of a herring – for the city of the future would be lit by the light of the Lamb. Lord, lead us to that light.

He was on his knees when they found him, feeding the fish that had refused to feed him, or such was the thought that passed through their minds as they shouted to him to lay off the Auld Kirk, the moonshine, when his stomach was seceding like that. Johnny remained riveted on his knees, mute and motionless as a bollard. They wandered up to him and, putting a drop more concern into their inquiry, asked if there was something ailing him. He moved neither lip nor limb. They looked qualmishly at each other before one of their number, Sauty the cook, laid his hand on his stricken shipmate's shoulder and, bending down and in a voice wavering on the edge of alarm, inquired again if he was all right. At which point Johnny slowly raised his head and opened his eyes, and as they peered down into them they knew that these were not the eyes of a man under the weather and far less under the influence. These eyes were too big, too bright, too moonshot for that; the fire in the water had entered into them, it was as if they had seen a vision of all the herring in the sea. This creature on his knees before them glowed with a phosphorescence that had been missing from their lives since last autumn.

They ran their eyes over him and then through him as if he were some strange fish that had been dragged up from the deep. What could it be, they wondered; what was it that was ailing him? Johnny Hallows. He of all people. On his knees on the deck. In the middle of the North Sea. In the middle of the night. Glowing. If he was communing with the spirits, these spirits of his were not distilled in this world. The firewater was not in his belly, it was in his soul; his face was pickled more in thought than in the unholy water. No, not thought. Rather was the old wanton not thinking so much as praying some matter over. Could that matter, they secretly asked themselves, each man not daring to address the question to other than himself, so inevitable and at the same time inexplicable was it, could that matter be his herring-starved soul? Could it be that he was vomiting up the sins of a lifetime?

It was a question calling for a little praying over itself. They stared down into Johnny's eyes. It was not his staring beyond them that was disturbing them so. They noticed a clamminess about him that so filled them with awe it distanced them from him, held them at bay as if he were a castaway in the throes of some unidentified fever. What if it was a fit he was having, an epileptic seizure? There was no man on board to hold him down. Strange that none of them had heard the epileptic cry; and yet what they were all seeing, was it not mightily like the ecstasy that was said to follow convulsions?

After a silence in which it was every man to his own jalousings, a voice rose out of the moonlit dark and said, with a hint of inspired desperation, that there was such a thing as moonstroke. Involuntary as a shiver, one man looked over his shoulder at the moon and then down again at Johnny. That was it. He had been mooning himself on the deck, as others might sun themselves; he had been bathing his soul in all that lunar moonshine. Was he not looking a shade blue round the gills? Throw him a cold towel for his head, somebody. And still they went on shaking their heads, all six of them, until, after more puzzling over what fearful affliction it might be if it was not the fits or moonstroke, somebody said that if he was feeling as low as that it might be better for everyone if he went down below for a while.

As for Johnny, he had neither ears nor eyes for any of it, so deep had he drunk of the spirit and so stiff with the mysterious libation had he become. Not a flicker of

concern passed over his face or his frame; not a
murmur of shock or shame was heard to come out of
him. And this despite their having caught him, actually
stumbled into him, on his knees on the deck in the
middle of the night and the North Sea, a heap of
helplessness like a sacrificial lamb. Could it be that the
lion was turning into a lamb; that Johnny had lost the
old identity by which he had known them and had
found another? Rather was the shiver of shame theirs
as, in a cold flush of pricking solemnity, it came to them.
They who had never laid eyes on the miracle of
childbirth were privileged to be witnessing, with those
pangs that are the natural offspring of empathy, the
miracle of rebirth in the womb of a new dawn.

No sooner had the light broken through, and they
began to bask in the wondrousness of the sight, than
Skipper Croll appeared in their midst and hovered over
the kneeling Johnny and said:

'It's too late for prayer – the herring's roasting in hell.'

As if the last word was a bell ringing out in his soul,
Johnny stirred; he raised his head yet higher, and then
his hands, and slowly he rose to his feet; he turned
around and, with the lightest of steps, and as if obeying
a still small voice in the reclaimed wilderness of his
heart, slipped past them, silent as the shadow of a
sleepwalker, inviolate as a dreamer who has caught and
enwrapped himself in his glimpse of tomorrow, and
went back down below to his bunk.

Into the hours of the morning watch he sat at the cabin
table, a pool of invisible light in the darkness. His
crew-mates, dog-tired after all their nights of feverish
chase and failure, were asleep with their clothes on in
their bunks. Johnny himself was feeling no less tired,
only he dared not close his eyes for fear of losing the
ecstatic vision that was in them. So ecstatic was that

vision that, although he had knelt alone on the deck for an eternity, it had seemed but a glorified moment. It was as if he had been confined for years in a dark room and had just woken up to find the sun streaming through the window. Roused from such an unenlightened sleep, the soul is in no state to surrender to thoughts of bed.

A dark glory-hole in his being lit up to reveal glimmerings of awareness that he had not realised were there. Whereas I was blind, now I see. They were stirring to the surface, these echoes of his half-hearted devotional past. The light shines in the darkness, and the darkness comprehends it not. He thought about his crew-mates curled up there around him in an unsound sinner's sleep. Only the thickness of a plank between them and eternity's shore. Throw out the lifeline. They would get their eyes opened when they awoke. Johnny Hallows, a not particularly good man in the moral sense, let alone a goody-goody one, would open their eyes for them. He knelt down on a couple of life-sustaining planks and prayed.

When, uncoiling themselves from sleep, they caught sight of him on his knees by his bunk, bowing and scraping to his Maker, they were startled into a silence so disquieting that they tried to avert their gaze, hoping, as they rubbed the sleep from their eyes, that the sight of him would be rubbed away as well. Only when Sauty said there was a mug of tea for him on the table did Johnny rouse himself; and they watched as, with the same light step that had taken him below, he climbed back on deck; where, scanning the sea and the sky, he seemed to be looking for a sign that had nothing to do with the weather. And as the morning stars sang together, as they had done on the day of creation, and a shimmer of life loomed all around him, and a calmness reigned as though the waves had been anointed with oil, he saw the sign for which he had been searching. The footprints of the Master were upon the sea.

All day the spirit poured into him and he drank as if he had forgotten how to say when. As the dew upon the grass and as a consuming flame was Johnny. What had been working on him for a year or so was coming to a head. He was in the throes of a happiness that all the herring in the world could not give. He had seen the light, the proverbial light. And would that he could turn this light on others that they might share it with him. Only how – how to turn this blessed, blessed light on others? And where – where was he to find the words, the gift of tongue? He was a man of deeds, not words. His seeing the light was itself a deed. (A deed, moreover, so beyond the sound and sense of the words that men spoke that it had struck him dumb before his own crew-mates.) And even if he had the words, and the courage to speak them, how could he stand up in front of a host of sinful men, be they crew-mates or strangers, with a bible in one hand and a cigarette in the other? How could he begin to tell them of this serene new light with a fag in his mouth? His lips trembled as he made his choice between the word and the weed. Down he went on his haunches again to pray for release. And when, an hour or so later, he got up off the deck, he fumbled in his trouser pocket for his packet of Woodbines and box of matches and threw them over the side.

That evening Johnny could have jumped over the moon. He had won release from a lifetime chained to a cigarette; and in the same breath, as it were, the fire was building up inside him, inflaming his desire to put the word instead of the weed to his lips from now on; the word whose glow would be greater than the lighted end of the wildest Woodbine.

'Come away for'ard here, the light is shining clear for you,' he was heard to shout as he stood near the bow, and they were the first sounds he had made since prostrating himself before the crew the night before.

'Lift up your souls to the moon that they may grow in beauty and grace,' he went on, as if trying to find his speaker's legs, his arms upraised, his voice so loud and clear that the fish in the sea could have heard it, if not acted on it, so sure of itself was this new voice that he had found.

There was something about the pitch and roll of the tongue; there was more than the wind in those tonsils, more than the sea in those eyes. If the light in those eyes was the mirror of the soul, then that soul was on fire. What the crew saw and heard began to vex the spirit. Had not Iley caught a blink of a rat feeding out of Johnny's hand in the rope locker? Johnny would have the very rats kissing the hem of his oilskin before long. It made a body peer down into the rat-hole of his own life. It made a body look for some kind of light. Could a man lose all heart and yet find his soul? Could a boat that had lost all hope find overnight a gleam? It had happened. It had happened right here aboard the *Bounteous*. Whence came that gleam, and how, and the fact that it owed its existence to somebody in their midst, made the crew uneasy and not a little afraid. And yet in spite of their fears, and in spite of their initial instinct to mock, their respect for Johnny Hallows as a fisher deepened in the light of the new regard in which they were beginning to hold him as a man.

He turned round to face them, something telling him that they were there – there with their heads bowed low. He held out his hands and sank to his knees on the deck. As he prayed for them, calling aloud each name in his anxious petition, he could feel the spirit moving inside him, flowing through every vein, flooding his being; strong man though he was, he could scarcely bear such sublime agonies, the sublime agonies of rebirth, of a bundle of joy inside him kicking to get out, bursting with the expectancy of glorious life. He did not have to open his eyes to know that the spirit was moving likewise among the souls that were bared before him. It was as palpable as plankton, the spirit that was working on him and them; it was as appreciable as the heaving of the deck. It was as if a wave were washing over the *Bounteous*, cleansing all on board. Johnny could feel it with every breath of new life that he took and then gave to them; he trembled with the fearful apprehension of it. They were growing more solemn by the minute, the men standing over him with their heads bowed and their caps in their hands; so that he was more gladdened than saddened when, more than an hour after he had knelt down to pray for them, he opened his eyes and rose to his feet again to find nobody there.

Down below the light was shining clearer still for them; and one by one, like ships in distress, they followed it. Iley was struck as if by a slung-stane and threw the Western he was reading into the boiler fire. Mack, lying back in his bunk with a bible in his hands and a thumping in his chest, a smiting of the conscience brought on by his letting his old folks down by going his own way after they had shown him to the Good Book, made a decision to head straight for their house as soon as the boat reached harbour and open the door and call out in triumph 'I've come home again.' They would know what he meant by that. Mack felt good, coming home again. Sauty the cook, dumpling of a man though he was, ran around as if he had seen the Holy Ghost and burnt his beam-end dancing into the stove with excitement. Wullsie, thrawn to the last, went through hell-fire and high water before hearing a sound which he took to be showers of blessing, in his elation at which he threw his half-bottle of whisky into the swill bucket and himself upon his knees in thanksgiving. And while all this recharting of life's course was going on among his crew, Skipper Croll, finding that it was not too late for prayer after all, stood on the deck vomiting up his past and chucking his cigarettes over the side on hearing a voice that was the sound of many waters calling to him.

At the surrender of his skipper, Johnny stood back and marvelled. One by one. Only one word could explain what he was witnessing. And how did you explain a miracle?

With half of the men won over to the light, he went to work on the other half. Above and below deck he prayed and petitioned for them, calling each by name as he had called the others – Ank, Spunk, Pow, Hamie, Stockie – and nothing brought it home to them more than when he said that they were all sitting in deckchairs on the *Titanic*. Launch the lifeboat! There was a ramstam rush to be saved. Almost as one man they fell off their deckchairs and on to the deck, fell before their Master and Johnny's opened bible (a gift presented to him 'appreciative like' by Mack), some exhorting their Saviour by name, others grunting and groaning as they wrestled with their souls, all groping for the vision that would lighten their darkness. And almost as one man the scales fell from their eyes and within the hour they were on their feet again and jumping about like sand-hoppers reborn.

It was as if the *Bounteous* had been struck by lightning; she was aflame from stem to stern. Johnny had turned a drifter that was heavily burdened with debt and sin into a salvation ship whose crew laid down their herring nets and followed Him – Him that could count every herring in the sea, Him that was the true anointed king of fish and of fishermen, Him that was the breaker as well as the maker of men. A miracle, i'faith.

From the swill bucket Johnny fished out the half-bottle of whisky that Wullsie had tossed away; opening it, he poured the evil spirits into the bucket, his face a beacon of anticipation headier than anything he had known when pouring himself a drink; and deeper, too, and more satisfying was his sense of celebration as, the whisky swilled out, the sacrifice completed, he placed the bottle on the cabin table while he scratched around for a piece of paper. In a pocket of his jacket he found a picture postcard of Yarmouth that he had not written on; then, digging out a stub of a pencil from a corner of another pocket, he sat down at the table and began to write. At the top of the postcard went his name and address, under which he wrote the name of each member of the crew, then the glad tidings that the men above, fishermen on the *Bounteous*, had been 'saved by grace at sea', followed by the date. He rolled the postcard into the shape of a fat pencil and placed it inside the bottle, which he sealed tight. Picking up the bottle, he climbed on deck where, to a hail of hallelujahs from the assembled crew, he consigned it gently to the deep.

As the bottle bobbled away to wherever the spirit of the waters willed it, Johnny sank to his knees on the deck and begged for the deliverance of the souls whose names were inside it, and for the delivery of its message into the hands of those who, no matter how strange the land in which they dwelt, would marvel at the miracle of it all. As Johnny rose to his feet, amid another hail of hallelujahs, he tingled to his very toes with the presentiment that this was but the intimation of a voyage that had scarcely yet begun.

Passing boats caught the sound of shouting and singing; a fishing smack making for the open sea was hailed with a rousing 'Hallelujah'; if the homeward-bound crew could have played a hymn for her on their siren they would have done so; instead they launched themselves into *Throw Out the Lifeline*!

'She's not washed in the blood of the herring,' Johnny said as the *Bounteous* approached the Brenston Deeps, 'but she's washed in the blood of the Lamb.'

And so, under a new banner of hope, with the hand of another Skipper on the wheel, and with a cargo more precious even than the blue-moon herring, the ship of souls sailed home. It had been a good fishing after all.

9

Johnny jumped over an upturned cran basket in glee. He leapt, almost wept, for joy. He felt so light on his feet that he could have sailed over the moon. His soul had taken wing. It rode the clouds above the sea. It swooped and soared over the town. And as it looked down it saw, not a port listing crazily to starboard, not a town as dead as a red herring, its people going about the streets like moles in their tunnels; his gull-winged soul knew nothing of the waves of hopelessness that were dashing against the town, drowning it in an apocalyptic silence in which everyone seemed to be waiting for the blast of a trumpet to signify the end of the world. Johnny was above such earthly woes. What he saw was Brenston in a blaze of light. He knew only a rush of wings. There appeared unto him an angel of light that hovered over the town, beating its wings and holding out its hands in solicitation.

Overcast though the sky was when the *Bounteous* tied up, the inner timbers of her crew had been given a magical coat of sunshine. For once Wullsie did not set course for The Anchorage as soon as he stepped ashore; instead he slipped soberly home to break the good news. Mack was as good as his word and headed straight for his folks to tell them that he had come home again. Mack felt good, going home again; home to his loved ones and to the One who loved him most. Iley and Sauty, with Ank and Hamie in tow, sallied forth with a

Sabbath tread to the Mission Hall to hold a prayer meeting. Pow and Spunk and Stockie sank to their knees on the deck and did their praying there and then. Skipper Croll wheeled off home, leaning on the arm of his missus and his Master. Which left Johnny, leaping over the cran basket on the quay and almost weeping tears of joy in celebration of his second birth, to marvel at how a man could come into such happiness and live. God had plucked out his sinful heart and washed it in a heavenly stream and put it back again pure. Johnny felt emptied of himself, obliterated before God. He had set off south as a commoner and had come back the son of a king. And no prince, in fact or fairy-tale, felt happier.

It was a happiness so transcending and yet so vulnerable that he did not want to speak to anyone for fear of losing it; and at the same time he wanted the whole world to know about it, that others may share it. What was he to do if he was not to hide his light, like the foolish man, under a bushel? Where was he to find the words to express his joy? Maybe there was no man in the world, nor words in the language, that could do that. It did not occur to him that he had not spoken in public before. Hallelujah, he shouted, loud enough for the public to hear. And from a joy unspeakable he wept, plain enough for the public to see. He wanted to sing as well as shout the good news; only he was afraid that in so doing he might grieve the spirit that moved him. A glorious feeling of being in the world but not of it came over him. It was there, all around, a presence. Every breath he drew was a silent prayer, every step he took was an act of worship. That he was walking on air seemed, for a wondrous moment, to be a miracle on the same plane as walking on water.

Mysterious as was the fact that not even the usually fruitful *Bounteous* had seen a cure of herring this autumn, there was no mistaking that she had come back with a cure of souls. The chosen vessel, Johnny found himself thinking, and no sooner had he thought it than he wanted to think it again, aloud. The chosen vessel. And not only the *Bounteous*. What about her crew — Iley and Sauty and Wullsie and Mack, Skipper Croll and them all — were they not also chosen vessels? Was not he, Johnny Hallows, like Paul of Tarsus, a chosen vessel? The young serpent had sloughed off his evil old skin and overnight had grown a new one, a skin of the spirit, and Johnny wore it like the finest raiment as he walked through the streets, a giant with the faith of a child.

A fine, gentle rain was falling as he reached the Burning Stone, a chunk of red volcanic rock set in the middle of the pavement overlooking the town Square, where little knots of people tended to congregate, more out of custom than curiosity, listening either to someone sounding the brass of oratory or more often to one another tinkling the cymbal of conversation. There were people gathered in knots there now, except that the knots were larger than usual, the figure of eight rather than the simple clinch, and surely they were more subdued than any company that the Burning Stone had ever kept. They hung their heads as if each was in a noose; they waited as if for the hangman to put them out of their suspense. Brenston was beyond reprieve. Even the Burning Stone itself seemed burnt out. If only The Steen, as it was intimately known, could speak. Many's the mouth that must have kissed it, judging by the fiery eloquence of those in years gone by who had stood up beside it and spouted forth to whomsoever would listen. It had been the stance for sword-swallowers and strolling fiddlers and strong men and barrel-organists and suchlike windblown flotsam as well as speakers, both native and missionary, for generations. Anyone with an act or a piece of advice to put across to the world did so at The Steen. It was the backdrop and the voice-box of the town.

Johnny could remember his folks telling him about a

preacher whose words had drawn sparks from the Burning Stone; the human tongue acting on the eruptive rock as steel upon flint; and the sparks becoming a flame and the flame a conflagration. Brenston was ablaze with the light of the Word in those days, his mother had said; The Steen was a veritable anvil for the Lord. Approaching it now in the vapoury rain, Johnny saw more of a dew on it than a consuming flame. Maybe it was the dew of heaven itself. No sooner had he thought so than he was overpowered by a strong light, a supernatural emanation, a vision of glory. With the suddenness of lightning he saw the sword of the spirit shining like white fire in that hulk of rock: Salvation the Excalibur waiting to be wrested from the rock of faith! As the dewy rain fell Johnny's circle of light widened round the Burning Stone until it seemed to encompass the knots of bystanders, the town Square, the whole soulless seatown. Brenston had to die before it could live. Out of the death of the fishing would arise new life for the fisherman. Johnny reached out for the sword and grasped it with both hands.

'The rain,' he shouted, his arms thrust out like those of a traveller dying of thirst in the desert. 'Feel the rain. It's different. Hallelujah.'

Skyward shot his arms and just as suddenly they dropped again. He held out his hands, cupped them, rubbed his thumbs against his fingers.

'Soft and fine like. Wouldn't wet a fish's back. Friends, Brenston rain's not like this. Hold up your faces to it and rejoice. It's the dew of heaven. And it's only the first drops.'

Pulling from his trouser pocket the Bible that Mack had given him, he searched the startled faces in front of him.

'This town, something tells me this town is in for showers of blessing. Oh, fine well do I know what you're thinking. The only dew Johnny Hallows sees is mountain dew. He's been at the bottle again. Friends,

I've got something to tell you. There's a bottle floating about outby with another kind of dew in it. Somewhere between this and the Viking Bank. If the fish could read the label on it they'd be drunk on just the thought. Not that the label will last long in that water; but the message, the message inside the bottle will. A fair tot of whisky there was in it, too, but Wullsie just throws it away and I picks it up and pours it out and sticks a message inside it and over the gunnels it goes. Well, whoever picks it up and reads the message inside will know that the crew of the *Bounteous* were saved by grace at sea. Aye, we made our decisions on our knees on a herring drifter in the North Sea. Half the crew at first, then the other half shortly after. All saved. We all put down our nets and followed. Glory, glory. The Great Skipper took over the helm that day. Lost our money, aye, but found our souls. Hallelujah.'

Passers-by stopped in the Square and stared at him, while the fishermen standing in knots here and there turned their prows to face the Burning Stone, and all of them opened their eyes wide, some of them their mouths as well, as if the object of their attention were a fire-eater from the pagan south. Johnny was surprising himself as much as he was surprising them. He was making a speech for the first time in his life, and he could no more believe his own ears than his hearers could believe their own eyes. Where could he have got the bawbees to drink, they wondered, and the whole town up to its gunnels, up to its very funnels, in debt? A pause to catch up with himself and he was off again, glorying in his new-found strength, afraid to stop, just as he had been afraid to start, lest he grieved the spirit.

'You think it's the end. No herring. The end. No, folks, it's not the end. It's only the beginning. Feel that rain. I believe it is raining righteousness. I believe this town will see the greatest harvest she's ever known. Aye, the greatest harvest. A harvest of souls, my friends. We will sow tears and reap a flood of joy. Hallelujah.

'Aye, we have lost everything; our souls are bowed down. Well, we're going to lift them up; we're going to lift them up, every one of us. We're going to cast off our burden and show the world a shining face.

'A few days ago I couldn't lift my head up for sin, for guilt. If you'd put my sins aboard a smaller boat than the *Bounteous* they'd have sunk her. Then I saw the light ... One night, turning for home we were, and the moon right bonny she was in a clear sky, how the light shone, the burning bush could not have been more wonderful, aye, and I knew I was being pulled out of the fire.

'Friends, I know a man who can turn your tears into pearls; I know a man who can show you the way to get rich quick. Real riches. True treasures. The kind that's only to be got Up Above. Where, we're told, no moth nor rust consumes. Get rich quick with God.

'Lass, hold up that head of yours. Hold up your faces to the rain, all of you. It's not your common or garden rain. Feel it. Smell it. Taste it.'

Johnny stuck out his tongue to taste it.

'Soft and refreshing, so it is. It's His showers of blessing, my friends. Oh, glory, glory. There's a blessing on its way for all of us. It may be here now. Let's get in the harvest. Let's get the harvest in before the fields are burnt black by the fires about to be sent down from heaven.'

Johnny lifted his head heavenward, as though to greet the falling fires. He wanted to feel and smell and taste on his lips the dewy rain, to look straight up at it so that it fell on him, soft and refreshing, like a benison, an anointment. The weeping sky was strangely aglow. He was encircled in light. His face upturned, his eyes the storm windows of his soul, he silently prayed. He prayed for Brenston, that it would be bathed in light, that it would be delivered out of the darkness and into a glorious dawn, that the bad would be made good and the good better. Lord, lift the dark clouds from our town and roll them out to sea. Blot me out of your book so long as you save this stricken town, these lost souls, these poor washed-up fishermen with their empty pockets and full hearts. Only one joy could compare with the joy of seeing the light, and that was the joy of leading others to it. He would point others to the cross even if it meant crucifying his own flesh. He felt like the man who took out a map of the world and prayed over it for the salvation of all mankind. Nothing did he desire so much as to see the whole world shaking hands in unworldly love. Like the man of flame of whom his mother spoke he would turn, if not an entire nation, then an entire town, to the light. Oh, that this season of famine would yet delight God with its fragrance.

Brenston folk were dour and deep and undemonstrative, a breed perversely slow to the quick, all the time weighing one another up, a clique who struck strangers as being cold enough to have the blood of the herring itself, if not of some queer fish from much deeper waters, running in their veins. For they did not feed contentedly on the plankton of life, they did not live in the more fathomable reaches of their nature: rather did they skim the surface of the sea-bed and react out of some dark cavern of their being. It was not that they were stolid so much as withdrawn. Suspicious of strangers at the best of times, they could at the worst of times transfer that suspicion to themselves. It was with a suspicion sharpened by shock that they listened to one of their number preaching in the street in a voice that would have blown down the walls of Jericho. If Johnny Hallows had become a new man, that new man was a stranger.

Dead, eh, the old Johnny, was that what he was

saying? He who had always been so ready to use his fists to settle a score with you, expecting you to swallow hook, swing and upper-cut a line about punching the Bible. When did Johnny Hallows ever read a line from the Bible? He did not possess a bible – it was Mack's he was waving around. Bottle labels were more in his line of reading. Hard man that he was, he needed the hard stuff if only to wash out his mouth. Was this not the same Johnny Hallows who in the Quayside Inn one night had drawn his knife on a Highlander? Aye, and there's the knife he drew, the very same knife, dangling from the sheath on his waistbelt. Dead, huh, the old Johnny. And by the hand, he would have us believe, of God, no less.

Most of the crowd kept their distance from the new Johnny as if he were a leper; the way some of them backed off he might have had the plague. A few crept closer to make sure that they were seeing and hearing aright, and their bewilderment could not have been greater had they been confronting a herring with three eyes and two tails. Children tightened their hold of their mother's hand and could not have looked more mesmerised had the Boneless Wonder escaped from Barnum's circus. Roll up, roll up and see the man wrestling with serpents. The old cursing, fighting, three-sheets-in-the-wind Johnny was preferable to this cloud-capped vision before them. Sword-swallowers you could take in one anxious gulp; bible-swallowers were liable to stick in the thrapple. Standing there waving the Holy Book high in the air as if it were a flag and shouting hallelujah, get rich quick, the rain falls only on the righteous. Surely he was drunk. Drunk or daft. Daft as a pennant on a windy day. Off his head, poor lad, and many another would be like him before the winter was out.

In the funereal wake of the failed herring harvest Brenston was in no mood to watch a man, least of all one of its own, pulling rabbits out of a hat or even herring-pie out of the sky. Such a man was as welcome as water in a sinking ship; and if for no other reason than that the town had seen and heard it all before. Brenston had been led a gospel dance in the past, folk birling around and embracing one another in some kind of jig that was meant to proclaim the death of worldly pleasures, but which was performed with what even those involved were later moved to confess was quite scandalous worldly pleasure. What good was this bread of life, anyway, when there was not a loaf on the table? The bread of this life surely came before the jam of a hereafter. Even more to the point, Johnny Hallows might have been telling them that the earth was flat, or that mermaids caused shipwrecks, for all they believed him. He might have been speaking in tongues for all some of them comprehended. And it was more than an incidental for those who did comprehend that, having grown out of the mermaid myth, folk were surely but a matter of time away from growing out of the Devil. Maybe the old Johnny Hallows had died right enough and come back as the Devil disguised in blue gansey, flat cap and kerchief. Devil that he was, and always had been.

'What ye selling, Jock, cockles?' a voice in the gathering crowd taunted him.

'I'm selling life insurance,' Johnny said.

'Christ's coming, Jock. And so's Christmas,' another, bolder voice mocked.

'I see the Devil's working overtime, too,' Johnny said.

'If Johnny gets any hotter, boys, we'll have to call the fire brigade,' Billy Bow, of the *Girl Eve*, game as the Devil himself, called out, and crackled with laughter.

'There's no fire brigade where you're going,' Johnny said.

'Johnny's thrown away his bonnet, lads. He wears a halo now.' It was Skatie's Bella, a woman known to be more of an imbiber than an imbibler, and as she shouted she waved an unsteady arm.

'There's no halo round a beer-mug, lass,' Johnny said.

'Tell us, Johnny, tell us. Where's the herring gone – to heaven?'

'You'll find no herring in the clefts of the Rock of Ages,' Johnny said.

'Have ye got your sky-pilot's licence, Johnny?' an old fisherman challenged.

'Aye, Dodsie, it's with the Master Pilot,' Johnny said.

'What's in the offing, Johnny Halo?' a voice boomed off the back of its owner's hand, its echo of the drunken woman hailed with horse-laughs and tee-hees.

'I see the good ship *Salvation* rounding the point, bound for Brenston with a cargo of life everlasting,' Johnny said.

'Tell us the truth, Johnny. Where's the herring gone?'

'I'll tell you where the herring's gone,' Johnny said, 'and it's not superstition I give you. In the old days – aye, and not so long ago, either – I could have stood here and had you burnt in effigy for causing a bad fishing. Or I could have dressed you up and put you in a barrow and wheeled you through the streets in procession if I thought you could bring this town better luck. D'ye mind on the Burry Man? Covered in burrs he was, with a hat stuck on his head and a fry of herring hanging by their tails from its brim. They'd sit him on a horse or maybe a barrow, or else make him walk, and they'd pipe him, or push him, or just follow him through the streets, cheering. If the poor cove failed to raise a herring they'd chase him out of town. Today, now, we wouldn't think of doing a thing like that. Superstition we'd call it. But think on this as you rue the empty barrels you left behind in the south: you came back safe, did you not?

'My friends, there's no herring in heaven. No more than there's herring down south. And I'll tell you why there's no herring down south: the English boats have been fishing on the Lord's Day. That's why there's no herring. Has any man here ever thought that the fish as well as the fishermen might need a rest on the Lord's Day? Fish's like you and me, they need to settle down, feel at home, rest their weary bones like all God's creatures must from time to time. If they don't get their rest they'll move on. Like they've done now, and look where it's got us. Friends, the One Above has moved them on. There's no herring because the good Lord has taken away His blessing as a punishment for those that fished on His day of rest.'

This was more like the Johnny they knew, sounding off about burning them in effigy and reminding them of the Burry Man and spreading the word that fish had the same rights as fishermen. Maybe the creature standing before them had not fallen off the moon after all; just a shade too much exposure to the moon's rays out there in the herringless sea – that would account for his throwing stones at them in the shape of sharp-edged words about his regenerate soul and blunt insinuations about their degenerate ones. When the moon was in the full, was not wit in the wane? What he said just then about the herring came over as if it might stand up to the light of reason. Might be better to hear him out rather than stone him to death like a saint, or nail him to the masthead of his boat, or shove his head in a brine tub – chastisements that had flitted across the wilder visionary eyes in their midst – or chuck fish-heads at him, except that there was no fish, and that was the root of it all, next year there would be no word of glory hallelujah when the sea was full of herring again. Aye, that was the cure for him and his kind. A sea full of herring.

And yet the more he stood there rejoicing in the rain, the less it seemed likely that a sea full of herring would cure him, and the more it seemed to his listeners that the new Johnny Hallows was less a man than a mania. The more he reached for heaven, the less he kept his feet on the ground, and the more convinced they became that he had suffered some terrible moonstroke. Some of them began to get the wind up and fled as if from the furies; while the more hardened shook their heads and wondered if they would have to cast him over the cliffs like a martyr. And all the time Johnny, filling out with the spirit, became more buoyant. Brighter still grew the light; he was borne on the flood of it, even into the gloaming. And as the circle of people around him widened, and closed in until it seemed that some were clinging like burrs to his gansey, and the baiting abated until it finally gave way to a stony silence, he laid forth like the son of thunder that he had become. It took dynamite to blast a way through hard, unquarried stone. The dynamite that had been in his fists as a fighter he now packed in his punching of the black, leather-bound book.

The kingdom of heaven is like unto a net, that was cast into the sea, and gathered of every kind. Johnny saw every kind, the good and the bad and the in-betweens, as one; he saw them with scales over their eyes, still blind to the light; he saw them as being like the herring, running away from the light. He would go on preaching to them until they could see what he saw, he would preach the whole night through if the spirit so willed it. The two or three knots of bystanders that he had gathered around him at the Burning Stone had become a multitude, and in the flood of eventide, just as he was beginning to feel like the fisherman who, at the end of a fruitless day, went home to his family and said that, although he had not caught anything, he had influenced a fair number, their apprehension of him changed, subtly but ineluctably changed. Maybe his words were beginning to go straight to the marrow:

'I'll kneel down right here, right now, in the rain if I think there's one soul that wants to be saved.'

Like the wind that has your ear as it sings in the shrouds, so to these witnesses was the surge and ripple of this voice with the sound of the sea in it: natural and supernatural in the same breath. And no less wondrous was the odour of the man: more of old nets than sanctity. Johnny Hallows was emerging before their eyes as something luminous, standing out in the deepening darkness like a pharos. Quicker than Saul became Paul did Hallows become Halo in the eyes of the Gentiles of Brenston.

The clock in the Square was striking ten, a time for respectable fisherfolk to be off the streets and saying their bedtime prayers, when Johnny heard the first amens. Thin and watery they came, punctuating his words and the soulful silence of his listeners.

'Amen ... amen ... amen.'

Stronger and more frequent they became until he thought he could hear the murmur of a contrite heart somewhere in the body of the kirk.

It was still falling, the dewy rain. All day it had fallen, on the just and the unjust alike. What were a few drops of rain to the fire and brimstone that would shower down upon their heads on the great Day of Judgement?

'You can't shut out God by putting up your brolly, sister,' Johnny reminded a woman at the back of the crowd.

Wet as he was himself on the outside, he was growing ever warmer within. And so, too, he could sense at last were they. He could hear the fizz and crackle as the sparks from his anvil were beginning to generate heat at the core of their being. And as he drank in thirstily that sea of faces around him, long and troubled faces, each one of them, he could see the water burning, the moon in their eyes, and he knew that the fish were ready to swim up to his net.

'There's a wave about to break,' he said, as a man might announce a heavy haul. 'There's a wave about to break across the heart of this town. And there's a heavenly wind behind it. Brenston's no more catch than an empty barrel with the bottom knocked out of it. The fishing's over. Aye. Dead's a herring before it began. So what now, what's in the offing, as the man said. I'll tell you what, brothers and sisters. Now is the season of grace.

'Last year, mind? Tail-end of the herring, aye. This time last year, mind? Joy and gladness everywhere. Everybody happy-like. Some, mind you, some among us couldn't walk for pride. How are the mighty fallen! Aye, after the pride, the fall. What a change. What a change has come over this town. Who would have dared to prophesy such a thing? After the feast, the famine. Just as in the days of Joseph.

'My friends, it's all there in your faces. Every face a wet and empty net. Soon as you go home tonight, have a look at yourselves in the mirror. It's as if your faces thought your heads were in the hangman's noose. I could be looking into the eyes of the drowned.

'Never, never was it ever like this. Never ever like this, cruel though the sea can be. Aye, cruel. Cruel at times. I've known men lose their false teeth out in that there sea. That was cruel. I've sailed with men that you'd think had made the supreme sacrifice, losing a finger. That was cruel, too. And there's not a fisher family in Brenston doesn't know what it's like to have lost a near or dear one, a father swept overboard on his way back from the fishing grounds, or a son going down with his boat not a pipe-spit from the shore. She can be cruel in many ways, the sea. We could fill the North Basin with all the tears we've shed because of her in the past.

'And now we're filling it again. Once more there is weeping and wailing and gnashing of teeth in Brenston. All of us here tonight have lost something. Some of you might say you've lost everything. Hold on a minute, all of you. Don't be going jumping in the harbour yet. I've got news for you. Good news. So good it cannot wait.'

With wet, thumby fingers he opened his bible. He read out something that was written on the inside cover.

'*Poor, but making many rich; having nothing, but yet possessing all things.* This disaster, friends, this disaster is God's way of speaking to us. He speaks through the storms as well as the calms. We are like ships at sea. No ship, and fine does the Brenston fisherman know it, can steer herself. She needs a master mariner to guide her. How many of you mind on those words at the Blessing of the Nets? There's no sea any man has sailed, no sea on earth, that can harm the ship that has the Master of oceans at her helm. As for me, friends, as for Johnny Hallows, the vessel the potter made was marred. So I asked Him to make it again. Oh, I may look the same Johnny Hallows on the outside; but believe me, there's a whole new man inside. Hallelujah.'

With his bible tight as a glove in his hand, Johnny punched the air. Then the new man inside him began to punch his way out.

'Yestreen I sailed on the *Bounteous* under a skipper you all know called Samuel Croll, and no skipper, say what you like, has graced the wheel better down Yarmouth way. Tonight, my friends, tonight I'm sailing on the good ship *Salvation* under a skipper you all think you know called Jesus Christ. I've struck my bargain at the cross: God has paid me my arles. And when the King of Curers arles you, it's not just for a season.

'Sign on, my friends. Step aboard the happy ship. There's room for all of you on the good ship *Salvation*; she's got a broad beam.'

Johnny paused to get back his breath. He had been shouting fit to drown the most sonorous of seas. Sticking his bible back in his trouser pocket, he took the weight off his waving arms at last. Then he lifted his bonnet and wiped his brow and face with the inside of it. He folded his bonnet and clasped it with both hands while letting his arms hang limply in front of him.

His head fell. Suddenly he was subdued. Meek. Shrinking as though from a delayed awareness of the divine gift he had revealed unto himself and of the fearful power he had unleashed upon others.

His fingers began to work round the twisted bonnet as a baker's might work a lump of dough before it takes shape as a loaf of bread. For an agonisingly solemn moment or two his hands were doing the talking. It was with a fumbling voice, a voice reluctant to rise from the dough that was his bonnet, that he resumed.

'No ... not for all the herring ... all the herring in the North Sea ... would I give up the joy I've found. Just catch me. The herring buries his head in the sand ... but mine ... mine is lifted unto heaven.'

And unto heaven Johnny, his resolve returning as abruptly as it had floundered, raised his head, and unto the sea again his voice.

'Christ's banner flies at my masthead. What about yours? You can't be a sitter on the harbour wall. Not any longer. You can't afford to be. Oh, I know what some of you are thinking – you womenfolk, especially. You're wondering where tomorrow's breakfast is coming from. Well, I'll tell you where. *He* will attend to that. He can see far, far beyond that. Seek ye first the kingdom. Don't be like the herring and run from the light.

'See that lamp over there? See, that street lamp. It wouldn't light up the nose of a clown on a mirky night. You can hardly pick out a light like that. Friends, a happy man shines forth like the sun; but an unhappy man, an unhappy man is like that lamp. Wouldn't you like to wake up tomorrow morning, not only with a shining face, but singing? Aye, singing?'

Johnny was trying to make a loaf again of his bonnet. There was a leavening in his voice, a new, quieter, fermenting seriousness.

'Joseph, who knew what famine was, wept over the sins of his brethren. I want to tell you I'm weeping right now over the sins of you, my brethren. And just as Joseph brought them down on their knees, so will I bring you down on yours. I'd sooner cut off my right hand than stop praying for you. Would you cut off your right hand for God? Would you pluck out your right eye for Him? I'm not saying these things because I'm a misery me. I'm not saying them because I've anything against you. I'm saying these things because I love you and the One who made you. I say all these things out of love.

'Don't ask me to speak with a book tongue: I'm a simple fisherman. A fisherman who's fishing now as he speaks. Fishing for his Master. You are my sea, my friends, and the holy gospel's my net. Hark, then. For I do not blow my own trumpet, but the trumpet of the Lord. Hark well, you men. You men who know too well that it's only a heart-beat and a plank between you and eternity out there in the deep. When her nose goes down, aye, when she goes down and you sometimes wonder if she'll come up again.

'Lads, have no more fears. Are you listening? For I've found a cast-iron way to ride a storm. Hold fast like a limpet to the rock of faith.'

Johnny slapped his trouser pocket where his bible was. Back on his head went his bonnet, then he pulled out The Book and began to wave it about again.

'I was a boy on a boat once when lightning struck the mast and split it in twain. Terror's not the word for it: I thought it was the end of the world. I've known grown-up men to be mortally terrified in a storm at sea. Then again I've known men who were pictures of calm out there in a corker of a gale. The terrified ones had nobody to lean on; the calm ones felt closer to God. Aye, closer to God, and the wind so bad you'd to put your

mouth to your neighbour's ear and roar into it to make
yourself heard, and the spray so thick midday was more
like midnight. Man, it's strange, the strain on the mind
during a storm at sea. I've seen one of the crew, as
steady a man, you'd think, as the next cove, go below
and put on his go-ashores, and the boat like some
rocking-horse that's bolted.

'There's only one word matters when a boat goes
down. There's only one word can comfort the folks
waiting at home. That word is saved. Saved. The one
little word that says it all. A fisherman in difficulties has
one wish, and one alone – to be saved, to get his hands
on that lifeline.

'Brother fishermen, the Devil is a wrecker luring us
on to the rocks to destroy us. Sure, it's natural to fear
your Maker when you're out there and a storm blowing.
Some of our boats just love water on their decks; we've
very near got to swim for it at times trying to make the
barest living. Them boats would fill a man with fear.
And that's just it. Our religion's like the fowl of the sea,
it's got webbed feet. Well, some of us, anyway. Some
folk's religion is well known for its sea-legs. It's a fine
sailor but it doesn't take much to dry land. Ashore, it's a
duck in dry dock.'

Even as the crowd shook their feathers in couthy
amusement, thankful for the merest glimmer of light
relief in their unrelieved darkness, and one or two
quacked in glee like ducks in a thunderstorm, Johnny
was already setting his jaw for a last appeal.

'Friends, you're all at sea in a sieve. The boat's sinking
and some of you are on the deck playing cards. The ship
of sin is sinking fast. Do you want her to go down with
all hands?

'To the lifeboat, my friends. Time is short and
eternity long. Now's the time, now's the moment to seek
the kingdom. Not tomorrow. Not the next day. Now.
Now, before you close your weary eyes for the night.

(Who's to say, my friends, aye, who's to say you'll open them again in the morning?)

'Fear not. Fear not, ye of little faith. The lifeboat's out and your Father's at the helm. He's holding out the pierced hand of pardon. Grasp it. For the Skipper's sake, my friends, grasp it.

'*He maketh the storm a calm, so that the waves are still; so He bringeth them to their desired haven.*

'Dear brothers and sisters, the new Johnny Hallows standing before you goes down on his knees to pray for you, and beseeches you to bite not the hand that feeds you the bread of life.'

So saying, Johnny fell upon his knees where he stood, knelt in the street and prayed. And seeing him there, wallowing and rejoicing in a puddle of rain, they looked at one another strangely, the strangers that he had called his brothers and sisters. And they murmured among themselves, and shook their heads, and tarried a while, and then slowly shuffled away. They were not around when the knuckles of the hand that clutched the Bible to the prostrate, imploring breast turned blue with cold.

10

When at last Johnny lifted up his head and opened his eyes, the sight that met him lit a flame in his heart. On the wet cobblestones, not half a boat-length ahead of him, was a figure. A woman. Kneeling. Alone and quivering, with her head in her hands and sobbing like a child on a doorstep. Out of reach of her though he was, he yet thrust out a hand in fellowship, at the same time raising his head heavenward in gratitude. For in this penitent figure in front of him he beheld the homeless soul, the Fatherless bairn left abandoned by the crowd, the new-born child of light that was the answer to his prayers.

Dragging himself to his feet, for he was wet and numb with cold, he went over to her. He bent down and laid a hand on her shoulder. She looked up at him.

'Lil,' he said, surprised almost to the point of disbelief.

It was Lil Gale, sister of Hannah. And with her eyes full of the wonder of one who has seen a shaft of moonlight in a bottomless pit. Johnny sprinkled a few words of prayer over her to the effect that one soul was worth more than all the rubies and diamonds in the world, and that he gloried in having found what money could not buy, the pearl of great price.

And when, on wet and watery legs, the priceless pearl rose, trembling now more through rapture than remorse, she spoke of the electric shock that had passed through her body, of the pins and needles that she had felt, of the Holy Ghost that was everywhere around her.

'God's your pilot now, lass,' Johnny said with an assurance that was twice blessed. 'Tonight there's rejoicing in heaven.' And giving her a short, shivery embrace, he said he would take her home.

His night's fishing was over. It was not that he had hauled his net and landed one fish; rather did he bask in the special blessing of a man who has hooked a herring on a line off the pier. The Burning Stone was burning again.

In the stony silence of the sleeping town they walked home, preacher and convert together. Johnny noticed that the rain had cleared and the moon was out. There was not a cloud in the midnight sky and a dew was rising into the clear, cold air. Darkness had enfolded every house. Not a light burned in any window. Only the moon and the odd gas-lamp in the streets shone the way for them. The moon and the light in their souls.

It was a long walk to the northern neb of the town where Lil and the rest of the Gales lived, and a long walk back to Sailmaker's Close. By the end of it Johnny, succumbing at last to a serene and triumphant weariness, was ready for his bed.

A blanket of darkness lay over the house. He groped for the orra pail at the back of the door and emptied his bladder in it.

To think that there was a Hallows anywhere in the Close who did not know that the *Bounteous* was back from the south, and with her whole crew, himself among them, trailing clouds of glory, was to shut one's eyes to the ways, stealthy as the motion of the tides, in which news ebbed and flowed in Brenston. If they were not expecting him, why had the old folks left the door unsnibbed? Not wishing to disturb them, he read his bible by the light of the moon. And before turning off that heavenly lamp he noticed a broch, a halo, round it. Was it not a sign of showers, a halo round the moon? He closed his eyes thinking of those showers of blessing that would come in the morning, and went to sleep dreaming of bringing in the shoals.

He rose early, as was his way every day of his adult life, except that on this special morning he was not going to sea, he was going to see the Skipper with whom he had lately signed on for the rest of his allotted span and beyond. He was going to look on the face of his Master before seeking out the face of man.

In the tremulous darkness before dawn Johnny knelt by his bedside in prayer. Then he lit the candle that stood on a plinth of its own wax on the kist by his bedside. Better not to burn the lamp, he thought; save the paraffin, soon it would be running low. Sitting on the edge of his bed, his head tilted towards the candle, he read his bible. Acts, chapter two. He was encircled in candlelight, reading about a rushing mighty wind, when his mother, drawn as a moth to a flame, fluttered into the room.

'A fine time that was to come home from Yarmouth,' she said sternly. In the chill draught of her entrance the candle flickered. 'What can they be using for bawbees now, think ye, at The Anchorage? You'll just have to take less to your head from now on, m'lad.'

Her figure looming in the shadow beyond the bloom of the candle added a starkness to the admonition in her voice. She peered round the room.

'Where's your gear? You haven't left it in The Anky by any chance?'

Firmly and yet gently Johnny said: 'Mother, I'm saved.'

She drew closer so that only the bottom half of her was in shadow now. There was challenge, even rebuke, in her voice.

'Am I hearing right, Johnny, or are you still speaking through the drink?'

Johnny dropped to his knees on the floor, both of his

hands round his open bible, and gazed up into his mother's face.

'Mother,' he said, begging her to believe him, 'I'm drunk on the wine of the spirit, just like Peter at Pentecost.'

She peered down into his eyes, observed him with the strictness of a Pharisee. Startled as she was to see him on his knees, a grown-up bairn tugging at her heart and skirts, she was confounded to find nothing in his face or form that mocked humility. She could not fault the light that shone forth from his eyes; so intense was it that it broke in a radiance over his whole face, the candle-bloom enriching and elevating it until she became aware of being in the presence of something uncomfortably close to goodness, a goodness that was surely next to godliness, a grace such as she could barely face.

She looked away and towards the window. She held her breath. She thought she heard the morning stars sing. Could they be singing the praises of her son? Disorientated, her eyes drifted back through the darkness of the room to the candle-lit face in front of her. He was drunk on something, whatever it was, and the very breath of it was strong and catching. If he was drunk on the spirit, like he said, she might never see him 'sober' again. So intoxicating was her joy and relief at such a thought that she could have fallen to the floor on her knees beside him. Instead she shook her head in disbelief and threw up her hands in exultation.

'Bless my soul,' she said. 'And they came and told us you were down at The Steen, fou as a whelk and raving about the state of the fishing.'

She went over to the window and looked out. It was not yet light. 'If only we'd known, son,' she said, wistfully.

Johnny remained on his knees. He bowed his head until he buried his face in his bible and prayed. He prayed aloud for his mother and father, his brothers and sisters, his uncles and aunts. He prayed that they might walk in the light before another day was done, before another day had even dawned. Cast their sins into the depths of the sea, he pleaded, just as you cast mine. He begged for guidance to help him prove worthy of being the chosen vessel. He called for heavenly blessings to rain down upon the town of Brenston that the people might 'row out and meet their Skipper and not wait for their boat to come home.' He cried out for the strength to 'take King Herring off the pages of our newspapers and put the King of Hosts in his place.' And as a last and most solemn word and testament he vowed to 'turn Brenston into a spawning ground for the Lord.'

Upon which high and venturous note he fell silent, not so much as a breath being heard, and when eventually he dug his head out of the Bible and opened his eyes his mother was on her knees beside him, weeping quiet tears of gladness, and through the little square window of his room the light of a new day was breaking.

'Lil's converted! Lil's converted!'

All over Brenston the cry went up. Lil Gale's name was borne along the streets like a leaf blown by a freshening wind. Round every corner, into every nook and cranny it went, creating a stir here, a sigh there. In the vicinity of the Burning Stone it had the effect of a trumpet-blast. Lil's conversion gave rise to a cry shriller and more soul-stirring than the shout that rang out when a man was drowned at sea. Not since God was last seen in all His glory in the town, awakening it from a sleep into which it had once more fallen, had the inhabitants of Brenston taken a thought and given it such an emotion.

Just when some of them had been talking of emigrating, of sending their sons on ahead of them to America, where a herring man and his spawn could live on more than the Shorter Catechism, Lil Gale got herself converted. She had discovered her own new land without looking beyond the seas. She had found it in the Square, under a stone, at the lightsome feet of Johnny Hallows. It was as miraculous as it was mysterious. Lil Gale was a seed sown by the wind.

And it was still blowing, that seed-sowing wind, as Johnny, showing a clean-shaven face to the Lord and those that he had created in his own image, slipped down to the *Bounteous* to collect his gear; after which he made straight home again to his room where, instead of unpacking his chattels, he fell to the floor and burst into prayer; at the end of which he opened his eyes to see his mother and father standing over him, his father regarding him as he might regard a cat in gaiters; for there was a strange light in Johnny's eyes which grew stranger as he turned, still on his knees, to face the window; whereupon, more in the tone of a gable-end weather prophet predicting a shower of rain than in the drone of a pulpit-pounder forecasting fire and brimstone, he said:

'We're going to have a revival.'

A man of the kirk rather than the camp-fire meeting, Jondy Hallows gave his head a shake and said: 'Converted? A son of mine converted? Herring will be falling from the sky next."

And as Johnny's head fell in silent prayer, his father, the very soul of scepticism, went on: 'So you've been seeing visions, hearing voices, down Yarmouth way. Did you see any herring in your visions?'

Johnny held up his head and his hands. 'No, father, but this morning a voice did speak to me in the night, and said "The town is yours".'

Johnny closed his eyes and his fists in petition. 'Lord,

give me the power to chase the Devil and all his works out of Brenston.'

Jondy shot a bedevilled glance at his wife, whose nod he took to be one of approval as much as confirmation of their son's declared intention.

'Chase the Devil?' he growled. 'What do you think the kirk's doing? We have a minister to take care of the Devil. You'll have to chase the minister first. No son of mine is qualified to take on the Devil' – his lip assumed a wicked curl – 'or even the minister.'

'Qualified.' Johnny faintly echoed the word, an echo as ironical as it was distant, and as he looked up from the floor at his mother there was the suspicion of a smile on his face.

'Johnny Hallows, B.A. Except a man be Born Again ...' Johnny's head dropped, and with it his voice. 'That's the only qualification.'

'Born again?' His father's echo was as mocking as it was near, and that wicked curl was round his lip again. 'I wouldn't want to be "born again" for fear I'd be born a lassie.'

Mother Hallows glowered at her man in a way calculated to abort any misconceptions he held about either rebirth or lassies, or both, and by way of further corrective she verbally stamped her foot.

'Johnny's had the call,' she said, with some stress.

Jondy shook his head several times, sighed and thought for a moment before he spoke. 'Are you sure he's not making a fool of himself?'

A floorboard creaked as Johnny rose to his feet. Placing a gentle hand on his father's shoulder, he said, in a tone of tender assurance: 'I don't mind making a fool of myself – for Christ's sake.'

There was a touch of defiance in his father's nod. 'Just as you say, just as you say. But remember this. Don't forget whose son you are.'

'No, father.'

A far-away look entered Johnny's eyes, a phossy intensity furred his voice.

'I can't forget whose son I am. No more than I can forget what I'm about to do. I'll tell the whole world whose son I am. And only one man will judge if I'm a fool or not.'

He went over to the chest of drawers to pick up his bible.

'I must go now. If I don't, I'll grieve the spirit. There's a boat adrift out there in a troubled sea and they're hanging over the side waiting for the lifeboat.'

He had reached the door.

'The Lord has lit a fire in Brenston, father, and he's called upon me to fan the flames.'

Man on fire that he was, Johnny left the room and the house and a silence such as only a blast from Gabriel's trumpet could have broken, and was gone; gone with the haste of a lifeboatman answering a rocket of distress; gone with the buoyant tread of the first mate of a gospel ship that was heaven-bent on catching the rising tide.

First, he would gather together his crew. He had only to call on them and they would be there. For his crew would be the boys of the *Bounteous*: Mack and Iley and Wullsie and Sauty and the rest of his reborn brothers, plain-one-purl-one fishermen like himself, who had been paid their God's penny, whom the King of Curers had already arled. Johnny would call on each of them in turn. Then they would all meet down at the Square. Where, in spirit if not to the letter, the *Bounteous* would be requisitioned, as she had been by the Admiralty during the war, except that this time she would be at the service of the Lord of all the Admiralties. In place of the three-pounder gun on her foc'sle would be the thunder of God's word at her prow. And she would be given a pennant, the pennant of the Lord flying from her masthead, and a new name, the *Salvation*.

She would be fitted out as a fisher of souls whose waters would be the Devil's deep. Her nets would be immersed in cutch made from the bark of the Tree of Life. And God himself would bless these nets. And Johnny would get up a head of steam such as no drifterman had ever seen and set sail to where the waters would be burning, radiant with the shoals of God. The Burning Stone would be his Smith's Knoll. And there would come a rushing mighty wind to stir up the grounds. And with a cry of 'Over for the Lord' he would let down his nets. And daylight would fade into darkness, and darkness pale into daylight again, and still he would be hauling. Pile in, he would say, you cannot sink the *Salvation*. And so great would be the multitude of blessings that the nets would be near to breaking. So many souls that Johnny and his crew would be measuring them by the cran. Their boat up to her gunnels in grace.

And under the street-lamps and the moon he would wash and clean and preserve the catch, steep each soul in the salt of the spirit. Gifts there would be for all the family when the fishing was over: not handbags or tricycles or dolls, but the gift of life without end; not sweetmeat rock, but the Rock of Ages in whose clefts no herring swam.

While his crew were knocking on every door in the town, spreading the good news about a meeting at the Burning Stone, Johnny was already in the Square launching himself upon a sea of faces. They were hud-dling in close to hear the hard man who had turned soft, rolling up to see the sword-swallower swallowing the sword of the spirit. How lean and anxious their faces were, Johnny thought, as he went to draw his sword. Above all, how anxious.

'You, Jimmick. Standing there with your head bared to heaven, gawping down into your bonnet. All you'll see there, brother, is the fruitless sweat of your brow. Lord, have mercy on Jimmick and all his bairns.

'Up to the thigh-boots in debt. Up to the sou-wester in sin. The dog may go without a bone, the cat without a saucer of milk, before another week's out. We may be sweeping the dust off the bakery floor before the first cheep of spring. But this I can promise you, all of you: Brenston will not go hungry for the bread of life. Aye, the cupboard may be bare, but as the old tin-miner said, him that wore his boots out for the Lord, you don't need teeth to eat the bread of life.'

Johnny's bible cleaved the air.

'*For what is your life? It is even a vapour, that appeareth for a little time, and then vanisheth away.* Aye, it is even the vapour that appears for a little time upon the face of the sea down Yarmouth way; the very breath of the waters that tells you there's life there, herring life, which is the breath of life to the fisherman. If that vapour can vanish from the sea, what hope is there for the vapour in the nostrils of man?

'Our days are swifter than the gutter's knife. Whither bound, fishermen of Brenston? You are swimming straight for the Devil's net, and with the chart of heaven in your pocket. Headlong like the herring into the net. It's just like a herring net, is hell, easy to get into, but hard to get out of. There's some of us here have dipped our souls in the tar-pot along with the warp. There's some of us here with souls as black as sails. If you want to get the blackness out of your soul, there's only one thing for it. Wash it in the blood of the Lamb. There's only one way to clear away the cobwebs from your heart. Clear away the spider.

'I remember my old Granny Hallows saying to us once, "I never meddle with the Devil or the laird's bairns." Meddle with him, the black-hearted auld nickum – I'd give him a shirtful of sore bones. Never again will I dance the night away, bobbing and birling to tunes like *The World is Waiting for the Sunrise*, and shuffling home just before the sun rises with my shirt soaking for the Devil.

'Aye, I've had my fling. It wasn't the sweet songs of Zion I sang then. Strewth, I was no angel. I've been before the beak. I've had more smoke in my mouth than would kipper a cran of herring. If the good Lord meant me to smoke, surely he would have stuck a funnel in my head, just like the steam drifter. But much as I bent the elbow, I've never bent the knee till now. A damp cloth was wiped across the slate and a lifetime of sin was gone. Just like that. Swapped my gansey for a robe of glory I have, my cloth cap for a crown.

'How about you? There's nothing God doesn't know about you, or you, or you. Or you, Jimmick. There's nothing he doesn't know about anything under the sun or the moon or the shoals of stars up there in the sky. You, brother. You may be able to tell me the age of a herring by counting the number of scales. But can you tell me how many eggs a herring has laid on the bottom of the sea? God can. Can you tell me how many herring there are – aye, all right, *were* – in the sea? How many scales there are – *were* – on all the herring in all the seas? God can. He can tell you how many herring there ever were, how many eggs were laid by all the herring that ever were. Not a single scale on any herring that ever was has slipped through His net.

'He who created the sun and the moon and the stars, and those oceans of space in between – He can see a sparrow fall in your backyard. Aye, the peerie-weeriest sparrow. In God's eyes the sun is just across the street; Neptune is over on the corner there, opposite Garvie the grocer; the moon is no more than a ball at His feet. Every snowflake He sends down to earth is different. In one bead of sea water there's more living creatures than folk in the whole of Scotland. The way of a ship on the sea, the way of a bird in the air. Think about it.

'Last night Lil Gale went down on her knees at this

very spot and was delivered from bondage. I put it to you that a sacred place is not where a kirk stands. Nor is it where a sparrow falls. A sacred place, my friends, is where a sinner sinks to the ground under the weight of his or her sin, and through his or her repentance is saved. For wherever a soul is struck down in God's name and is raised up to a new life, raised from the living dead, there do angels gather, and a cross marks the spot where Christ is.

'Where Lil Gale fell to the ground, stricken by conviction, and rose like a herring to the light – there was a sacred place. You are standing right now at that very place.

'Hark. It's the beat of the Archangel's wings. Hovering. Closer and closer. I can feel the breath of the Master in our midst. Heave to, my friends. She's rounding the point, the lifeboat of the Lord. Jump to it. Seize the lifeline and scramble aboard.'

It was the prayer that did it. It was the bowing of the heads in the silence that followed the mighty wind-rush of words that finally moved them, moved them in mysterious ways.

Not that they were unaffected by his words. This man whose tongue they knew of old to be so sharp that it would have gutted a herring was speaking to them with the tongues of angels. He was speaking with a voice that would have pinned ruffles on the stars, that would have turned herring scales into mother-of-pearl. No fisherman had ever spoken before like this fisherman. Could this man really be Johnny Hallows? Could this man who had found the words to squeeze a heart out of the Burning Stone be Jondy's Johnny from Sailmaker's Close? His voice booming out fit to shiver the timbers of Noah's Ark.

The faces of the crowd soon lost their look of

bemused surprise and took on the crushed look of oak leaves pressed between the pages of Jeremiah and Lamentations. His tongue was a flame licking at their consciences, and they shrivelled up. Some of them tucked their heads under their armpits as though fearful of coming face to face with the truth. Weaving like Jack Dempsey in the ring and moving just as lightly on his feet – the opponent in the red corner was, after all, a slippery customer – Johnny, his well-seasoned barrel-chest heaving with the burden of his message and with lung power enough to inflate a fleet of net floats, poured forth such a thunderspate that his call for prayer was as a lifebuoy offered to the outstretched hand of a drowning man.

If the onding of words had them by the ears, the silence after it stopped, and they closed their eyes in euphoric prayer, had them by the throat. For only then did the words of Johnny, rumbling on as an echo in the reverberating silence, take root in the stoniest soul and the faces shed their look of leaves pressed between the holy pages as the sap returned and a great rustling, as of a wind in the trees, began. God was in the still small voice more than in the thunder.

Deeper and deeper they prayed until the less silent became their prayer. Some prayed in ever-louder whispers. Some prayed and broke down. Some prayed through a veil, if not a valley, of tears. One man clenched his fists and shouted 'Lord' in a voice racked with grief. A woman tore her hair in remorse. To starboard came a cry of 'Save me'; to port a bellow of 'Hallelujah', followed by a bleat of 'Amen' from the whole flock. Out of the abundance of the heart the mouth speaketh. As the quick was touched, the tears came in fountains. Girls wept upon each other's necks. One of them slumped to the ground, pleading for forgiveness. Others swooned away peacefully, their mouths closed on the inexpressible, as though body and soul were floating on invisible waves.

For a full five minutes the crowd prayed. Their eyes

shut the while, they stood and unbosomed themselves in sobbing voices, or lay on the ground in a shiver of contrition, if not in a dead faint. At the back a man broke into song. It was Skipper Croll belting out the chorus of *Throw Out the Lifeline*! Sauty the cook, standing by Johnny's side, picked it up and before the pair of them could throw out another line almost everyone who was still on their feet joined in and began to repeat the whole chorus, Johnny's baritone sounding and resounding above the rest. In as many tunes as there were sons of Abraham they sang, the crows along with the nightingales.

If they were not in one voice, they were clearly in one mind. When Johnny opened his eyes the glow on his face was a reflection of the glow that he saw on the sea of faces in front of him. Not only was the water burning; not only was the sea shimmering and swarming; not only had the crowd assumed the luminous look of the lost shoals of Yarmouth: the lost souls of Brenston were glistening as they found his net.

No more were the heads of these herringfolk buried in the sand: they had come up to feed on the plankton of the spirit. There must have been a couple of hundred people in the Square, and they glowed like the phosphorescence Johnny had seen on the sea. He had opened up a channel through which their sins were washed away and love flowed into their hearts. Eyes which had been as blank as the windows of an empty house were suddenly filled with light from within.

He thought of Lil Gale. True enough, it was the sign of a gladsome season when the first fish shaken out of the net was a female. *Throw out the lifeline and save them today*, he half-thought, half-sung to himself as he tried to remember a line from the hymn. White handkerchiefs were waving in a signal of surrender. Fire was falling from heaven and setting Brenston alight. Men who had been standing up straight as pokers at hell's fireside were melting in the heat of this intense moment. Strong men shall bow themselves, and bow themselves they did. First on one leg, then on the other. The eggshell covering their souls cracked under the blows that had rained down from his hammer upon this anvil of the Lord.

They fell at his feet, the strong and the weak together, more like innocents slain by a swordsman than something beaten out by the hammer of a soulsmith. And the heavens were rent with the cries of salvation. Johnny let them get their cries out as a mother would those of her infant child. There was nothing so inwardly cleansing as the hot, heartfelt tears of repentance.

He closed his eyes again in earnest, unspoken prayer. The Blessing of the Nets was over. The gospel ship was sailing. The first catch was a great multitude of blessings. It was going to be a Yarmouth of the first water in the herring yards of the Lord.

11

For twelve hours he hauled and the fish sang as they swam into his net. Bigger became the crowd as folk, summoned by the church bell that was Johnny's voice and burning with the curiosity of the disbelieving, congregated to watch the children of disobedience, the children of wrath, repent. They craned their necks to see the thirty or so bodies lying on the ground in the Square, slain by the sword of the spirit; lying flapping like fish on the deck, some of them fighting like mackerel, many of them gasping as though suffocating on the sulphur of hell.

It was a sight that had the onlookers themselves gasping, choking on the vision of their own kith and kin grappling with the demons that possessed them. There was something out of place, and for some it verged on the mortifying, about folk in the throes of worldly death and in the pangs of spiritual rebirth making a public exhibition of themselves.

While it all stuck in the craw more than any sword-swallowing the town Square had ever seen, nothing stuck more in the minds of the bystanders than the fear that a momentous time had come, and that the moment was right as it was right for a germ to strike down a body and start an epidemic.

With their hallelujahs and their amens the crowd had keyed themselves up to the frenzy of the herring they seemed no longer to mourn. The hour of decision had become six hours, the six hours twelve, and the twelve one long momentous moment during which a town that was under sentence of death began to glimpse a shaft of light, began to play host to angels, to behold visions of crowns of glory and of mansions in the sky and of the jasper walls of the New Jerusalem – began, in fact, to put on the air and grace of a town under sentence of life.

Gully Bow, who had chewed tobacco of the blackest Strathbogie blend all his days, spat out a half-chewed plug and wiped his lips clean on the sleeve of his gansey.

Dod Rann, whose blackened briar was never out of his mouth, not even, the neighbours swore, when he was in bed, and who was known to all the town as Smokie, pulled his grown-up baby's comforter out of his mouth and dashed it to the ground where he stood, stamping on it as though he were putting out a cigarette end. There, trampled for ever into the dust of the town Square, was Smokie's urge to smoke. He had found his true Comforter.

Old Girzie, who could not count more than a dozen herring, thumped his chest and counted his blessings. It was all in there, he announced, what words could not express.

Polly Denes tried to find the words that Girzie was lost for as she half-sang, half-wailed *Happy day, happy day, when Jesus washed my sins away.*

And while Polly's vehemence threatened to do violence to heaven, a boy went skipping down the street shouting in the bell-like tones of a town crier: 'Conger's wife's converted! Conger's wife's converted!'

In and out between the prostrated forms Johnny moved, touching each one on the shoulder and saying 'Jesus died for you,' and one by one they rose to their feet, and it was as if they had acquired new stature. By and by they linked hands and sang *Will Your Anchor Hold?* Young Billy Bowster ran home for his melodeon,

and when they sang to it the Sankey favourites their
voices could be heard half a mile away. Everybody in the
Square joined in the singing; even the stray drunk on
his way home had his own grace-note to add to that of
the reborn soul who was drunk on the firewater of the
spirit.

Midnight came and still they sang. They sang fit to
waken the sleeping as well as the dead-in-Christ. Johnny
wanted to go on preaching and not go to bed; but they
had got the spirit so bad themselves that they would
have drowned him out with their anthems and
choruses.

Not that he or they were thinking of their beds as,
having taken off on the wings of a final, soaring prayer,
they marched down Baltic Street singing *Let's All Gather
at the River*. Some, almost hoarse from shouting and
singing salvation, did not go home, at least not before
knocking up their relatives and friends and neighbours
to tell them what had happened to them. Others went
home, only for the neighbours to poke their noses in to
see what all the commotion was about; and what the
nosy neighbours found was noisy families singing and
dancing, their voices carrying out of the windows and
into the streets and down to the empty, unlistening sea.

Down to that sea they marched next day, those who
could not sleep for joy that night. From the Burning
Stone they marched, Johnny at their head and on their
lips a battle hymn. *When the Roll is Called Up Yonder I'll
be There*, they sang as they passed doorways full of
bystanders with bless-my-soul faces and eyes and ears
that all but shied away from the sight and sound that
met them, for both were terrible as an army with
banners. Some of the more inquiring spirits fell in with
the more devil-may-care and stepped out of their
doorways and formed a parade of their own, tailing the

marchers all the way to the shore, where for a good hour they stood back, looking as forlorn as gulls in a mist, and shivered and flinched as one by one men, women and children walked partially clothed into a sea as cold as naked steel. There must have been about fifty or so recruits in Johnny's army and another hundred or so witnesses to their attempt at setting up what their leader called 'a beach-head for Christ.'

'We are already baptised in the fire,' Johnny shouted above the roar of the winter waves. 'Now to be baptised, as the Lord commands, in the water.'

As he spoke the spray off the sea sprinkled their heads in token baptism. He waved his bible in token rebuke. 'We are not here to be sprinkled but to be immersed, as the Lord commands. We are not here to bathe our bodies. Baptism is a cleansing of the mind and the spirit.'

And the first to cleanse his mind and spirit was Johnny. Taking off his bonnet, his gansey and then his boots and hose, and passing them to Skipper Croll, to whom he already handed his bible, he strode in his trousers and braces into the water up to his waist while old Dan Dowdie, a cousin of his mother's and an elder brother-in-Christ, waded out in sea-boots by his side. To lusty lungfuls of *Pull For the Shore* from those awaiting their turn to be cleansed, Dan grabbed Johnny by one arm to steady him in the swell, placed the palm of his other hand on the crown of Johnny's head, and as another wave broke pushed him under and pulled him up again in one movement; then he helped him back on to the shore, where Johnny shook himself like a dog after a paddle and panted like one as he hastened past the still-singing choir, one of whom threw her coat round him; and up the foreshore he went, past the cowering figures of the dumbstruck watchers as he made for the kippering shed behind the sea-wall and a shift of dry clothes.

Fired rather than dampened by Johnny's example, his troop of followers began to nudge in front of each other and edge closer to the water in a race to see who would be baptised next. No sooner had Dan Dowdie waded out again up to his thighs, at which point he turned round and beckoned to the others to step forward, than he became a busy master of ceremonies, ducking fifty or so heads under the billows. Skipper Croll's head was the first of them; then followed those of his crew, after which it was the turn of the multitude.

Dipping their gooseflesh in that bitter sea, drowning their old sinful selves – submerging, they were washing away the past; surfacing, they were ushering in the future – fifty or so men, women and children emerged anew, emerged as white as the driven horses. And if their skins were white, too, with the cold, their souls were tingling with a secret, sacred warmth.

PART THREE

Glow and Afterglow

Johnny Hallows died that day and Johnny Halo was born. Ever since he got back from Yarmouth, when Skatie's Bella, butting in with her bar-room bawl from the back of the crowd that first day round the Burning Stone, charged him with having swapped his bonnet for a halo, the not unaffectionate corruption of his surname had gained increasing favour. With his baptism in the fiery sea his rechristening by the townsfolk was confirmed before the world. From now on even those for whom he had been plain Johnny every day of the week, save on those more stiffed-necked occasions when he was Jondy's Johnny, would be disposed to add, if only to be upsides with the rest, the new baptismal surname of Halo. It was Johnny Halo here and Johnny Halo there, and as such did his flame and fame begin to spread; the flame spreading faster than a man could run away from it.

For the next few weeks Brenston burned with a lowe never before seen on northern land or southern sea. A holy sea-fire engulfed the soul of the herring town. On the deck of a boat, in a neighbour's house, at a street corner, on top of a pile of nets along the quay – give me a place to stand, any place, seemed to be Johnny's message, and I will move this town, if not the world.

In an unfinished house he began to move it.

In a house in Firth Street without roof or doors or windows, a house abandoned by its builder in the wake of the herring failure, he began to move Brenston until it was no longer of this world. Sitting on the rafters and window-ledges while the wind blew about their ears and legs, a crowd off the street hearkened to Johnny bringing home to them some other unfinished business: what about their own houses, were they in order?

Driving rain drove them into a tarred shed.

In that shed, among ropes and floats and suchlike gear, meetings went on in the light of a solitary oil-lamp and broke up as the first lark was ascending to heaven.

The crushing need for more room forced him up into a net-loft, which he proceeded to turn into a workshop for the kingdom of God.

From house to house he went, recruiting for the Lord.

In the humblest but and ben, with a sailcloth from an old sailboat decking the floor and the fish and flour barrels scraped clean in the struggle to live, a man who had stolen coal to keep his frail old mother warm repented.

With but as well as ben being converted into a prayer parlour, families wept the cold out of their hearts until the floors were wet with their tears. When a woman told her neighbour that her very cat at the fireside had been converted, the neighbour replied that the parrot next door was learning to say its prayers.

Johnny pub-crawled as he had done in his youth.

Venturing into the dark places where once he had got fighting drunk, he invited the customers to step outside and fight for the Lord. One publican poured his entire stock of whisky down the sink, smashed all his glasses on the rocks, threw the bar sign in the sea and reopened the place for prayers. One regular spat at Johnny, and Johnny wore the spit on his chest like a medal.

At the dance-hall he tripped the Light fantastic.

Under a sky of such twinkling splendour that the Milky Way might have been a reflection off the sea on one of those three-hundred-cran nights down Yarmouth way he stood outside the door and addressed a crowd who shuffled their feet and sang *Oh, Johnny, Oh, Johnny, Oh!* until Johnny invited them to shake a leg for Jesus. He emptied the hall and they all waltzed down the street to the strains of the catchiest hymns.

Outside the Labour Exchange Johnny laboured.

Every day a crowd would gather there looking for work, and there he would be every day working for the Lord. Men with faces bitten by hunger and eaten by hopelessness, their heads almost buried in their boots, would lift up their eyes as Johnny fed them, fresh from the oven, the bread of life. It was no good offering a gospel leaflet to a hungry man unless it was wrapped around a slice of bread.

Brenston was on the march. Satan on the retreat.

Every day opened with a hallelujah and closed with an amen. Meeting melted into meeting. By the time the evening praise ended, it was almost time for the morning prayer to begin. When Johnny started preaching the dew-rise of dawn was on his face, and he was still preaching when the dew-fall of dusk was in his hair.

Hear Johnny at the Mission Hall. 7p.m. All Welcome.

At first it was announced on sandwich-boards humped through the streets by three or four members of the crew of the *Bounteous*, then it was chalked on the pavements along with a text or two (Wullsie going out at five o'clock in the morning with his chalk), and finally it appeared on bills printed by the local newspaper and posted all over the town and in the surrounding villages. If the number of folk that went into the Mission Hall to hear Johnny were herring in a barrel, there would be no room for the salt. That Hall became a glory-hole in the house of the Lord, a conversion factory that never closed.

Some folk said that the walls of the Hall shook, and that

you could hear the crack of Johnny's thunder in the next town, if not in the next county, or even in the next world. If a passing ship could not quite make out the words that were setting the sea on fire, she might have picked up the sound of the singing as a town of many denominations blended into one congregation.

From outlying towns and villages they came in what became known as the hallelujah trains. From far-flung places they came to see the strange happenings for themselves. Folk came in invalid chairs and with white walking-sticks; they came from factory and workshop, where they stopped machines or downed tools and left for the meetings, bringing their tea-flasks and piece-boxes with them. A man who came to town for the day on business forgot all about his business and was saved. Johnny's crew-mates became human brushes sweeping up drunks in the streets and depositing them in the Mission Hall, where they wept the tears of the tankard before walking soberly up toward Johnny and the penitents' form. Sauty the cook went his rounds ringing a ship's bell, summoning the town to the banquet of glory in the Hall.

Off its food with excitement, Brenston was in danger of going off its level head as well. A partition was knocked down in the Hall to let in more people; chairs were placed in the aisles and along the platform and still the overspill flooded the back rooms. So tight was the squeeze that Johnny himself had to wedge his way in. In order to make way for the unsaved, the saved were asked to stay outside. And having burned the midnight oil of the spirit, the saved and the unsaved alike followed Johnny home from the meetings, hungry for more of the word.

Neighbour rushed to neighbour with news of the slain. Line boats at sea pulled alongside each other, as was their custom so that their crews might swap accounts of how the haddock was going, only this time

the first words squalled into the wind were the names of
the latest recruits from the legion of the lost. While the
newly reborn were so full of life that they would not go
to bed, at least not before they had strolled along the
Muckle Shore singing hymns, the stricken could not
sleep, and Johnny was called out to attend to them. A
physician of the soul, he had more patients than a
doctor in an epidemic.

What was this if not an epidemic? Everybody was
going down with the falling sickness. Some of the
smitten were fevered for days, others for weeks. Hearts
had to be broken and voices cracked before they could
be made whole again. Strong men betrayed the
symptoms when they began to blow their noses in an
attempt to hide their tears: the handkerchief became
the signal of surrender, and the signal of surrender
became the flag of victory.

In turning the town inside out so that its heart and
soul were exposed to the light, Johnny Halo was
purging it of more than sin; in the eyes of the law he was
cleansing the streets of crime. The police approved as
characters who were considered disreputable were
brought to their knees before the mercy seat of His
Worship in heaven. For crimes were confessed to as well
as sins; confessions that neither painstaking pumping
nor brutal beating would have extorted. Only one
drunk came up before the police court in a period of six
weeks, he being neither a son of Brenston nor a man of
the sea. It was the quietest winter in the long, retentive
memory of the law.

It rained sulphur and fire until Christmas.

So hot under his dog-collar did the minister of the
North Kirk become that he threatened to call the fire
brigade to put out 'this consuming fire from hell.'

You could have warmed your hands on the preacher's

words. In the raging blaze of them there was more than a flicker of blazing rage. Johnny's tongue became an eternal flame licking at the core of everything around him. Every meeting was as highly charged and, for those of a jumpy persuasion, as scarifying as an electric storm. It was as if Johnny were wired to a bolt of lightning or, so divine was the spark that he struck, plugged into the sun. Through the transforming agency of his words he would provide the light and the power to regenerate the town.

He keelhauled the kirk.

'What kind of religion is this that comes on and off like a hat? Standing there like stookies, dressed to the nines, hats to turn a statue's head, white hankies peeping out like a rabbit's tail, not a hair out of place in the house of the Lord. Hold on to your hats, I'm going to tell you something no minister has ever told you before. No more can you be sure of going to heaven by going to kirk than you can be sure of going to kirk by going down the Kirkgate.'

He mastheaded the ministers.

'So the kirk's dying – dying for a revival. And who'll revive it? Have you ever heard of a bishop starting a revival? Have you ever heard of a minister saying he was saved? To have the word is one thing; to have the spirit is another. The clergy have all gone through the Bible, but has the Bible gone through all the clergy?'

Stupefied, wry-eyed faces.

'In the hands of these learned men the Bible is like a sun-dial by moonlight. Theology, that's what they preach. What's it got to do with Christianity? The same as botany's got to do with flowers, or astronomy with the stars. Botany's rewritten, but the flowers remain the same; theology changes, but Christianity abides.'

Scandalised, they thought: He'll close the kirks.

'Course, they've been to college. They've got a string of letters after their name as long as the numerical fleet of Yarmouth. Sister, your wet tears are worth a whole library of their dry volumes.'

Wine, too, tasted the grape-shot of his wrath.

'As a wise old skipper used to say, there's never any trouble at sea: the troubles begin when you throw a rope ashore. For us lads on the *Bounteous*, soon as we got her tied up, it was full steam ahead to The Anchorage. We'd the throat of a fish and the head of an ass. The amount we drank would have floated a flagship. If you placed all the drinking-glasses in this town one on top of the other the rim of the topmost glass would just about touch the lips of the man in the moon.'

Poor as kirk mice were the rich.

'Squirrels, that's what you are. Bright-eyed and bushy-tailed when it comes to worldly possessions. Poor little rich fools that you are. You possess all things except the greatest thing of all: charity. Rich you may be, but you wear the filthy rags of sin. It's easier for a rich man to go through the eyelet of a sail than enter the kingdom of heaven.'

He was heckled.

'Me, I'm only a poor fisherman-preacher.'

'We know – we've heard you.'

'If Christ came back, Bowie, what would you do?'

'Play Him at centre-forward for Brenston Thistle.'

'Are you saved, Ruthie lass?'

'I've been vaccinated.'

'You may laugh. *For as the crackling of thorns under a pot, so is the laughter of the fool*. You may laugh your soul into hell, my friends, but you'll never laugh it out.'

'If you were a ship's boiler, Johnny, you'd blow up.'

'And you, I could catch a cold standing next to you.'

'Away to the butcher for thrupenceworth of brains.'

'And will I say they're for you, Yarco?'

And to a drunk with a well-oiled larynx: 'Your tongue keeps rapping away there, daft as a gate on a blustery day. Brother, it takes this crowd all its time to put up

with me, never mind you. Folk like you who come here
to mock will yet remain to repent.'

And as for man ...

'Have you noticed all the nice things written on
gravestones? Where are all the sinners buried? Saint
Paul wouldn't recognise his fellow man from some of
the things you see on yonder stones in Brenston
Kirkyard. No disrespect for the dead, but I believe Paul
was nearer the mark in the third chapter of Romans.
Man's portrait in X-ray. Behold him, deadly as a snake,
more treacherous than the herring, his soul as black as
the Earl of Hell's waistcoat.'

In the thick of this face-slapping storm the weather
grew sullen, a wind got up and in its blowzy way ran its
fingers through the sea. Dishevelled, the sea rose in a
towering rage; the harbour foamed at the mouth. Along
the North Breakwater the sea and the sky decided to
meet at the front doors of the houses. Half of the
roadway was swirled away and into parlour and privy
water swooshed. Brenston was blue in the face.
Cowering before the ire and fire of Johnny, it now had
to flee from the path and wrath of the sea.

His meetings swelled. While the boats were kept at
their moorings, their crews were kept at the meetings.
Folk called it an act of God. Not in sixty years had the
town seen such seas or felt such winds; not since the last
great revival, those with a belief in signs remarked. It
was more than a gale, Johnny told them, as if they did
not know it. It was a visitation. A judgement.

To the whole town, trooping to the Mission Hall to
hear the word, it was as if Johnny had provoked that sea.
Was it not strange that in the eye of his rushing mighty
wind of words there should come this rushing mighty
wave? Even as Johnny was slaying his sinful brother, the
sea was raising Cain. Was it not somehow sent?

They shivered and shied as he pitched into the storm.

'Caught in a storm like that out there, the sea coming at you like an octopus, you're seasick, homesick and sick of the sea, and lucky is the man who can string two thoughts together. Battered about in an easterly, and running for the harbour mouth, you point her bow between the two piers, and with one mighty heave you're home. You could kiss her stem, aye, even her stern, you're that relieved. Then a mighty calm descends. How much mightier the calm that descends when your eyes behold the city of gold and the harbour bright, when life's storms are past for evermore as you reach at last that heavenly shore. I'd rather be lashed to the wheel with the waves dashing over me than go without God for a single day.'

All over the Hall, all over the town, all through that weekend of hell-fire and sky-high water rockets of distress went up. Not just a ship here and a ship there but whole fleets at a time were sending up flares that said Save Our Souls as the storm of wind, wave and word got to them as never before or, as those with venerable memories said, not since a cooper named Jeems Turner delivered them out of bondage in the days of the open luggers.

Almost as beside itself as the sea was Brenston as it scrambled for the lifeline; so fired up did the town become that on the Saturday in the Square it made a bonfire of its wicked past. Having piled a medley of items, reminders of their unbelief, from prerequisite plug to prized pea-shooter, on top of the organ in the Hall the previous night, men, women and children cast this and other worldly gear on to the unworldly pyre. Briar pipes and tobacco pouches, golf balls and clubs, playing cards and draught boards were offered up by the men; dancing shoes and necklaces, flashy clothes and ribbons, novels and artificial flowers were consigned to the flames by the women; and ludo and tiddly-winks and snakes and ladders were gleefully thrown in by the children. Nothing that only a few hours before had been held dear, but which now they saw to be standing between them and grace, was spared the sacrifice. Some celebrants stopped just short of tearing up the planks of their sinful houses to feed the fire that was purging their hearts and purifying their souls.

Fanned by the high winds, the flames leapt and devoured the articles of faithlessness until the sky was an incandescent red. There was more smoke and fire in the Square that night than there was in a whole row of houses at the height of the winter, and a harder winter the hoariest patriarch could not remember. And round that glory blaze they formed a ring, men, women and children; and they all knelt in prayer and sang choruses, sang like kettles building up a spout of steam and then boiling over, tears gushing in all directions. *I Surrender All* was sung until the ripples of it circled the town itself. In that baptism of fire the world of the surrenderers was dissolved into a molten ball, and when it cooled, long after the last ember had died, everything was changed.

13

Brenston, perceived as a hotbed of contagion, found itself in quarantine. It was given a wide berth by the rest of the world, or at least by that part of the world that was ruled by the Devil in exile. To the worldly it ceased to be a bearing on the social compass. Rather was it to be steered clear of as a ship would steer clear of a dangerous reef; the danger being not that you might be lost, but that you might be saved.

Joyless were the tidings that the Devil had brought with him out of the town from which he had been forced to take flight. Brenston, said he, was not a place any more: it was a state of grace. No longer was it a down-to-earth seatown hard as bone on the fibrositic shoulder of the eastern seaboard: it had been lifted up so that it was suspended somewhere between heaven and earth. And not only had the people changed: the very granite walls were giving off a shimmer, the whole place had taken on a holy haze.

Travellers spoke of a town that had seen a ghost; they talked about a supernatural wind that had blown everybody from for'ard to aft; they swore that they had witnessed a miracle, and by the sound of it – that it was as if a high wind from the east had blown through a timber yard and fashioned a boat – it might have been the creation all over again.

A town so scourged by north-east winds that it went about with its head down and its hands in its pockets was making a national spectacle of itself by looking heavenward and beating its chest in repentance. On bus and boat, in street and fish-house, at work and play, on land and sea, by day and by night: bodies falling before God and their opened bibles.

Bible sales multiplied like the seed of Hagar. Brenston slept with one under its pillow. Shopkeepers kept one on their counter so that they could lay a hand on it and, with a bow of the head, bless each customer in turn. No such comfort bestowed by the merchant who, rather than stop selling cigarettes, lost his customers and had to close his shop till the clouds of glory rolled by.

Feeling the draught no less than the public houses were the two picture houses, the manager of one of them praying in the columns of the *Northern Star* for 'all this hallelujah madness' to blow over. Such states of sobriety were reached that some folk gave up drinking tea because it was a stimulant, a poison, and therefore an enemy of the spirit.

Tobacco, smoked or chewed, taboo; football games cancelled; secular songs bowing before hymns as choirs sprang up at every street corner; dogs and horses, brought up on the Devil's mass, no longer knowing what their masters were saying to them; men calling each other brother, women each other sister; neighbour unable to pass the time of day with neighbour without breathing the name of their Maker; visitors to houses asked to join in prayer when they entered and again when they left; fishermen talking about their souls as openly as they talked about the fishing.

Because the Great Skipper would not approve, men cancelled the insurances on their boats. So as to have money to hand over to the mission field, they mortgaged their shares in these same boats. Nothing impressed the sceptic more than that a town so canny that it was said to look at both sides of a penny before parting with it was giving it away on an impulse and a promise. Nothing was thought of or talked about unless it was clean and pure and of the spirit. While the local Member of Parliament was craving the attention of a sparse crowd on the subject of the conservation of herring stocks, Johnny Halo was holding rapt a teeming throng on the subject of the survival of their souls.

So big had he become, this man who was raising Brenston heaven-high, that the sky was the only roof that could contain his meetings. And not only the sky above Brenston. If the herring-fishing turned a man into a migrant, so did the business of soul-fishing. Soon Halo was jumping on a push-bike and wakening up the sleepy villages round about. And before long he and his crew were boarding a fish lorry and travelling from place to place.

They lit fires all over the coast. Broken and depressed villages were rekindled, fuelled by an inflammable spirit. Blessing came with an autumn ripeness, with the fullness of a harvest moon. It was what the Covenanters had called a bonny-bairn time. It was as fruitful, as spontaneous, as natural, as glorious as spring. And, in the withering eye of the winter witness from outside, no doubt just as transient.

As for the man himself, when the law fined him for the lights failing in the fish lorry there was a whip-round among his followers, and not only was the fine paid, there was enough money left over to buy new bibles and hymn-books. When he went into lodgings so as to ease the burden on the house of his father, for whom the tides of joy were an ever-encroaching turbulence to which neither his hearth nor his heart was yet disposed to open up, his converts sustained him. They would knock on his landlord's door and hand in parcels of food. His landlady would go to the door to find a dead rabbit dangling by its hind legs from the knob. She would take it in, skin it and stew it, and when it was served a special grace would be said. They handed in money, too, to pay for sending a missionary to the Dark Continent. And there were young ladies who bickered among themselves over the far-from-incidental matter of whose would be the privilege of blackening and polishing his boots.

Children followed in his wake in the hope of touching his hand as if so doing would somehow vaccinate them against the Bogy Man. They were settling their quarrels in the playground and, with a good deal more reason than rhyme, they invented a new game. Let's play at converting, they would cry, as if it were hopscotch, or tig, or marbles. What fun the kids had stopping cars in the street, drumming on biscuit tins and chanting at the drivers: 'Christ is coming, you must be saved.' They were so good, the kids of Brenston, so good as they disported themselves in the backyard of the Lord, that when they played marbles they did not cheat.

In the beginning the kirks saw it as no more than fire in a smoke-house. Moonlight on a fish-house door. Until all of a sudden it blew up into what one of their pillars crossed his heart and claimed was a psychic wind hulla-ballooing through the town; putting, according to the most moderate observers, the fear of God into every living thing, cats and parrots no exception.

The kirks declared a blight on the harvest.

Halo was preaching the people mad. He was a danger-ous agitator and as such should be driven out of town. The herring tribe had lost their heads. Inter-marriage had made them unstable and therefore unable to with-stand the hysteria of revival. They would listen to a monkey with a mutch on its head. If Halo told them he had seen a skate flying over the Breakback Rock they would believe him. He was sweeping them from the moorings of reason and balanced judgement. He was giving them no time to think.

Instant salvation. Thirty minutes to waken the dead.

Such harvests did not last. Early ripe, early rotten. A windblown apple fell short of a hand-picked one. As a fisherman Halo ought to know that one sole caught by the hook and line was of a better quality than twenty caught by the net. What went for the sole of the sea went also for the soul of man. All that this soul fisher had caught with his net was immature fish.

In the kirk of the Reverend Balfour Gall wrath burned like incense. So flushed with hostility was the incumbent of Burryhaven Episcopal that you could have cracked a match on his face. Famine had brought them to their knees, he declaimed, not this silver-tongued herring fisherman; prostration was through lack of food and sleep, not this street-corner crusader. If the herring fishery had been as much a success as it had been a failure nobody would have given a snap of the fingers for their soul.

To the Episcopalian lash of Mr Gall was added the Presbyterian scourge of the Reverend Atholl Selvidge. Someone, submitted the man who graced the charge of Northcliff Parish, should throw a net over the head of this man and haul him into the madhouse before he turned Brenston into an open asylum. How could he be allowed to preach unchallenged to such crowds? And as for the flocks that were straying from the kirks to taste the new grass, they were committing more than the sin of promiscuous hearing, such black sheep had bats in their belfries. To the doctor who complained about his patients receiving the 'glorious chloroform' Mr Selvidge had a prescription of his own to recommend: cold baths.

Throwing light on the dark side of events, the newspapers stoked the fire of damnation that showered down from high and mighty pulpits the length and breadth of the land. There were reports of 'pulsations', of a 'psychic disturbance', of people driven to the cliff-edge of madness. A man ran screaming down to the sea in his nightshirt; another smashed a chair to smithereens because a minister had sat in it, and next day was removed to the asylum. Some poor, deluded soul stepped off the pier and almost drowned because he thought he could walk on water. A woman claimed that her handbag had been stolen at a meeting. Doctors warned that the late nights were detrimental to health and were leading to the neglect of children. Families were not so much divided as riven asunder. A reporter posing as an evangelist in the hope of getting an inside story was set upon by a crowd using banners as barricades and weapons of persuasion, his motor car kicked and stoned out of town.

They stoned Johnny, too, the bullies who had tried to wreck one of his meetings. They stoned him as he made his way home the night he went for the ringleader's throat. Be quiet or leave, he had pleaded with them in the Hall, and they laughed at his weak words. He called for a hymn, which drowned out the noise of them while it lasted. Then they started up again. He called for a prayer. He had got halfway through it when, with the four trouble-makers at their most troublesome, he opened his eyes to see half of the meeting fidgeting and looking about them as though they were too scared to pray. Down he went to where the four were sitting and asked one of them to come out. They sat tight and laughed. You, he said, beckoning to the ringleader. A hush fell over the meeting; everybody was on the edge of their seat. Those who shut their eyes in despairing prayer did not see Johnny's hand shoot out for the bully's throat and twist his muffler until he gasped. Amid flailing arms Johnny hauled his man into the aisle, where he shook him as though he were shaking herring from a net, and next thing both of them were rolling on the floor like drunks in a bar-room scuffle. Women screamed. Some ran out of the Hall. The man from the *Daily Post* saw irony in all hell breaking loose just as the meeting was reaching out for heaven. Not until Johnny had frog-marched his man to the door and bunged him out into the street, and the other three rowdies had sheepishly joined their leader outside, was order restored.

In looking, as was their wont, for motes in the moon's eye, the newspapers seemed to be running a crusade of their own. From the day that a photograph captioned 'The Burning of the Idols' appeared in print all over the country, the glory story was the subject of daily, though far from reverential, devotions by the scribes. Brenston was leading with the highest number of conversions, one chronicler informed his readers, for whom a league table was produced that would not have looked out of position on the sports page. Scores of converts had gone forward, another report alleged, because their friends had done so, or because it was the fashion, or because of false shame. Senior citizens read that many of their number went to the meetings for warmth, in order to save fuel at home; while the womenfolk were taking their knitting with them, one fisherwife being observed to enter the Hall with a newly begun stocking and to leave it with the heel well turned.

To the town's young men it was something less than news to learn that they talked about going to 'The Show', that one of their main pranks was to roll stones down the roof of the Hall when a meeting was on, and that inside the Hall they sat themselves behind unsuspecting women, the ends of whose shawls they set about tying to the backs of the forms so that when the women stood up to sing they were bound in knots, held together like a string of fish.

For the reader of the public press women were running out of their homes in nightgowns and bare feet during the sleeping hours and throwing themselves at the feet of a man with chloroform in his handkerchief: a man known variously, depending upon which journalistic hymn-sheet you followed, as Johnny Halo, Johnny Holy, Herring Johnny and Hallelujah John. Drunks were going for drunks who would not stop shouting as this man who could say something three times without anybody noticing was doing just that and bringing his fist down with the force to break a board in the pulpit. Anonymous and abusive letters were being sent addressed to 'Saint Johnny'; and a parcel of horse-dung was popped through his letter-box. From the mouth of a cave, according to the *Evening Gleaner*, there came the strains of hymns and the screams of souls in purgatory. One glance into the furnace as he stoked the boiler was enough for one boat's engineer to flee from the fires of eternal punishment. A man stood at the door of his house, doffed his bonnet and preached to passers-by the imminent end of the world. Teachers were chucking in the chalk when they found that they could not contain the fervour of their pupils.

To the correspondent whose letter in the *Brenston Beacon* said that the time had come to get out the straitjacket a reader replied that similar noises had been heard in ancient times. A mad fellow they had called the young prophet who anointed Jehu; mad, according to Isaiah, was how they looked upon any man who departed from evil; mad was Jeremiah in the eyes of Shemaiah, who thought he should be put in prison and in the stocks; a fool was what they saw in a prophet in the days of Hosea, and a hallucinating spirit in a spiritual man; crazy was Paul in the mind of Festus; a devil possessed John the Baptist; while demon-driven and deranged was Jesus, whom the Jews accused of being a raving lunatic. To which litany of transcendent madness another letter-writer addressed himself and asked if, from the cradle years of the Christian faith, it had not been so that the children of darkness had always called the children of light mad.

Searching for a light in his own darkness, a commentator in the *Northern Star* came up with the paraphrase that, since all along this north-eastern coast folk lived within a stone-cast of high-water mark, their fortunes reflected the crests and troughs of the sea, the pattern of their lives a series of waves rather than a constant current, and in the fluid state of such an economy no new high or low could be experienced without the Plimsoll line of public emotion going up or down as the tide ordained.

Like a man betrayed Johnny confronted his crucifiers.

It was with misgivings that he submitted to the interview in the *Weekly Informer*, for as he told its representative, who rejoiced in the title of Our Special Commissioner: 'I don't want my name plastered all over the papers like a prize-fighter. And I can't say I warm to the idea of being translated into print by ungodly persons.'

Unashamedly quoting the strictures, Our Special Commissioner, describing his subject as straight as a spirit level, proceeded to plaster Johnny's name not only all over the front page of the *Informer*, and the prize-fighter face that went with it – the whole splurge made all the more circusy by being embroidered with the names and faces of his crew – but all over an inside page as well, as Johnny dealt with the questions fired at him while the ungodly person firing them occasionally filled the space between the previous answer and the next question with anecdote, both authentic and apocryphal.

Have you always wanted to be a preacher?

'I'm not a preacher, I'm a messenger of God.'

How did you become God's messenger?

'He took Elisha from the plough, Peter and Andrew and John from their nets, and me from the herring-fishing.'

How is it that you, a man of the sea, are able to take a sermon, a sermon with which, as you yourself might say, a minister would send a congregation to sleep, and preach it so that you transform the lives of scores of people?

'Your ministers are speaking to the times: I am speaking for eternity. I use penny words: they use shilling words. When a man talks about the bionomics of herring you may be sure that that man cannot catch a herring to save his life. So it is, then, when a man holds forth on the new theology. You may be sure that that man cannot save a soul – no, not to save his own one.'

Where did you find this gift for words, this hitherto undiscovered power that has suddenly materialised in you and has brought Brenston to its knees?

'I haven't brought Brenston to its knees: the herring has. I just happened to lead it in prayer. As to where I found the words, I believe it was the words that found me. *Then said I, Ah, Lord God, behold, I cannot speak: for I am a child. But the Lord said unto me, Say not, I am a child: for thou shalt go to all that I shall send thee, and whatsoever I command thee thou shalt speak. Be not afraid of their faces: for I am with thee to deliver thee, saith the Lord. Then the Lord put forth his hand, and touched my mouth.*'

What have you to say to the minister who wrote, in a recent letter to the *Informer*, that your preaching did not go very deep?

'To anybody who thinks that I'd simply say this. Take a look at a bottle of milk. Is not the cream on the surface?'

What is your answer to the charge that you are preaching the masses – as a town councillor puts it – 'out of their misery and into the madhouse'?

'What's wrong with going mad for heaven? People go mad through drink and gambling and debt and war, but no mention of that in your paper. What of the thousands that are in the asylums through demon worship and spiritualism and the like? No mention of that. The mad ones among us are not the ones that are wrestling with their souls: the mad ones are the ones that are running away from the good fight. Mad? There's nothing wrong with our heads. It's our hearts that have changed.'

What will happen to the converts?

'I am a fisher of souls, not a processor. I catch the fish, I don't cure them and pack them and prepare them for the table. Once we've caught and landed them we leave the rest, the processing if you like, to the kirks.'

Are you planning to campaign elsewhere?

'God is my planner. Whatever He wills I will do it. Man is powerless to plan affairs of the spirit: you cannot organise the Holy Ghost.

'Right now I cannot leave this place; it is so full of glory. We've spent a long winter in the wilderness. We have all come home by weeping cross. The fruitless fig-tree is crying out for dung.

'I believe we are entering a springtime of the spirit. Ben Mor is being shaken by the prayers of the fishermen of Brenston. This part of the coast has become a place of light: the land of Goshen. Love has been increased tenfold.

'Brenston may be in ashes, aye. But that's only half of it. It's going to be in sackcloth as well before I'm through.'

In the course of an endless spate of questions Our Special Commissioner noted the silver watch-chain that Johnny Halo was wearing – 'a gift from a man whose life he had changed' – and informed his readers that every watch Halo wore was apt to go cuckoo, such was the electricity generated in his body. 'God is my time-keeper,' he quoted him as saying. And describing his subject finally as 'the dispenser of a local anaesthetic called "gloryform",' he reported that, in losing a stone in weight through his tireless preaching, Johnny

Hallows had gained for himself a new celebrity, his rechristening having already been commemorated in the launching the other week of a fishing vessel glorying in the name of *Johnny Halo*.

14

It took only one shepherd to leap the dyke; then, with a diffident baa here and a dragging foot there, the whole flock of shepherds followed.

Moved by the interview in the *Informer*, the Reverend Fergus Boyd, a young man with letters after his name, who knew it all from books and could deliver a solid sermon, strayed one night into the Mission Hall, where he had occasion to bend down and listen to a prostrate child praying; in the course of which he straightened himself and stood rock-still, as might a man on the brink of a boundless leap, immovable in his conviction that what he had just seen and heard was the work of God. Still in a state of shock after he got home, he knelt down in front of an armchair before ultimately praying himself into prostration, becoming like that wondrous child on the floor; where, for an eternity, he was to remain until he came to, a new man, resigned to the realisation that no longer was he the assistant to the incumbent in the churchy charge of Westhaven.

Judgement day had dawned for the kirks. Sour grapes no longer hung heavy in the vineyard of the Lord.

No sooner was the Reverend Mr Boyd's awakening adorning the newspapers than his fellow blackcoats, some of whom had been proving more difficult to overcome than the Devil himself, wandered into Johnny's meetings out of curiosity as much as duty to their congregations and were themselves awakened from their apathy or put to rest in their antipathy. In the humble confines of the Mission Hall they saw the upheaval for the first time in the spirit as well as in the flesh, and were amazed. Marvelling, as they came away, at those who could not read the letter of The Book being so versed in its spirit; and agog at this unlettered fisherman holding an audience for seven hours in the palm of his salt-scoured hand when they could barely hold theirs for an hour.

From all over the country scholars and theologians made an almost ungodly stampede to see the 'spiritual strip-tease' and 'emotional debauchery' for themselves, and went away muttering words like 'spiritual refreshment' and 'moral reformation.'

Nor was it just lip-service. Not only had the kirks begun to pray for Johnny: they opened their doors to him, invited him to speak within their sacred walls. And these kirks he filled from altar to vestibule. For the first time in their lives elders came into grace. While ministers marched to the Mission Hall at the head of their flocks and behind a brass band.

Johnny, who had trodden on many a toe before, came within a hairbreadth of treading on the heads of the bodies stretched out at his feet as he walked down aisle after conscience-smitten aisle. Having taken the spiritual cold out of the town, he endeavoured to take the chill out of its churches. Freer and less formal the services became. There was no need for the bells to ring since the faithful were already sitting in their pews long before the bell-ringer had left his house. And from pulpits that hitherto had counselled against a man who had caused more rupture than rapture in the life of the town, the remaining sceptics heard such things as signified that he had converted the very kirks themselves.

Far from being mass psychology or crowd consciousness, the new word came down from on high, this was the genuine spirit. This was that which was alluded to by the prophet Joel. This was the latter rain that the apostle James had spoken of, that yielded the long-awaited fruit. Whereas the kirks had only knocked on the door of the people's hearts, this reformed fisherman had the key to open them. And why was such divine truth concealed from the wise men of the church and revealed through the mouth of a man whose university had been a herring boat? To make the wise men humble, to teach the church humility. Johnny Halo walked in the truth. The hand of God was in all that he did. His gift of speaking like that could only be godly. Humbleness and pride, the lamb and the lion, dwelt in this man. This man who was as proudly humble as a herring on a king's plate.

The most high-minded of Johnny's flyters, those who had been prescribing cold baths to combat the fever, could be seen baptising converts on the beach. When dog-collar met dog-collar in the street one would shake the other earnestly by the paw. Those who had never left their pulpits since the day of their induction were emboldened into winging from pulpit to pulpit, spreading the evangel. Not only had the people of the straitened town taken to their bended knees: the very men who should have been leading them in that observance had themselves been brought to their hassocks.

Brenston awaited Johnny's loudest hosanna.

Great though his conversion of the kirk was, and greater though the list of the slain became, there was no doubt in the mind of saint or sinner what his greatest conquest was. It was the rounding up of the one who had strayed so far over the hill as to be beyond human recall, the returning to the fold of that black sheep who, in the heat and bleat of the spiritual lambing season, had sought succour in the lowest pastures of pleasure, in the demon dip and the wanton frolic. Nobody had trampled his pearls into deeper mire, nobody had gone awhoring after more gods, than the painted Jezebel whose room on the top floor of the tenement known as The Gullery had in a couple of seasons grown from a window-box into a garden of earthly delights for those men who liked their whisky neat and their women with a dash of moral dishevelment.

Heaven's rapture could hardly have exceeded Brenston's when she who had been clothed in the scarlet of sin walked free in the whiteness of purity. It happened on the heels of such a pentecostal gust of air that Johnny was heard to exclaim at the end of more than one meeting: 'We've caught some cran tonight.'

Out of such a haul might have emerged the catch of the season had not she who was regarded as the biggest fish of all in the sea of sin decided to give herself up. And seven days later, in the afterglow of her rebirth and in a Hall packed as for a spiritual strip-show, Hannah Gale gave her testimony.

'You all know me. And my business. It's taken a lot of reckless living and a famine to get me standing here tonight, giving my testimony. The thief at the foot of the cross, remember. It's never too late to change. Never mind how bad you've been. If there's hope for me, there's hope for all of you. I was what the Bible calls a harlot. Well, Jesus himself says harlots will enter the kingdom before some priests and elders.'

So composed did she look, Brenston's Prodigal Daughter, that she might have been talking to a friend at her own fireside.

'It's not been easy for me. No man could have pardoned my sins, they were so great. Such a burden, I think I did well to carry it. From the soles of my feet to my head I was mixed up in it, the oldest sin in the world. Folk would come up to me in the street and say I was giving Brenston a bad name. Fishermen visiting the place had their own name for it. "Hannah's Port", they called it. Soon as they came ashore they looked me up and put wads of notes into my hand for certain favours. Twenty clients one night. Rolling up in taxis. My partner in sin, Maizie, a young lass that had run away from home, had to be treated for the bad disease. How I missed it only the good Lord Himself knows.

'I'd rather my hand was cut off than lose my sin. Aye, I was like Judas, I'd sooner have been hanged than believed. If anybody claimed they were goody-goody, I'd have scoffed at them. If Jesus walked down the same pavement – forgive me, Lord Jesus – I'd have crossed to the other side of the street. I was scared to go near a kirk for fear I met God. I could never have faced Him. Like the bats, I hated the light. They'd taunt me in the street, my old school chums. "Eternity's round the corner," they'd say, nodding in the direction of the Burning Stone. "So's the Quayside Inn," I'd answer back, my heart like flint. "You Jezebel that you are," they'd say, a fist flashing in my face like a gutting knife.

'It was only after I threw a friend out of the house one night for prigging with me to go with her to a meeting that I began to be troubled. The more I heard about the revival, the more unhappy I was. One day I saw a cow eating grass in a field and I wished I was that cow, for then I'd have no soul to worry about. Every morning I'd wake up in hell. I didn't want to live and I was too scared to die. I couldn't pluck up enough courage, Dutch or otherwise, to jump into the harbour. I think I was beginning to realise my sins had nailed Him to that cross. I felt bound with ropes.

'Now the bonds are loosed and I have the good Lord to thank for giving me one last chance. I'd my coat on that night, ready to do my usual rounds of the harbour, when this friend turned up at the house again and asked me to go along with her to the meeting. I don't know why I didn't throw her out again; I don't know why I agreed to go with her. Business, in any case, was bad, the fishing being as it is. Anyway, I had the war paint on and was reeking of perfume. Like a lot of women, I thought a dab of scent would cover up all sin. "Take your knitting with you," my friend said, "so's the neighbours will think you're going to somebody's house for an hour." Just like Nicodemus, we tried to hide the real purpose of our errand, so ashamed were we of being thought anxious about our souls.

'I arrived at the Hall with a fag in my mouth, and when I saw Johnny standing there I just had to look away. There was a light in his face that seemed to shine right through me. I didn't just snib the fag out, I stamped on it. He was preaching from the ten virgins. "How many of you here tonight," he said, "will have oil in your lamp if the bridegroom comes in the midnight watch?" Then he said something that sounded as if he was picking me out. "I'm not speaking to the ninety and nine," he said, "I'm speaking to the one that's lost, the one that's strayed, and I'll walk to the mountain-top till I've found that lost sheep." That was me, the lost sheep. And you all sang *The Ninety and Nine*. And a young chap who'd been clanging a bell at the back of the Hall came forward, crying for pardon.

'There were more like him, coming forward. And more singing. And more praying. I sat there till I could take no more. I got up to go when my friend grabbed hold of my hand and pleaded with me to stay. I wanted to run out. Then Johnny started to speak again, and next thing I was crying. He seemed to be speaking to me, to me alone. Why should Jesus care about me, a sinful wretch like me?

'The first thing I did when I got home was throw my packet of fags in the fire. Something was working on me, and I was afraid. For a whole week I couldn't sleep at nights for thinking about it. I was in torment. I was so worked up one night I smashed everything I could lay my hands on in the house. Everywhere I turned, he was there, the Devil. I took off my shoe and flung it across the room into his face. I crawled on the floor. I felt like Eve without her fig-leaf. I wanted to hide in a corner I couldn't find. I got out of bed in the middle of the night and walked along the shore looking for the answer. God has caught me in my curlers. I knew the game, my particular game, was up.

'There's a new man in my life now, and his name is Jesus. And I tell you, in the very short time I've known him I wouldn't change places with the Queen. To think that if it hadn't rained last Wednesday night ... if it hadn't rained, we might never have met. I'd taken my shoes off so's not to let the neighbours in the tenement know I was slipping out to the meeting by myself. Not till I got to the Hall door did I put them back on. Every seat was taken, so I stood with a crowd at the back. Again it was all meant for me, everything Johnny said. *"I will take the stony heart out of your flesh,"* he said, taking the words from The Book, *"and I will give you a heart of flesh."* And straight at my stony heart he aimed the next words that I've cause to remember: *"I find more bitter than death the woman whose heart is snares and nets."* And then, when he said the roughest diamond can be polished by the spirit, that cheered me up. And again when he pointed to The Book: *"Though your sins be as scarlet, they shall be as white as snow ... If ye be willing."*

'Oh, the words he poured out that night. All of them meant for me. And yet in the end it took only ten, ten words to make me see what all the others meant. Aye, ten words, just. It took ten words, if you remember, to create the world. *In the beginning God created the heaven and the earth.* Well, it took ten words to create my new life – to give me a new beginning. *"She that liveth in pleasure is dead while she liveth."* That was all I needed to hear. I stood condemned. The life I'd been leading was a living death. When the meeting broke up somebody said it was raining. Raining hard, and many of us without coats. So Johnny decides to keep us in till the rain goes off. And while we're waiting a score of souls are saved, and Hannah, the wildest of all the Gales, as my mother used to say, is one of them.'

Hannah of the Herring Moon. Whom Satan sought to defile and destroy. Hannah the Harlot. Behold her now. Hannah, the gift of God.

Johnny remembered the flame on her cheeks when first they met; the autumn flush on her face while she gutted the herring at Yarmouth. That flame, that flush was as a wax-light flickering on a sickroom wall to the bloom he saw the night she cast off her coat of scarlet and walked, pure as the rushing wind, into whiteness.

Like a gas mantle, her face. Such a glow that more than a shade of it had made bold to mantle the already glowing face of Johnny.

As quickly as it took to bend the knee, the change had come. There she was on the floor, beating her breast and weeping rivers. Tears sputtering down her face like sparks from the blazing faggots that were her eyes as she petitioned God for help. Somebody dabbed her cheeks and brow with a handkerchief. Johnny, remembering the seven devils that were cast out of Mary Magdalene, went to her. And while she locked horns on the floor with the ghost of her past, her eyes closed as though blinded by some intoxicatingly strange light, the congregation sang for her and prayed for her until eventually, perceiving the Devil behind her, bound hand and cloven foot, they began to clap their hands in triumph.

Hannah's throat tightened; her lips parted. The knife plunged and the seven scars were excised from her soul like the guts from a herring. To her lips she took the cup of salvation; the taste of milk was in her mouth, and sweeter it was than the deadly pickle of the malt. She who could have papered her room with temperance cards she had signed over the years was turning at last from the table of Mine Host to the table of the Lord of Hosts; she was stepping out of the wine-vault and into the vineyard. And exhilarating it was for Johnny to behold.

When she opened her eyes it was to reveal a face dismantled of its former agony and serene as a pane of glass. Something in these eyes, and in her grip as she shook his hand, told Johnny that the rough diamond had found the priceless pearl. Her tears had been transformed into stars before his eyes. She whom they called the Painted Lady was wearing a new, comelier make-up, and more fragrant it was than the spices that the Queen of Sheba gave to Solomon. He discerned a light in her soul, a light that drew its brightness from a luminous, numinous love, and a lightness in her heart, a lightness that was not of this heavy-laden world. Just as a gleam of moonlight on the water could make him catch his breath, so did this shimmer of immortal loveliness, this divine phosphorescence that was moving upon the face of the waters of the spirit, flooding and transfiguring the countenance of his regenerate Hannah, and endowing her with a new and burning vision.

*

From the moment she went to the door on the first morning of her new life, and saw lying there a bunch of white flowers, Hannah experienced a happiness that she wanted to proclaim until it was heard in the hallowed halls of heaven, proclaim as though she had indeed changed her name to Hosanna. Could heaven be more glorious than this? Was she not perchance sleep-walking; drifting maybe on a magic carpet? She was so glad, and all the world seemed to be glad with her. She wanted to ride on a white steed through the town in triumph. Golden bright were the pavements, and the granite walls turned to jasper. In the distance the light was silvery. By the Suddron Kirk the trees were a heavenly host. *I am the Vine, ye are the branches.* She was walking on a cloud. Alive to a new plane of being, she was dead to the mockery of the world.

To Johnny's lodgings she went, seized by a strong yet tender urge to offer him some token of her gratitude. If certain young ladies had a mind to blacken and polish his boots, why not she? She would minister to his weary feet, that's what she would do. These blessed, wandering, anchored-on-the-rock-of-faith feet. She could have kissed them, washed them in her tears, wiped them with the hair of her head and anointed them with fragrant oils. Her face still mantled, the bloom on it still garden-fresh out of Eden, she prepared a foot-bath and asked Johnny's landlady for the best towel in the house. Nudged on by the landlady, Johnny assented. And so, by washing his feet, Hannah became unto Johnny what Mary Magdalene had become unto Jesus: a faithful dog at the heels of the shepherd. Hannah would have been there, too, last at the cross, when they crucified her Lord. She would have been there kneeling at his feet in the shadows under the dead stars.

A few nights later God's servant and his handmaiden stood before a huge chest in front of the Mission Hall platform. Hymns were sung and a sermon preached in which Johnny claimed that there was not a single instance of infant baptism in the Bible. Hats and coats were removed from off the chest and its lid opened. It was full of water. A man with his sleeves rolled up stepped forward and, mouthing a snatch of scripture, dunked Hannah backwards into the chest until her head went under. Panting and shivering, she surfaced.

'Hallelujah,' a voice shouted from the body of the

meeting.

It was her sister Lil. Skirt and blouse dripping, Hannah was led away to an ante-room, there to change into a new shift of clothes to go with her new person.

'When I lifted up my head,' – Hannah's voice had grown softer, warmer, surer the further she had got into her testimony – 'I could have looked into the face of Jesus. Whereas I was blind – aye, some of you may say blind drunk most of the time – now I could see. "Every tear is a pearl," Johnny was saying to me quietly as the tears streamed down my face. "Every tear is the dew-drop of a new dawn." I felt so happy I wanted to go to heaven. Aye, straight away. So happy, I could hardly sleep that night. For a couple of days before and after I made my decision I could neither eat nor sleep: I was too troubled before, and too happy afterwards. Soon as I got home I gave myself a good washdown, so I was clean in body as well as mind.'

Next morning she got up an hour earlier to read her bible, to talk to God. For the first time in her life, she said, she could pray. Not the parrot prayers she had learnt at school but personal, private words with God. Words about such matters as those who had disowned her.

'My own family, my friends, even the folk of Brenston – all of them had cast me out. Well, I forgive them all. They may not forgive me, but the new man in my life has, and I rejoice. Day and night I pray for them, all of them, that they may be changed like me. As for my family, we're reunited again, they've taken me in after my years in the wilderness. We sit up till daylight, me and the folks, talking about salvation. I've burnt my worldly magazines; I'm even learning to play the organ. Nothing scares me any more, not even mice.

'Whatever's happened to her, the whole town's wondering. Hannah Gale's got a nice new dress on and she tires herself out going round the doors with tracts. I'm a good girl now, I tell them, and if they take a good look at me they'll see that the wrinkles have gone from my face. God's peeled off the mask of pleasure I've been wearing all my life, and revealed the real face behind it. Sin was keeping me from the Bible before, and now the Bible's keeping me from sin. What'll you do with yourself now, an old drinking chum asked me the other day, as much as to say that not only was he at a loss to understand what's happened, but that I must be at a loss, too, as to what to do about it. Well, Mully, I said to him, I think I might just start translating the Bible. Into life.'

And before the eyes of all the Mullys of the world Hannah held up a cork, a souvenir of her conquest over the bottle; and confessing that she had been one for a drop of whisky in her tea instead of milk, she smiled as she said that, like the Cornish miner Johnny spoke about, her teapot had been converted as well. When the hallelujahs died down Johnny called for a prayer in which he thanked God that Hannah had chosen the fragrant life, and that His word was now a lamp unto her feet and a light unto her path; after which he offered up the petition that others might follow in that path and put a hand up for Jesus, remembering that he had put two up for them.

*

It did not come to pass. Hannah did not grow her hair to her knees and, true to the prophecy of the old wives of Brenston, weep dew-drops at the feet of Johnny. She did not have his foot-bath ready when he returned from his wanderings. To his catch she did not add the salt of the packer. Not for her a whithersoever-he-goest-I-will-go act of penitence, she the vowel to his consonant in the hymn of praise to their Master.

Such was the thoroughness of the Gales that the change that had come over Hannah was not yet complete. A whole new woman, she needed a whole new change. So rather than hit the sawdust trail as a prize trophy of the man who had once before been the light of her eyes, as the old wives had prophesied she would, Hannah set sail for a clean start in the New World. Not alone, as she was to assure family and friends before departing. God would be sailing with her.

15

What else could it be if not the crack of doom? A boat from Burryhaven was blown up by a mine off the Breakback and went down with all hands. A boy from Sandness was drowned while fishing for his supper off the rocks at Brenston. A snowstorm such as had not been seen for years set in, and as an afterclap a flu epidemic in the county town of Seahaven claimed thirty lives in one week.

While the questioning mind brooded on those things, mystified as to why the Lord should repay the redeemed in this way, the bite of the famine deepened. Cold, cold was the moon in the wolf-month of January. Just as it turned a deaf ear to the baying of a dog, so it turned a blind eye to the plight of his master. So hard had life become in this world, the unshriven felt no less than the shriven, that things were bound to be better in the next.

It might have been the next world that Johnny was living in, for all that Brenston saw or heard of him. True, his voice of late had sounded raw and hoarse, so it was no surprise to hear that he had finally lost it. And difficult though it was to imagine him without a tongue – like imagining the sea without its roar – it would have been none the less reassuring to have had him around, moving, a silent sermon, mute and yet glorious, among them. Maybe his being reduced to a whisper was an impediment he found altogether too embarrassing;

maybe a voiceless Johnny was a powerless Johnny. Whatever the reason, he shied away from the meetings.

If he had stayed indoors, ministering to his vocal cords, it would have been understandable. But he took himself off to places far removed from the crowds. To wild places inhabited by the master-works of nature and empty of all people save for himself; to solitary places where he might feel not merely alone but Alone; to god-forsaken holes and corners where his congregations were the beasts of the field and the fowls of the air. While he wandered, lonely as the moon on an arctic night, from place to place, seeking the company of no one, and no longer looking for his lost voice but on a mystical pilgrimage the nature of which was known only to himself and the invisible presence who was his constant companion, it seemed to many a Brenstonian that his withdrawal from the scene of his conquests was absolute.

Word of him drifted in on a tale-bearing wind, each tale taller than the last, so that the pedlars of rumour felt obliged to observe that maybe more than his voice had cracked up.

He had done a moonlight flit, they said. He had gone to live in a cave. He was tramping the fields and scouring the hedges for lost sheep. He was seeing the water of life in a puddle, God's footprints on the sands, and little children gambolling on the hill of the heavenly Lamb. He was calling the moon his brother – and she a lady. She it was who had drawn him in the beginning, and she it was who would claim him in the end. Nights you would find Johnny Halo baking cakes to the queen of heaven.

It was true that he had gone to a cave. One day he went down to the cliffs, picked up a plank on the shore, and walked with it into the cathedral-like cavern known as the Devil's Kitchen; there he knelt upon the plank, clasped his hands and prayed. Before he stood up again

the incoming tide was all but lapping his feet. When he
left his face echoed the cathedral calm of the cave.

It was true that he had tramped the fields. Falling
upon his knees and raising a prayer in his husk of a
voice as he ploughed his lone furrow for the Supreme
Reaper. Seeing the spirit of God in a snowflake and
hearing it in the whirring wings of a bird. Different,
every snowflake that fell on him; different, every
snowflake that was sent down to earth. He thought of
the shepherd boy who became king and of the
carpenter who became King of kings. So much was he at
home in the open that he could have roofed a ditch and
lived there. Once, physically spent, he nodded off
behind a hedge and slept like a stone.

It was true, too, that he had bathed himself in
moonlight. One evening, lying in bed at his lodgings, his
eye caught the moon eavesdropping through his
window. She was bigger and bolder than any moon he
had ever seen. She filled his room with a pulsating light
that filtered through him until it burnished his soul like
the brass on his bedstead. He could not sleep. He leapt
out of bed, knelt before the window and prayed; the
words flowing out in a fevered tide, husky words
flashing and flaring in the phossy light.

Turning his face to the moon, he reached out his
arms as if to embrace her; and immediately dropped his
hands and head. What he was seeing was only a glint,
only a hint of the light of heaven. How pale and
penny-pinched the light of the moon was. How wan and
watery was the glow on those beguiling moon-seas off
Yarmouth. Compared, he thought, to the deep, blissful
radiance of the heavenly illuminations. There was light,
and there was Light. He was walking away from the
former towards the latter. For a darkness had been
creeping up on him under cover of light: the darkness
that was none other than the sunshine of revival in
which he had been tempted to bask. There was only one

antidote to the blaze of publicity, only one escape from the falsity of fame: to seek the light that shone in the soul that was in tune with the harmonies of heaven.

With these harmonies he was in such tune that in his song the wild cat lay down with the day-old chick. Spiritually as well as physically he was on the move. Further and further out of self and deeper and deeper into Jesus. More and more on his knees. The walls of his room stained with the breath of prayer.

Away from the crowds, he was a dove set free. Liberated from the cage of vexation by the spirit taken wing. The eye of the understanding filled with light.

His feet swollen from all his walking and standing for hours on end, he remembered the words of Moses before he viewed the promised land (and thereafter, being full of days, died): *Thy shoes shall be iron and brass; and as thy days, so shall thy strength be.* Johnny was wearing his feet to his knees. And in so doing he had viewed his promised land.

Every morning, come hail or hale water, he climbed the hill above the town, the hill up which he had scampered as a boy to see the Yarmouth boats leave and return, and on the brow of it he stood and wept for Brenston.

Light, glorious light

Then one night he got lost on the cliffs.

'Ahoy,' he shouted through a chasm of darkness, his lungs swelling out, the air inside them almost rattling his ribs.

No answer. Nor yet an echo. It was the darkness of the infernal pit. Bottomless, towering, and with no horizon. It was as if the world were a void again, without shape or form.

'Ahoy, there.'

Nothing. Nothingness. Worse by far than being in a storm at sea, for there was nothing happening to take the mind off its helpless, hopeless extremity.

There should have been no other feeling but fear; yet instead there was a heart-pounding headiness as, inch by perilous inch, he crawled on all fours back up the cliff to safety; upon reaching which he gave out a blood-curdling baritone bellow, less in relief than in response to the realisation that he had attained more than his physical safety; for in losing his way, he had found his voice again.

Not that he needed a voice, living the life of a herring as he was. Barely did he need a body, sustaining himself as he did almost solely on the bread of life.

That body he would have neglected more were it not for those converts who saw to it that gifts of food continued to arrive at his lodgings. Rarely at home though he was to accept such charity, he left a firm instruction that any monies offered were to be refused. So that when the poor of Brenston collected for him they were told it was their souls he was after, not their bawbees.

And again when the villagers of Greensea raised fifty pounds for him, they were told to give it to the poor. One of the poor, as old woman dressed as if to scare the crows, handed in an envelope, and when Johnny opened it he found a shiny new sixpence. In the spirit of the widow's mite it had been given to him, and in the spirit of the widow's mite he passed it on to his landlady.

A seagull turned up at the door one day.

Skipper Croll it was who had caught it: with a net this time rather than the gun. It was in a bag, alive and flighty, when he handed it in. Johnny's landlord released it into an old rabbit-run at the back of the house. There it would be safe and fresh for the pot. A bonny bird, too, it was, if a bit on the young side to have seen many herring seasons; and none the worse for having seen this one. Johnny could have it for his Sunday dinner.

A couple of days went by before the lodger saw it. It

was screeching and squawking and flapping against the wire netting of its cage. Feathers were flying off it as it fought to be free.

Johnny would sooner have starved than eaten that bird. On the morning when it was due to have its neck thrawn he went to look at it again. No longer was it the bonny young bird that Skipper Croll had handed in. Only the feathers on its wings and tail remained: there was nothing left to pluck before it went into the pot.

His own feathers ruffled at the pitiful sight, Johnny reached out and plucked it from the cage. Inside his gansey he hid it and made off in haste for the shore. There he set it down upon a rock, where it flapped its wings, gave out a last mocking shriek as if the Devil himself were taking flight from its body, and flew off along the shore and out of sight.

For a few minutes Johnny stood motionless, searching the sky. He saw himself as that gull. He saw the whole town as a flock of gulls in a cage screeching and squawking and flapping their wings for their souls to be set free. Then he remembered a rhyme he had learnt in Miss Macarran's class at school. It was about a robin. What if the same words applied to other birds? What if that gull in its cage had set all heaven in a rage? Against the rock upon which he had placed the reborn bird he leant with bowed head and closed eyes, and for a few more minutes soared on the wings of prayer.

As he walked along the shore, a strangely birdless shore, his mind went back a couple of years to a day at sea when the sky was falling in on the *Bounteous*.

Skipper Croll, keeping an eagle eye as ever on the water around him, looking for the sign that could mean a change of luck, spotted the merest rimple on the surface. A pair of tiny wings seemed to be making for the boat. A straggler who had been blown off course. And who, too tired to keep his beak above the waves, had been caught by the crest of one of them and tumbled into the sea. A mite of a thing on the mighty main. So played out that he would surely die if he did not stop for a breather. His sky, too, was falling in. Fast.

Anyone on the *Bounteous* who regarded his skipper as uncompromising as a crab's claw was about to learn that he was as benign as a kipper at heart. For the skipper did not reach for his gun. Instead he answered some inner call that dictated that he should go to the rescue of any living thing that found itself in peril on the sea. Turning the boat round, he eased her towards the ounce or so of feathers quivering on the water; then, leaning over the side, he scooped up the stricken bundle and, taking a rag from his pocket, dried him.

A laverock. The bird whose body was always in the clouds and his spirit higher still as he scattered his song over the fields of light; who kept on singing all the way heavenward until his song became one with that of the angels. A bird of the wanderlust, was the laverock. Where he came from and where he was going nobody could tell. Appearing from nowhere, only to vanish to somewhere. For ever reaching for the open places. A herring with wings.

Nestling him in his cupped claws, Skipper Croll stowed him away in the wheelhouse until the warmth returned to his body, until he found his wind and wings again. Meantime the crew began to haul their nets, and long before they had finished they had visions of a catch laverock-high.

It was a couple of hours or so after the last net was hauled when the skipper, his boat pot-bellied with herring, went to the wheelhouse to see how his feathered waif was doing, the bird that had brought him such good luck.

Flaff went the wings of the peerie-weerie creature, as through the door he shot, a bolt into the blue once more. Rising in the air, he drifted around the boat, raised his voice in a watery trill as if to say thank you for the rest, thence, a vibrant ball of energy again, clapped his wings, soared higher and higher until he was no bigger than a seed, and vanished into the thinner air of the southern sky.

Mack it was who set the crew to wondering among themselves; wondering, one of them at least, if their sudden strike of fish was a reward from the Master for saving the life of one of the most blithesome of his winged minions, the one that sang at his gates, when it had found itself in troubled waters.

When a story flew round the town that he had taken to talking to seagulls, that so well in was he with all the birds of the air that they let him come closer to them than any other mortal, Johnny was still present in the body, if absent in the spirit. He was still around when, in the columns of the *Brenston Beacon*, a reader wrote that he was reminded of the saint who talked to the sparrows – the seraphic one who was as pure as he was poor, the little brother in lamb's-wool for whom an exaltation of laverocks sang as he fell asleep for the last time in his shanty on the plain below his beloved Assisi – and envisioned Johnny as of the same order, as a Knight Errant of the Lord's Table, a latter-day Saint Francis of the Herring Yards.

He was not around, however, when, four months and two days after he had launched the whisky bottle in the sea, there arrived at his lodgings a letter from Denmark which his landlord got a curer to translate; the sum and substance of it being that the terse message of hope inside the bottle had touched a lady in a land across the sea more than all his sermons had touched some of the ladies in the houses across the street where he lived.

He was not around to receive these tidings because when his landlady went to his room one night to place in his bed his clay hot-water bottle he was not there. Nor was he around the next day, nor the days or nights that followed. One morning he had gone out, and never come back.

Where he had gone to nobody knew. No message, no sign was left with anyone. Riddles were not unknown in these coastal townships. Boats had been swallowed up at sea, never to be seen again, and bodies thrown up on the shore, and plaguing them right now was the profoundest of all riddles, the sudden and surely unnatural passing of the herring.

Such was the uncertainty and suspense engendered by the latest loss that the voices of discord were at concert pitch. Johnny had fled town. He had fallen into the sea. He had done an Aimee Semple McPherson on them. He had gone to save the birds. He had died of exposure in a ditch.

Whatever the truth of it, he had taken to oblivion like a laverock to the sky. He had vanished as unfathomably as the Yarmouth herring. Leaving an entire community to stew in its own pickle, to try to salvage something from the dying fires.

Of only two things about the whole swirling mystery were the faithful sure of in the town whose rebirth was to many an even greater mystery: if he was still alive in the flesh, he would be travelling light in the Lord; if not, he would have gone to his rich reward.

Either way, they found comfort in the knowledge, the certain knowledge, that be he in the world or out of it, Johnny Halo was in a state of inviolable grace.

PART FOUR

Hallowed Ashes

Autumn was coming round again, drifting in like a haunted tide, so haunted that just to be reminded of it sent a wintry chill down the backbone of Brenston, and before the most sanguine of fishermen could point their bows south to what they prayed to God would be a revival in the fortunes of the herring, some of the greenest leaves on the tree of life were already on the change. For what had happened to the salt herring was happening also to the word of God: it was beginning to lose its savour.

Crippling though it was for the good ship *Salvation* to lose her skipper, it was the manner of his going that weighed down the rest of her crew and her passengers. Like a thief in the night he had stolen away. If he had expired in the pulpit before their horror-shot eyes the shock could scarcely have been greater, and certainly no more lingering. Some tried to weep him back, their faces swollen with the grief of their loss. Amid the public lamentation the unafflicted were moved to remark that the town had lost an idol; while to the sorely afflicted the only comfort lay in reaching out for that ultimate straw of the soul that is lost for an answer: that it was all part of the equitable, if inexplicable, divine plan.

The rumours ripened over the ensuing months.

They ranged from the flippant to the fanciful by way of the speciously fortifying. Johnny had run off to join the Salvation Army. He would turn up, just wait, on another part of the coast, like the herring. In his prayers he had seen visions of eastern empires and had answered a divine call to India. No, not India; those who claimed to have been in his inner circle held that his star had guided him to China. Had he not once privately confessed to an interest in the mission field?

For a while Johnny's inner and outer circles followed their star through the desert as the tribe had done in the days of Moses. For six months or so they walked the way he had walked before they began, discreetly at first, to fall by the wayside. No sooner was the shepherd gone over the hill than the first of the bleaters started to stray. Then, as it sank in that the *Salvation* was becalmed on the waters, that her skipper, like the raven of Noah, would never return, the tidal wave slid back and those who had been carried aloft on it slid back with it.

Firmly ensconced though the ecclesiastical cuckoo was in the evangelical nest, there was no kirk in the land that could keep warm the fervour of Johnny Halo's converts. In vain they cried out for help. Carefully, methodically, painstakingly the kirks tried to rebuild the fire; but there was no one around to light it.

Hard as they tried, the clergy could not prevent the love of many waxing cold. Their congregations became as lukewarm as the Laodiceans. In the fullness of time the indifference was such that evening services on the Lord's Day had to be abandoned. Brenston did not have to wait until such a time before it woke up to find that the morning dew had turned to night frost; that God had caught a chill in one of His houses in the town; that He had come down on a fleeting visit after all, as the prophets of gloom had always maintained, and could not be persuaded to stay.

Where the spirit went to only the Almighty and His

mighty adversary knew; but as mysteriously as it had arrived it departed, just like the herring; the herring whose fall had given rise in the souls of men to a fierier phosphoresence than ever was seen on the face of the sea.

And, sure enough, revival came to the fishing.

Not with the speed of fire on the water; not in a blinding flash upon the southern sea. It came slowly, steadily and with a bounteousness never before known to those reapers who had sown untold sorrows in the less than teeming waters, the too often economically shallow deeps, lying off the north-eastern shores of Britain.

Many a wintry autumn was to go by, and many a moonless night, before the good times rolled again; the world had to go to war a second time before the sea gave up its living treasure in quantities worthy of the name of boom; and when, sixteen years into the peace, the boom began, the herring was to swim only in the memory, only in the minds of those whose hair had turned to a scaly silver.

Forty years the revival was in coming. And again life's course was changed.

Affluence spread like a virus. Having known want, Brenston took to its harvest floodtide with a relish that to the rest of the world was as obscene as it was enviable.

Long since had the herring gamble ceased to appeal. In its last days it had got to the stage when a boat would come in packed to the gunnels with fish that had taken her crew hours to haul up, only for the catch to be dumped back in the sea because the market was glutted. Things had reached a pretty pass when, taking the industry seriously no longer, the gutting quines confessed that they did not go south to make a living any more, they went to meet new boy friends. Besides, a new generation had been born that did not want to get its hands wet and dirty.

So a palate was evolved that put eggs before herring. A prejudice surfaced out of which factories would sooner can pears than the fruits of the East Anglian sea. And as the autumn exodus from the northern ports diminished and disappeared, so did the markets; the countries upon which the fleet had traditionally depended for their customers deigned to wet their own hands for a change; and the way these countries fished, they were more interested in pig meal than wholesome fare. Then, to crown it all, did not the Russians land at Yarmouth? Talk about carrying water to the sea ... With the biggest buyer becoming the seller, the last dash of salt had been added to the wounds of a fishery that in its prime had seemed immortal.

Dramatically, if gradually, Brenston changed.

It changed from a barrel into a box as the drift-net men who had hunted the silver darlings on the surface of the southern sea by night became the seine-net men who went after the white fish on the northern sea-bed by day. By a fluke the new wave of prosperity, as it rolled on from one season into another and from one year to the next, became freakish. For when, thirty nautical miles to the south, the premier port of Seahaven decided to raise its landing dues, one boat after the other signalled her protest by pulling out and pushing off to Brenston; where they all stayed, turning what had for long been a dire strait into a bay of plenty.

To take the extra traffic, Brenston's fish market and slipway were extended; and even then there were times when second sales were necessary. More berths were built. More boats, too. And the harbour deepened. Old craft were modified to keep pace with the new. Every year the landings of white fish multiplied. No vessel operating out of Brenston had to look for customers. First they came from Seahaven, and then from the

Continent. Boats plying the entire length of the east coast turned to the new white fish port of Brenston as a mecca. As no less did the buyers from across the water, who began by sending over their refrigerated trucks to carry away the quality fish that was being landed, and went on to set up processing factories in the town.

Strange as these new craft and their crews were, the changes that came over the old and familiar fishermen were stranger. It seemed that the safer their boats became, the less grew their fear of danger, and of God. Nor did folk who could afford to buy a new pair of shoes, and then throw them away when they got tired of them, need souling and healing any more. Gone was the evangelism that split houses in half. Long ago had the last soldier of Christ deserted. Broken up, after having been sold and her name changed to the *Nimbus*, was the boat that had been called the *Johnny Halo*.

If a spiritual wall had been built around Brenston, the outside world had broken it down, leaving not a trace. God was as dead as the steam drifter, and to those who had gathered round the Burning Stone in his name the term Holy Stoners was applied, and as the years wore on it got to be a term of disbelief more than derision.

The Devil rose again, and danced in the Kirkgate. Sin swept through the town like a pestilence. Into a pit of godlessness the backsliders fell, and from out of that pit you could smell the sin, plain as the waft from the kippering kilns on the hot summer days of yore.

So loose, so wild, so brazen were they in their wickedness that for all the world could tell sin itself was being sinned against.

As bountiful as the fruits of the sea were the fruits of the flesh as Satan laid hold of Brenston. It became a barrelhouse of backsliders, a golgotha of died-again Christians; its heart as empty as its pockets were full.

Having shut the door on the kingdom and thrown away the key, Brenston became known as the town whose halo had slipped.

What the founder of the Holy Stoners had built was a sandcastle that began to break up soon after his converts had been gathered into the body of the kirks. For in these stained-glass houses the gospel was drained of its blood; and with the pulpits seen to be weak, the pews became empty. Those who had not been backward in coming forward when the Burning Stone was speaking to them in tongues of fire proved just as forward in going backward when the wave of righteousness receded. As one of them was later to put it, he was loath to sit down on a cold, hard seat in kirk for fear that he got piles before he got back his religion.

Down the years, as the moral code got slacker, so the religious code of the kirks got slacker in order to accommodate it. Unless the divine word was watered down there was no goodness in it. There was no virtue in being fundamental in these new times. No longer did the Bible hold the place in people's lives that the Highway Code did. If, in that one-season spiritual Yarmouth heaven knows how many moons ago, the old-time religion had saved a few souls, the new-time religion seemed to be more concerned with saving principalities and powers. Ministers were politicians trying to redeem the social system rather than rescuing individual souls. Only ten minutes or thereabouts of a sermon in a service lasting two hours; the old hymns no more, murdered by musical groups who had their listeners dancing in the aisles. When the novelty wore off, the congregations fell away.

Churches that once had been too small were proving too big. Cancelling evening services was for many the first step on the road to closure. One kirk was deconsecrated and converted into a dwelling-house, its pulpit a toilet, its chancel a dining-room, its vestry a kitchen. Another became a garage, yet another a byre. Throughout the land places of worship were no longer sacred. There were sightings of kirks that had been turned into an electricity sub-station, a bookmaker's office, a warehouse, an auction room, a farmer's store, a pram factory. Surely the millennium was at hand? And yet if Christ returned to earth, would He have a house to go to?

Forty years had been enough to change the people. They were not inter-marrying so much, there was not the same inbreeding and therefore character. There was not so much brotherly love about. Life was not as plain and simple as formerly; on the contrary, it was quite fancy. And it was confounded by the onset of an age of violence.

Nor could people get as worked up about their trespasses as the sin-busters wished, or as their forebears had got. They were not disposed to turn against themselves so readily as in the past. Something was there, psychology or science or some such ferly, that made them immune to the electric or electronic shocks of the bible-belters. The very idea of sin, of conversion, of a God of love was over the green hill and far away.

So the fires that had consumed the coast a generation ago had left behind them these ashes. Something had upset the divine rhythm of the souls, something that had nothing to do with the ice-caps melting, and not all the navigational aids of the modern soul fisher could sniff them out and haul them back on board. Where were they, those two hundred or so converts of forty years ago who had become missionaries abroad or ministers in the south? They would have been more gainfully employed at home, in a town more in need of saving now than it had been then.

That hour, that moment had come again when nature was ready – was there not something of the kind every generation? – for a fresh rush of the spirit to the heart of man.

17

Johnny arrived in the fall.

Slowly and unsurely he walked down Baltic Street. There was more autumn than spring in his step as he tried to find his bearings. Lingering here, loitering there, looking this way and that, he made his wary way along the curve of the street that once he bestrode like a Colossian bearing an epistle from Saint Paul.

Familiar, that curve. Still the curve of the crescent moon. And yet everything else was strange. Everything a blur of change.

Everything had taken on a polish that was not there before. Not just the buildings. There was a polish, too, about the people in the street. About the way they spoke, the way they dressed, the way they carried themselves.

These were not the fisherfolk he had known.

They were not the same tribe at all.

They did not have the look of people who would eat herring; or of people who had ever seen a herring. They looked more like what the old herringfolk had called the outside world.

In the act of drawing in air he felt the sharpest sensation of change. For gone was the very breath of the place, the yoam from the kippering kilns, the tang of nets freshly steeped in cutch. He could have been in Chattanooga, Tennessee.

His ears, too, brought it home to him.

No gulls crying overhead.

So tangible was the change that with every step he touched it. On the soles of his feet the change stamped itself. For if the air of the town was different, so was the ground upon which it stood. Gone were the cobblestones upon which he had walked and talked and prayed. Replaced by asphalt. It could have been Half Moon Street, Toronado Springs.

Between earth and sky there was change. Pausing in front of the North Church, he learnt from the notice-board that it had merged with the South.

Puzzled into a state of animated disbelief at not being recognised, he kept giving the older faces in the street second looks. One passer-by, returning his stare, swithered in his stride, and with more challenge than curiosity in his voice said:

'Do I know you?'

'Halo,' Johnny said, almost bashfully.

'Hallo,' the man said, mystified, and walked on.

Leaving Johnny to flap and flounder, a strange fish washed up on a strange shore.

If only one face from the crowd of forty years ago had popped out at him, if only one voice from the past had whispered in passing 'It's Herring Johnny,' then might he have begun to feel that he had come home again.

Where had they gone, the people who had bent their knees before him? To a better land, he guessed, many of them. A host of herring men, especially of the older school, had no doubt slipped their cables.

And what of his old crew and cronies? Skipper Croll he knew had passed on. The rest, as he was learning for himself, had dispersed.

Leaving him alone to these strangers rushing past him in Baltic Street. Criss-crossing and colliding with one another like the currents of the Five Ways. Adrift. Broken free from their moorings. Every pulse, it seemed, racing.

He could remember nothing like it, not even when the town was running up a temperature at the height of the herring fever.

He guessed where they were going.

They were all on their way to a fire.

The fire of hell.

That he, too, had changed did not occur to Johnny as he walked anonymously through the town whose heart and soul in darker days he had stormed and captured with the fire and flood of his message.

In a pearly blue suit, white shirt, grey silk tie and shiny black shoes, he did not have the look of a person who would eat herring; or of one who had ever seen a herring. With half-moon spectacles, cuff-links and tie-pin all giving off a glint of gold, he looked more like a bank manager than a saver of souls. Gone was the wholesome reek of herring, albeit herring smoked in hell-fire, that his clothes had once exuded. About his colouring there was the suspicion of a foreign clime; his face as pasty as a pastry lightly done, where once it was as brown as the sail of an old English smack. And a pearly grey trilby. Such a thing sat ill on a head reared on cloth caps washed by the sea and ironed by the wind. That this man would not know a pulpit wheelhouse from a canvas dodger was to be surmised, too, from the way he moved. For in his walk there was no hint of the fisherman's swing. Rather was it the studied tread of something out of a seminary.

If this old man was once the fisherman-preacher in a gansey, then he had changed beyond recognition. This man was groomed. It was the grooming of a stranger; of someone who had seen a few places, met a few people, read a few books. He had undergone more than a sea change. It was an oceanic transformation. He who had stolen away like a thief in the night had come back like a herring in the moonlight. With stardust on his shoulder.

What had happened between his going and his coming back had been somewhat distantly and soberly related in the latest two issues of the *Brenston Beacon*. In answer to a call from over the sea, he had crossed the Herring Pond partly at King George's expense, Uncle Sam having called upon him to forsake his nets and follow him. Mr Hallows had wanted to go to training college to 'learn the Scriptures proper' and have the rough edges of his preaching smoothed out and polished so that he could speak to any gathering anywhere in the world. And he had always secretly admired American shirts, anyway.

For a time he was a door-to-door brush salesman in Tennessee. Bucked up and backed by friends, he eventually satisfied his desire to go to bible college. Two years later, still considering himself a 'graduate of God's university', he was ordained as a minister. Using his pastorate as a base, he launched upon a crusade to 'unite the States in prayer'. Halo being reckoned too saintly a name, too ideally glorious, the Reverend Mr Hallows's sponsors got him to change it to Zion.

In every state of the American continent, the *Beacon* said, Johnny Zion had sojourned and spoken. He had his own radio and television shows. He headed an organisation called the Right Hand of God, for which a team of hundreds worked. He ran a magazine and a school for evangelists. He had learnt to fly his own plane. Reducing the population of hell by half a million, as the Right Hand of God calculated, had been no easy task physically. It was to take its toll of his health, and one day about a year ago he was forced into semi-retirement. This was what had given him the opportunity to come back to Brenston; this and the invitation of the Reverend Fergus Boyd.

Mr Boyd, having found grace through Johnny Hallows forty years before, and having retired gracefully to the outreaches of Seahaven, had been

approached by an elderly lady belonging to his former
charge of Westhaven about a dream she had had in
which the fisherman-preacher appeared again in what
she called 'this sin-sick town'. Having located Mr Hallows's whereabouts through an old divinity classmate
living in Baltimore, Mr Boyd sent the appeal, with a quiet
prayer for its success, across the Atlantic.

Living in comparative obscurity, and having reverted
to the name of Hallows now that Zion was no longer a
name in the sky-signs, the evangelist accepted the invitation to spend a week's working holiday at the kirk's
expense. Both his parents being dead and his surviving
relatives scattered, he would be put up in the manse of
the present incumbent of Westhaven, the Reverend Mr
Last.

It would be forty years to the month, the *Beacon*
reminded its readers, since Johnny Hallows first stood
before them in the rain round the Burning Stone and
told them they were in for 'showers of blessing'. It would
be forty years since he sowed the seed in that fertile soil.
High time, the reporter observed, if not long past it, to
look at the crop.

Mr Hallows had always wanted, according to the
Beacon, to 'see the old town again in the fall', even though
he had heard that the glory of the herring was no more.
And the lady he had met on one of his coast-to-coast
crusades, and whom he had later married, would be
accompanying him on the trip.

Had he, in the intervening years, changed much?
Older readers, the *Beacon* warned, would no longer know
him by his voice. It was richer and deeper even than of
old; the transatlantic accent being of such a thickness that
only a gutting knife would cut it.

The Reverend Johnny Hallows rose to speak.

'Thankya, Mr Last. I ain't so sure Johnny Hallows

needs no introduction to the good folks of Brenston, but thanks jus' the same for all your warm words of welcome, and not least for the hospitality of your home. Thankya. We sure appreciate it, my wife and I.

'Now, if there's one word describes why I'm here, here again among my ain folks, that word, that one word, is return. No fiery cross in the sky brought me here. No letter written in blood, neether. No, jus' a simple request from an ole fren and sister-in-Christ, Jessie Jane Watters by name, who's right here with us tonight, sittin' right over there.

'Sure, I remember Jessie Jane. When I got her invitation through Mr Boyd and a mutual fren back home in the States, I knelt down and prayed for her. I prayed for all the others who made their decision last time I was here. And I prayed for myself, too, thanked Gawd for His gifts, you bet I did, for it was here He first made me see the light.

'For a long time I've wanted to come back to Brenston. Back to see how my ole frens, who were young like I was then, have grown in grace. I wanted to hear again, I told myself, Jessie Jane pray like she did that night on her knees in Skeely Jock's house in Coggie's Lane. I wanted to shake hands with her and the rest of you.'

Westhaven Church was barely threequarters full, the congregation swollen by two or three coachloads of kirk folk, accompanied by their ministers, from outlying districts. If many had come out of deference to convention, in respectful answer to the advertisement that had been running for three weeks in the entertainment pages of the *Beacon*, others had come out of a deeper-seated curiosity, to see and hear the man who they had been taught to believe had changed the lives of their parents and grandparents. Although some had brought hymn-books with them, there were still not enough to go round.

Among the platform party were Mr Last, the minister of Westhaven, and his lady of the manse; the Moderator of Seahaven Presbytery and his lady; the Provost and Lady Provost of Brenston; and, unseen but no less a felt presence than any of these personages, the Devil and his mistress. Johnny leant against the pulpit, gazing over the half-moons of his gold-rimmed glasses and down at the upturned, inquisitive faces.

'Forty years it's bin. Forty years since I left the ole town for the challenge overseas. Forty years nearer judgement. Forty years nearer eternity. Well, it don't seem more than forty months. Don't time fly? Ain't time short? Will you be waitin' another forty years before your long night ends and the mornin' comes?

'Rip Van Winkle slept for twenty years up in the Catskill Mountains. When he woke up everythin' was changed. His gun was rusted over; his wife was dead; his house was a ruin. He'd grown a beard. He'd become Rip Van *Wrinkle*. And he covered his face with his hands. Nobody knew poor ole frenless Rip save for his daughter, who took him in.

'Brenston's bin asleep, too. It's bin asleep in sin for twice that long. It otta be coverin' its face with its hands. Is it any wonder, folks, I can no longer figure out the ole place?

'Sure, you had to widen them streets to take all them nice automobiles; and the sidewalks, too, to take the boom-town population. Brother, those sidewalks. They're a whole lot harder on the feet right now than when I was poundin' them as a rookie preacher.

'Things like that you gotta do. But there's one thing you done you otta never done. Why do ya have to go widen the road to heaven? That's one road you bin better to leave like it was.

'Why, they're playin' bingo in the ole church I used to go to as a kid. It's never seen such crowds. They're queuin' up to sit there with their eyes down prayin' for their numbers to come up. Dunno 'bout you, but jus' the thought of it sends a cold shiver down my spine.

'You've all bin like naughty children while I bin away. Well, maybe not all of you. But I didn't come over in a herrin' barrel. I can smell sin real strong here. Man, it's so strong you gotta rub it out of your eyes, yeah, jus' like we did the kipper smoke back there in the ole days.

'And there's houses of vice. Boats of vice. There's one gel sez she earns more in one night on one boat in the harbour than her father earns in a whole week at sea. And what are those boats floatin' on? You guessed it. Scawtch and water.

'There's folks advertisin' in the papers for frens. This ain't the town I knew. But you ain't heard nuthin' yet.

'In my time I've called for the conversion of the church itself, and it's prob'ly lost me an invitation to the vicar's tea party, but the way you've converted some of your churches here – why, one's a bingo hall, another's bin turned into a storehouse. It looks like the sinners convert the kirks in these parts. That's what happens when you let your church become a social club. Before you know it, it's a bingo parlour.

'Now spose I was to hold an open-air meetin' out there, and call for a prayer like I used to, you wouldn't hear my words for the noise comin' from the juke-boxes next door. It might be the only kirk a lotta them out there ever bin to. When they tell me there's more pulpits than parishioners in this town they prob'ly got it right. I bin figurin'. You got Sunday sailors, Sunday drivers, Sunday painters, Sunday this and Sunday that. You got 'em all. Everythin' 'cept Sunday worshippers.

'Mr Boyd here, Mr Boyd introduced me to an Amurrican stoodent the other day. Fella from the University of Pennsylvania. He's over here doin' research into folklore. You otta hear what he sez. He sez he's met the Devil right here in Brenston. The Devil, he sez, commutes between hell and Brenston daily. He figures he'll end up with a doctorate in diabolism. Well, folks, I jus' could not believe my ears. Satan blackenin' the good name of this town. *My* town. It's so bad, my stoodent fren sez, they're callin' the noo cemetery that's opened along the south road there Devil's Acre.

'You, too, my frens, have returned. To the Devil. Better the Devil you know than the Gawd you don't. Right? Brother, if I was goin' to hell I wouldn't go on roller-skates. You'd have to drag me there. Akickin' and ascreamin'.

'Now if you men of Brenston can take your likker neat, you can take what I'm gonna say neat. Like a man.

'You bunch of hell-raisers – I'm still pullin' no punches, see – a heaven-raiser has come to save you from your sins. Johnny Halo's returned to give you back the years the locusts have eaten. And jus' as I have returned, so I want you to return. I want you backsliders to return to the fold, and the unconverted to return to the book of their fathers. Myself, I was longin' to come back. How 'bout you?

'Sure, it's good to see the ole town again. It's good to see it back on its feet. You remember when our boots, as well as our boats, leaked? You remember when a certain fisherman's family – no names, lest we embarrass someone – didn't have a single pair of boots between them? And one night his wife prayed and prayed for a pair of boots for one of her boys, and her prayers were answered the next day?

'This town's gone from rags to riches. Okay. But in terms of the speerit it's gone from riches to rags.

'This revival, this bonanza, is not of Gawd. Sure, you got full employment. And big wage packets. And everybody smartly dressed and goin' about like they scooped the soccer pools. But are you happy? I walk the streets, but I don't see many smilin' faces. And this is a boom town. Ae prosperous town.

'S'matter of fact, you never had it so good. That's

what the leader of your country sez. Could be he's bin listenin' to them Democrats. In my adopted country the Democrats were sayin' the same thing a coupla Presidents back. Your mayor here – I beg your pardon, sir – the Provost here tells me he doesn't go all the way with Harry Truman or Harold Macmillan on this. I guess I see why.

'You don't wanna *be* good, you wanna *make* good. Like the Democrats, your heads are swellin' with success. You gone and added an L to Gawd's name: gold is your gawd now. The golden calf. Could it be you spell prophet a different way, too? There's more money around than folks can handle without drinkin' themselves kooky and breakin' up their homes.

'A fren of mine asked a fisherman how come he was able to run his flash car. "I don't run it on glory hallelujah," he said. I got news for him. There's no goin' to heaven in a sedan.

'This town ain't boomin', it's slumpin'. Sure, it's grown. But the people in it ain't. Sure, I can see progress. A lotta progress. Backwards.

'To think when I left this town every head was bowed in prayer. Look at you now. Scurryin' aroun' with your heads in the air. But you ain't happy. You look like you're waitin' for the crack of doom. I left you waitin' for the crack of a new *dawn*.

'What's gone wrong in my absence? Where's that joy you knew when you gave your life to the Lawd? The crime rate fell in that year of grace. The police said they'd time to do a bit of sinnin' of their own for a change. I'll tell you what's happened. Brenston's moved nearer the North Pole. Gawd's in the ice-box with the white fish.

'Right now there's a lotta talk about pollution in the sea. Have you ever thought about the pollution in the soul of may-an? I don't like to see a trout stream turned into a sewer. But that's what's happened right here in

Brenston. *The dawg is turned to his own vomit again; and the sow that was washed to her wallowin' in the mire.*

'Soon as I arrived here somebody said I should've come with a gun in my hand, I'd need it to clean up this town. Tell me, I said, when does the next stage leave for Dodge City?

'Pardner, I told him, the gospel is mightier than any gun. Anyone who was aroun' forty years ago will tell you that.

'As for cleanin' up the streets, they're sayin' it in Brooklyn as well as Brenston. We gotta clean up the streets, they say, there's too much crime about. Let's clean up our minds first and maybe the streets will look after themsel's.

'Some of you may think I'm tryin' to sell you some kinda detergent. Okay, I'm sellin' you detergent. Only this detergent's for your soul. The word of the Lamb washes whitest, my frens.

'I know a very rich man who'd pay any price to get right with Gawd. I knew a man who was so protected by the Lawd he could hold a rattlesnake in his hand without bein' bit. Preachers have bin killed doin' that.

'Ole Abe Lincoln, now. He believed in prayer. For eleven hours he was on his knees talkin' with Gawd while the Battle of Gettysburg raged. There was a fisherman in the States, guy from a place called Martha's Vineyard, who could quote you the whole Bible from memory, startin' at any specified chapter or verse.

'Why don't you, my frens, shake the dust from your bibles? Why don't you try openin' them at Jeremiah? Chapter seven, verse twenty-four. *But they hearkened not, nor inclined their ear, but walked in the counsels and in the imagination of their evil heart, and went backward, and not forward.*

'When I left here two score years ago, followin' a dream in which I saw a modern Tower of Babel, and took it to be Noo Yawk, for it was to Noo Yawk the speerit guided my feet, this coast was ablaze. I can remember when the crowds stood six deep down this very aisle. Everybody was beatin' the drum for the Lawd.

'When I pass a certain storehouse today, do I hear the sound of storemen at work? No, sir. No, ma'am. I hear the joyous sound of voices singin' the praises of their Maker. Do I see those ole kirks as garages, warehouses, bingo palaces? No, sir. No, ma'am. I see them as they once were, workshops of the speerit.

'We Scawts have shed blood on the heather for our religion. And you gone and put that religion in the ice-box along with your fish. Okay, keep it there. Keep it in the ice-box and try the fresh variety. Try Gawd as if you jus' fished him up this day.

'Who wants yesterday's fish, anyway? Nobody in Brenston. Nobody 'cept maybe the fertiliser factory. We don't want that old-time religion, people say to me. We don't want the religion of a hundred years ago. We don't want the religion of forty years ago. Maybe the churches were fuller then than they are now, but we still don't want it. Why don't we want it? Because it don't fit the bill any more; the world's changed.

'I believe the young folks desperately want ae speeritual experience; but the graven image of their father's Gawd is not for them. What they want is a personal, livin', dynamic Gawd, ae faith, ae code, to live by.

'Jesus Christ didn't like the establishment any more than they do. Sure, times have changed; but the message is the same. And it beats tryin' to work out your own salvation.

'Way back in the days of the depression the folks of this town pulled together. Today, in these times of vulgar affluence, the folks of this town are fallin' apart. We pull together in adversity, and fall apart in prosperity. Jus' as we couldn't take the poverty of a disastrous herrin' season forty years ago, so we can't take the new-found riches of this white fishin' boom, with all its attendant evils, today.

'So we turn, as if by instinct, to somethin' that is changeless. Gawd. Make no mistake, in this town you are goin' through changes the likes of which you ain't ever known before. You are bein' disinherited. Never has the need been so great to turn to Gawd, the Changeless One.

'*He that trusteth in his riches shall fail.* You may be smart, but there's none so smart as the gen'leman in scarlet 'n black, Ole Nick himself. Don't gamble away your soul to him. Jus' remember the depression years. It can happen again. The sea has taken its revenge for overfishin' before.

'Someone took a hold of me backstage there and said, funny thing 'bout you Amurricans, when you come over here you're more concerned 'bout where you came from than 'bout where you're goin'. Funny you should say that, I said to him. When I first went over to the States they were not at all sure where I came from but, may-an, they knew where I was headin'.

'I don't have to ask you folks where you came from, any more than you have to ask me where I came from. But I do have to ask you where you're goin'.

'I see a gen'leman there lookin' at his watch. I wonder what time he makes it. Time for me to be goin', I guess. My body-clock's still on Eastern Stannard Time, I reckon. I got a lotta catchin' up to do.

'D'you know, brothers and sisters, what time it is in Amurrica right now? Don't be lookin' at your gold watches. We got four time zones in Amurrica. Five, six, seven, eight hours behind Brenston, dependin' where you happen to be walkin' the dawg. That's accordin' to the time zones. Accordin' to my watch it's the same time in Brenston as it is in Amurrica. Sure. It's the eleventh hour.

'I believe there's a greater famine here now than there was forty years back. This boom has brought a new dark age to these parts. I detect, how can I put it, a certain uncertainty; I sense ae mood of restlessness. That is why I think this town is ripe for a new revival.

'*For it had bin better for them not to have known the way of righteousness, than, after they have known it, to turn from the holy commandment delivered unto them.*

'You have forgotten your knee-drill, my frens. You have gotten so set in your ways, it's as if religion was some sort of cement.

'When a fire goes down the glow on our faces starts to fade. If we want that glow back we must stoke the fire, get it goin' again. That's what we're gonna do this week.

'We're gonna take the chill out of the room in the house of the Lawd, and put the fear of Gawd back into Brenston.'

18

Never a shout of glory, not the sound of a footfall. A blanket in a wash-tub would have caused a bigger stir, a swish on the ebb more commotion. Johnny might have been preaching to empty seats for all the ripple of a new wave that he raised. The north wind would not come, nor the south; the spices in the garden would not flow out. The town that would have floated a fleet with its tears forty years ago could no longer be moved.

From his first word to his last, and for those no less eloquent moments between finishing speaking and sitting down, the congregation stared at him, clear-eyed, cold, calculating. He had noticed a youngish man in a middle pew nodding off, and had taken him for a shift worker. Yet no shift worker, however tired, had dropped off listening to him in the old days. Far from sleeping through his sermons, many a witness to them claimed that it was because of his sermons that they could not sleep at nights.

He had not, and maybe should have told them so, come as a conqueror. He was not looking for a civic reception. It did not bother him that no crowds swarmed round him as he entered and left the church. But those faces of stone in front of him, faces that were still bugging him after he got back to the manse – if just one of them had come forward, if just one had sought his counsel privately in the vestry afterwards, it would have been more than a gesture, it would have been a merciful bounty. Instead of gaping at him as if his breed were all but extinct. Instead of looking as if they had just cast their bibles on the bonfire.

Whether they were waiting for a death-bed preacher, or whether the natives were out to convert the missionary, he could not reckon for sure. Whatever they figured, they were making him feel as welcome as water in a riven ship. And that went for those who thought they knew him better almost as much as for those who did not know him from Adam.

Cold and clear-eyed even as they sang one of the Sankey hymns, they tried to fathom him out. There was a bounce about him, a certain assumption that took those who remembered him of old by surprise. Maybe it was the twang. The way he spoke was the most affecting change of all. His voice rising and falling, polished and professional-like, the old pathos trained out of it. It was a trained voice. And he had gotten round the mouth with an American dishcloth. God was no longer Goad, he was Gawd. Lass had become ma'am, and man may-an, and spirit speerit. He had asked them to sing to one of Sankey's toons.

Before they had gone halfway through that hymn they felt they were more than halfway towards working him out. This was Johnny Zion, or whatever they called him over there, not Johnny Halo. This johnny did not sound as if he had ever brandished the sword of the spirit; those hands did not look as if they had ever held a marlinspike. Salted herring and potatoes with their jackets on were foreign to this New World Johnny who called himself Hallows. Sleeping on a hayrick, or on the floor of a friend's house, would not become such a man who, having kept the shop on the corner, had gone and opened a chainstore. A man who, having missioned round the world, was rolling in it. A bigger noise now than he had ever been, and that was saying something. Anonymous at home but, lo, a prophet abroad. Maybe he should have tried going to sea when it was blowing a force eight just to see how long the creases in that suit of his stayed in.

As they skailed out of the kirk their ears rang, not with anything in the way of a resounding message from the pulpit, but with the silence of a judgement pleading to be released from suspense. It was a fine address, as fine addresses went. Like Mr Last's own sermons, it went to the head rather than the heart. Compared with the old Burning Stone days, it was as a fresh herring to a dyed and boneless kipper. Older and wiser in the ways of the world, the young fireblood from Sailmaker's Close had been turned into a performer. A performer whose business was to work up a revival rather than draw down one. That was just it. A revival was not something you worked up; it was something you drew down. There could be no fire without its falling from heaven. Johnny himself had said so. That belief it was above all that had made him what he was.

Which, to those who knew the old Johnny, was why this visit was as man-made rain to an April shower. If a voice had called him back, it was the Voice of America. This was a visit. Forty years ago it had been a visitation. A couple of items in the local paper about a certain Reverend Johnny Hallows revisiting 'the scenes of his former triumphs' ensured that no great excitement was to be generated before his arrival. Billy Graham would not have done what Johnny Hallows was doing – entering the town with scarcely more ceremony than when he left it.

With the likes of Sandy Groyne, who forty years ago threw in his barman's towel and his lot with the landlord whose inn dispensed a purer kind of spirit, and who to this very day was still playing the organ in church, admitting that Johnny was not the same, that when he had left them he was all obedience to the spirit, that on the physical side, too, the tide of change had left its mark on him, that he had gone away made of Brenston granite and had come back made of Mississippi clay, his hands as soft as a kitten's purr and his face as suety as a doughboy – with the likes of Sandy Groyne coming out with such things, it was difficult for those who knew only the legend, especially a legend that had led them to half-expect a veritable godling to fly in under his own power, to understand what it was that had inspired all the awe, both in themselves and in the old-timers that knew him.

In this vice-gripped town they spoke in tongues of many tribes, and not one of them was the language of Canaan. While some suspected that whatever key Johnny had used to unlock people's hearts he must have thrown away when he crossed the ocean, others swore that this one-time fisherman was preaching a style of life that had all but gone the way of the herring, and that nobody had the spirit of a fly in a windflaw to preserve it. In anybody's tongue it was clear to the new, herringless generation that, because Johnny had converted the poor, it did not follow that he could convert the rich.

Nothing, then, had he to sell them, this brush salesman from Tennessee. He was just another overseas branch of Barnum and Bailey. American as apple-pie in the sky, his pie-jaw had made him so rich that to him the dollar was the real Almighty One. And who, his harshest critics asked, might be oiling his palm? Had he been sent by the Central Intelligence Agency to administer the opium? *And many false prophets shall rise, and shall deceive many.* America had more false prophets than Brenston ever had true believers. Men who had died in the spirit and were reborn in the flesh.

Called in like some fast-drawing lawman of the Wild West, the stranger calling himself the Right Hand of God could not clean up this town if for no other reason than that his right hand had lost its cunning. He was too slow on the drawl, his aim was not what it was, and his ammunition was as live as a dead herring.

And yet wherever the Reverend Johnny Hallows spoke, as the guest of a different church every night, he was assured of a congregation, if not of a reception any less cold or calculating than the one endured in crucifying silence at Westhaven.

He resorted to saturation bombardment by leaflet. Tracts, written by Johnny Zion and published by the Right Hand of God Inc., were dropped through letter-boxes and handed out by ushers at the church door. After reading a tract, Johnny told one meeting, the man who led the air attack on Pearl Harbor repented and went on to win his wings as a sky-pilot.

Having thus softened up the opposition, Johnny tried to appease them with words of reassurance. Money was not the root of all evil, he told them, it was the love of money, that was what Saint Paul warned against, that was where the songwriter had got it wrong. If they were to look up Deuteronomy they would see that *The Lord giveth the power to get wealth*.

He continued to allay their fears with the reminder that a tree was known by its fruits, not its fertiliser, though from what he could see the trees that had borne such tender fruits way back in the depression were now so barren – 'after the dew, the mildew' – that a little fertiliser, if not a spot of insecticide, would not be out of place.

Slow down, he advised and admonished them at the same time. Why, a man could run a mile in less time than it took to boil his breakfast egg, and he liked his eggs soft.

Did they know that in South America the conversion rate – and he guessed he was not talking about converting pesos into darlars – outstripped the birth-rate?

That wind out there. They were reckoning without

that mighty harsh wind. One day the chill north wind would come and blow away their materialism. Then, make no mistake, Brenston would begin to feel the draught again.

For three nights he spoke and each night his breath froze as soon as it left his lips. Still the spices would not flow out. If he had started off with the thought that all he had to do was to remove the dust-sheets that had been protecting the town from the fall-out of the permissive explosion ever since the day he left it, he was in for a rude awakening. Under the dust-sheets he was beginning to think there was nothing more than dust.

Was there, he wondered, something wrong with the seed? It came from the same packet as before. What about the soil? It was difficult: the ground was stonier than it used to be. Maybe the seed he had scattered would yield a harvest that others coming after him would reap. Patience. He would have to have patience. Instead of always looking for quick results.

Deliberating over it, he could not believe that it was the wrong season for sowing. Or the wrong time for God. God had not changed. In no wise. God would not desert him. Could they have changed? As much as this? Was it he who had changed? Sure, he no longer had the smell of the sea about him. But nor had they. They were so cosmopolitan he expected to see foreign coins in the collection plate. Their emotions no longer naked, they were seeking refuge behind an outer shell that no words of his could crack. To these folks the idea of sin was obsolete. Were these his people?

He prayed for a sign. Just one sign.

True, he had no vision of souls in torment. Nor any call to light prairie fires. He began to see his mission as not to convert the sinning so much as to revive the saved. Brenston was full of retired, or at best semi-retired, Christians. If there was enough of the fisherman left in him to know that to every tide there was a turning, there was enough of the Brenstonian left in him to see that so great had been the ebb, it had left no water in its wake. Hell had dried up the place. He was fishing in the Dead Sea.

His faith in mankind shaken yet again, he thought of all the souls he had won over in his lifetime, from his first days as a cracker-barrel preacher to these last days of his electronic ministry across a continent. Genuine trophies of grace they had been, too, not the counterfeit kind planted among the crowd by rogue evangelists, as he feared was sometimes happening nowadays (the speaker's friends being hired to come forward as converts when the appeal was made, in the hope of getting an unresponsive audience to do likewise). Forget it, he thought, and sighed. He was not one to hold communion with the past. That he was looking back now had, he hoped, everything to do with where he was and what was happening to him. It was an understandable indulgence in the circumstances; and it afforded an abiding comfort that could not but lift his spirits.

What was happening to him he knew had happened to multitudes of preachers down the ages. Christ himself had known the feeling. Maybe he had overfished, maybe he had exhausted the grounds. Maybe if he were to hold his next meeting, not in a stuffy old church, but at a street corner, or in the Mission Hall of happy memory. Maybe there was still a sermon to be got out of the Burning Stone of even happier memory. To the Burning Stone, buoyed up by the past, he went.

And there in the Square he felt at last that he had come home again. He chose a text that he had often spoken on with great effect in the old days. And his listeners seemed to be hanging on his every word. These, he felt, were his people: the fisherman in the street, the innocent bystander, the ungathered host, the unaffiliated witnesses to the Word. These were the true heirs of the woman who had forsaken her wash-tub for the cleansing of her soul and who, he was happy to learn the other day, had lived the rest of her life without stain and was now in heaven. These were the descendants of Gully Bow, who wrestled on the ground with his soul, only to be lost at sea three years later; and of Billy Bowster, who had the whole Square singing to his melodeon, and who became a missionary in foreign fields. Here were the vindicators of the trust shown by Jemima Monk who, from the day that Johnny left the town until two years ago when, at the age of ninety-three, she went to her reward, had kept her door unlocked in the hope that one of these days he would return. Not only had he returned: he was about to return in triumph.

As he spoke the circle widened, and presently a dewy rain began to fall. Or rather it drifted almost sheepishly down, soft as lamb's-wool on the cheeks. More like a mist that had been maturing in casks since those first heady days round the Burning Stone, it was a rain unlike any other on earth; and it told him better than any sight or sound could that he was back among his ain folk in his ain countrie.

Right now it might have been the breath of God. For he was holding them, as he had held their mothers and fathers, and even their grandmothers and grand-fathers, in the hollow of his hand.

Before long he saw white handkerchiefs fluttering in surrender. He saw Dod Rann's spitting image stamping on his pipe. He saw strong men falling on the cobbles, tearing at their hair. And he heard again the old hallelujahs, the weepings and the wailings, the voices bursting into song. Lifting up his eyes, he saw that the heavens were rent. Across the Square the waters were burning, radiant with the shoals of God. He saw a bonfire and a ring of people feeding their worldly possessions to the flames. The sky was aglow and every house ablaze. Brenston was on the march along Baltic Street, and the newly reborn were wading into the winter sea, washing away all record of their sins. Then he looked at the Burning Stone and saw, in the midst of a circle of light, an anvil. From the anvil came sparks. Showers of blessing.

It was with a heaven-kissing confidence at the end of his address that he invited those who wanted to become Christians to step forward. And when not a soul stirred he knew that his eyes must have misted over in the rain, that what he had seen had been all in the mind's, or rather the spirit's, eye; and that what he was seeing now, and seeing for real, were not the rough stones that he had quarried and dressed and made ready for placing in the temple all those herringless moons ago – the temple that the churches were to have built before the bulk of the stones fell back into the quarry – but the hard-edged, unyielding hunks of granite that had replaced them, stonefaces so cold and austere, so unreachable that they could only have come out of the darkest, most impenetrable pit.

His spirits dampened, he called for the closing hymn. There was a deafening silence. It seemed an eternity. Long enough for him to begin to look upon it as a reprimand from God. Speak, someone, he begged under his breath. *Sing.* They had found his appeal to come forward impossible not to ignore. Very well. His head fell. Maybe he had been working too hard. Was he not, after all, supposed to be retired? He had been so busy of late, he had forgotten how to catch a cold. He had forgotten how to catch a soul. And in his own home town, of all places.

It was not just the embarrassment. There was also a feeling of impotence. He could understand how Samson felt when he lost his hair. More than that, there was a chilling sensation of failure. Followed by a creeping sense of disownment. For this was their judgement. *Before the cock crow, thou shalt deny me thrice.* And after the cock crow, thrice again. There was no divine unction this time. Not a drop. The Burning Stone itself had backslidden. Coming back to Brenston after having left it forty years ago was like moving into a dark room out of a lighted one.

God be his witness, he had not hungered for the headlines back in the old days; but their absence now seemed like a conspiracy of silence. He had come as a brother, and they were treating him as a stranger. He had arrived under what the old-time fisherfolks would have called an ill-starred moon. How else to explain the loss of his bible, the one that opened and closed with a zip, which he had left behind in one of the churches, a thing he had never ever done before in his whole ministry? A skipper who lost his gear at the fishing grounds, he remembered his own Skipper Croll once saying, was losing his touch. *Quartus, a brother.* He would not rate even that brief mention when his story came to be told.

He lifted up his head. He who had preached to millions suddenly was lonely. God had taken his hands off his life, and turned his lips to clay. His good work lying right here in ruins before his eyes.

There was nothing for it but prayer. Public and private prayer. Private, especially. He would go to his hill at once and genuflect. With the dawn would come new hope. When the morning came it would be different. His vision would return. He would put away defeat and rejection and take new heart. He might even receive his second call.

Before the next day was over the skeleton was out of the closet; the fundamental impediment stood revealed. Before bedtime the muted fears about that which in the main was preventing a felicitous reunion between the town and its celebrated son had been given a positive voice as the authorised version was laid before the world.

What it was that was holding Brenston back more than anything else, what was alienating it, making it harden its heart so that it hesitated to take Johnny into its trust, started out as a murmur at first, a whisper among neighbours that grew louder with each succeeding sermon until finally it reached, by way of his hosts, the ears of Johnny himself.

Almost since his arrival in the town rumours had been fouling the air, transatlantic undercurrents disturbing the waters. Had Johnny himself not backslidden? Was he not a wolf in sheep's clothing? What about his own fall from grace? Did he reckon that word of it had not reached Brenston?

Since there was something that he was failing to declare, something that he was keeping back from them, they were obliged to judge him as less than candid. Among all those high moral words of his there was not a mention of his own lapses. Was it a deliberate evasion? If so, it was an act of betrayal. He had broken faith. When he addressed them it was with one foot in heaven and the other in hell. He was all veneer, he was trafficking in the varnished truth. While she, canny soul-mate that she was, sat tight by his side. Tight-lipped and two-faced, the pair of them.

The longer they shammed and shamed Abraham, the fishier and the frostier the atmosphere became, the murkier grew the light in which the townsfolk saw them, the coarser the tales that were told out of church, and the closer Johnny's hosts came to seeing the snipers carry out their character assassination.

It was to stay the assassin's hand, to clear the air of fret and frostiness, that Johnny's wife rose to her feet and addressed the evening meeting. Her aloofness had been no small factor in the chill that had attended the meetings. While not expecting her to twirl the baton like some elderly drum-majorette, everybody yet wished that she would not sit so mum at every meeting, twirling her gold wedding ring (on one occasion at the same time as her husband was twirling his), or fingering the silver brooch shaped like a bible that adorned the lapel of her jacket.

It was the turn of her listeners to trifle with their trinkets as she emerged from under the cloud that they had formed around her, and found her voice at last. She began by making an appeal to the young women of the town. Her voice, as was no less than expected, was as American as pecan pie, flavoured as it was with such odd-sounding things as rout when she meant route, leezhure instead of leisure, larn for learn, and dooty and cenner and ae-live, and by her placing the accent on the second syllable of adult.

She was more than a luuvin' wife to Johnny, she explained, she was his aide as well. She had been all over the world helping her husband with the Lawd's work. In a busy life together they had found time to bring up two sons. Both of them had received Christ and become ordained, and right now were missionaries in Latin America.

Following which biographical driblets she came – and with no noticeable loss of her matronly elegance or queenly dignity – to the point as to why she had taken the floor.

It seemed, she said, that things in the town had changed so much they did not know even themselves any more. What, she wondered, had become of Hannah Gale?

Hannah Gale. At the sound of the name her older listeners swapped anxious, embarrassed glances. For to them, even to this day, casting up such a character, replete with its reminders of a low-water mark in their lives, and moreover casting her up in, of all places, a house of public worship, was tantamount to mentioning the unmentionable before the ancient fisher god, Tabu. Yet how welcome was the relief as the one name that they had been waiting to hear all week from platform or pulpit was mentioned at last.

'She was one of ya … remember?'

Sure, they remembered. In spite of their having tried to forget her for four decades.

'She stood right here forty years ago and gave her testimony … remember? Well, I'll tell ya what happened to Hannah Gale. She went to the States and became Mrs Johnny Hallows.'

Throughout the Mission Hall there was a shaking of heads. A shaking of knowing heads. Even Johnny nodded. A nod that was well on its way to being a bow.

'Forty years have passed and the Devil still has not won me back. Hallelujah. The glory is Gawd's, my frens. And now … now I jus' wanna say how wunnerful it is to be here. To come back to the place I was reborn in. Back among my ain folks. It sure feels good. May Gawd bless ya all. May he do for you what he has done for me. Thank ya and hallelujah.'

Although she had not told them anything they did not know already, they were bewildered. Their bewilderment was all the greater for their having heard what they had wanted to hear at first hand. From madam herself. Why had she taken so long to announce who she really was? Why had Johnny shied away from introducing her? Were they both afraid of what Brenston might make of it? Grey-headed, old-world Brenston had long ago made something of it. That it smelt of a plot. That it had all been staged. Hannah Gale's conversion. Her testimony. Her elopement to America. Johnny taking ship after her. Getting wed in a tabernacle somewhere out west. A couple of moonlight flitters on the make. It had all long since smuggled itself into the anecdotage of the town's old quarter. But not till now had Brenston heard it from one of the parties concerned.

He having assumed the new name of Zion, she apparently (and affectionately, too, so it was said) became known as Mrs Zee. And now she was plain Mrs Hallows again; or, as she was more familiarly if less affectionately known in these parts, Hallelujah Hannah; or, less affectionately still, the Painted Lady. Not so much done up like a dyed kipper as she once was, she had become a classier kettle of fish, more like cod dressed as salmon. That salty tang to her tongue was gone; and no bad riddance, either. Sitting by her husband's right hand, no doubt to give him immoral support, she and he made, as the Devil said of his hooves, a bonny pair.

And that was what those newspapers of the intemperate kind thought, too, as they ran, under bible-black headlines the following day, what they called the revelations of a hot-gospeller's wife ('I was Hannah Gale'), and amplified them with the reactions of the home town she had scandalised.

So unwelcome were the attentions of the scribes and Pharisees of press and television that Mrs Hallows had to flee from the town and seek sanctuary in the country. With Brenston itself harbouring a small town's hunger for the skimpiest tit-bit of scandal, and with its appetite gingered up by the world at large showing a partiality for the same morsels, the town had a banquet. That it left a lot more of Johnny than a few bones for the vultures to pick should have surprised nobody chaptered and versed in the ways of such things; for to such a witness, the merciless exposure of a public figure's infirmity not infrequently has the reverse effect to that intended.

And so the voices rose and multiplied as they pitched

against a celebrated son's discreditors. From under their bushels emerged those lights who felt that their own apprehension of morality had been challenged; from nowhere appeared those who were instinctive defenders of the shorn lamb; and from everywhere came those whose besetting sin was apathy, along with those who for this or that reason had steered clear of the meetings. Hankering after Johnny's version of the story, they packed to overflowing his meeting on the following evening, when the air of expectancy was vaguely reminiscent of the days of old, except that the expectations forty years later were of a more temporal kind.

Without all this widespread incidental interest to augment it, the event in the Mission Hall was no less a rallying call for those who, guided there by a force no more compelling than their sense of occasion, wanted to attend the last meeting of Johnny's week-long mission in Brenston.

Forces of a more potent persuasion had pulled in the man sitting in the second row from the front behind a camaraderie of press photographers. It was not so much the spirit that had guided him there, more willing than the flesh though that spirit was; rather was it a personal interest in the proceedings, in the man who was conducting them especially. Advanced age had not blunted his spiritual curiosity, far less dimmed his memory. Nor had it subdued his sense of excitement, for he sat forward in his seat, edgy with anticipation, tickled and at the same time not a little fearful that at any moment he would be recognised by a speaker whom he had neither seen nor heard from for forty eventful years.

Not that there was much likelihood of Johnny picking out his old crew-mate on the *Bounteous* after all these ravaging, irredeemable, lifelong years. Johnny, in the throes of delivering a few finger-wagging home truths about Mary Magdalene, was in no mood to wave to friends, old or new, in the congregation. Wullsie himself had difficulty squaring what he saw with what he remembered. If he had met Johnny face-on in the street he would not have been able to place him. Such, he mused, was the toll exacted of the human flesh by time and tide, and whatever else had befallen them, himself and Johnny, never mind Hannah Gale, in this respect at least they were still, the pair of them, in the same boat.

Which was more than he could say for the way Johnny spoke. Were Wullsie a blind man, or were he to close his eyes and just listen, he would have to take the speaker for someone unknown to him, the voice for something out of a Hollywood picture. If Johnny looked like a stranger, he sounded like an alien. Far from being on the same boat, speech-wise, the old crew-mates were not even on the same sea. And yet, divided as they were by a common language, they were united in a common spirit. Surely that would be enough to see them back on the same old couthy conversational wavelength when, immediately after the meeting, Wullsie went to the ante-room and reintroduced himself.

He would tell Johnny how he had crawled out of his sick-bed to get this far; how, a few years older than Johnny, he had contracted rheumatism as a young man, and at fifty had been forced to give up the sea. His ailment having crippled him more and more down the years, he had long ago retired from the shore job he had taken in a net factory. A stage had been reached when he was prepared for, if not resigned to, the inevitable lot of a bed-ridden invalid. Only by a superhuman exertion of the will had he managed to hobble along to the meeting. Whatever foreign bodies had taken up permanent lodgings in his bloodstream, they had not infiltrated his soul. Since his conversion aboard the *Bounteous* forty years past he had stayed true to his own

and his Creator's word. Johnny would be mighty
pleased to hear that.

To hear such a thing might just cheer him up in his
hour of trial. What with the way the meetings had been
going and the aggravation over Hannah, there was not
much cheer for him on his first trip home since the
glory days. When his old chum chugged and creaked
into view Johnny would get the jolt of his life, as if
Wullsie had dropped from the clouds; especially as
Johnny, on the day that the newspapers put about their
lurid stories, had been due to look Wullsie up, having
been led to believe that his old crony was poorly and for
some time back had been confined to the four walls.

Johnny's memory would get a jolt, too, as Wullsie
reminded him of the day he commandeered his kindred
spirit's whisky bottle, and emptied it and popped into it
a postcard listing the names of all the crew, and tossed it
into the sea. That a lady found it four months later in
Denmark would be news to Johnny, for it was on the
day that word came through about it that Johnny went
clean out of their lives, leaving no message even in a
milk bottle or anywhere else. Of the crew that became a
band of brothers working for the revival, Wullsie would
tell him, five were still alive at the last roll-call, of whom
only one remained in Brenston. Iley and Hamie being
lay preachers down south; aye, the same Iley that fell
out of The Anchorage and into the harbour, Johnny
himself hauling him out; that same one was working
among the drunks and derelicts of the Gorbals.

Remember, Johnny, how you used to call us your
chosen vessels? And how you talked about being the son
of a King? And, how right you were, too, as a man with
two birthdays? Happy birthday, he would say to Johnny
as soon as he met him. Maybe Johnny would say happy
birthday back. For they were both a mere forty years
old, spiritually speaking. This month. October. Wullsie
on the thirtieth. He would no more forget that day than

he would his physical birthday. And according to what folk said about the age of forty, life for both of them was only just beginning.

For Johnny it was, certainly, or so it looked and sounded as he raised a fair head of steam sailing into the challenge set by Hannah Gale and met (for both of them) by Mary Magdalene. It was a text on which Wullsie had heard him preach before, if not with quite so much passion; and yet his delivery was such that the echoes came rolling back. Although there was still no sound of the sea in the voice, a strong sea-swell, not altogether Atlantic, was creeping back into it. Wullsie felt that the tears that had once punctuated Johnny's words were returning; they were fighting back.

Through the mist of it all he thought he could see again the young Johnny Hallows, Jondy's Johnny from Sailmaker's Close, jaunty in his cap and gansey, strong as Gurdie's horse while he hauled a fleet of bulging nets at the Knoll Buoy, his brow wet and fevered, his eyes glinting in the light of the moon off the water. He saw him, too, with his bonnet in one hand and his bible in the other, hauling aboard the souls at the Burning Stone, his eyes as big as the moon, a light as bright as a shoal of herring anointing his face. And he saw him walking arm in arm along the Denes with Hannah, the pair of them as intertwined as the strands of rope she had knitted on his gansey.

Wullsie peered over one shoulder and then the other at the faces around him, and what they told him was that they, too, were being confronted by a different Johnny; one that no longer troubled them on account of his having acquired a deep drawl and a private aeroplane and having run off and married the sinfulest woman that ever walked the quays of Brenston. There was a look on these faces that hinted that Johnny had finally found his way back to them, his way into their hearts, his way home. He was afloat again.

Afloat after having been stuck fast on the shoals of a backslidden coast. After having fished all week and taken nothing. Maybe at his last meeting, at the eleventh hour, his luck was going to change. Just as he was about to turn tail like the herring, and vanish again across the water.

It was too late. He might have known better than to begin his crusade when he did. On a Friday. Nobody set sail for the autumn fishing on a Friday. A gull would not build its nest on a Friday. It was unlucky, so they said. Johnny should have known that. And tomorrow he would be setting off again. On a Friday.

When, in the withering winter of his life, Wullsie recalled the events that followed, it was not the day of the week so much as the time of the year that was enshrined in his mind. They would have remarked on it themselves, those glistening shoals of people who had swum into Johnny's net when the moon was young and fair and swarming over the herring. To them there would have been no better time than autumn for the soul of a herring man to make its migration. This herring man in particular.

'You once had oil in your lamps,' Johnny was saying at the time, and Wullsie had never known him sound so vehement or look so luminous. 'Now you got electricity ...'

He got no further. Having spoken, as Wullsie could now see with hindsight, like a dying man to dying men, as though it were not just his last meeting but his last testament, as though he would be going from preaching to judgement, he stopped in mid-breath, put his hand to his head, made a sound that was half-groan and half-gurgle, slumped, and slid out of sight behind the pulpit.

'Merciful Lord,' a voice cried out behind Wullsie.

Two of the platform party carried Johnny, to the accompaniment of a popping of flash-guns from the battery of press cameras, into the ante-room, and several anguished minutes were to pass before Mr Last, the minister at Westhaven, took the pulpit to say that a doctor had been found among the congregation. Meanwhile would they all join him in a prayer in which he would ask God to give Johnny, his faithful servant, strength.

Three or four more harrowing minutes went by before the town that had been slowly beginning to warm to its celebrated son was told from the platform of his peaceful passing, of his crossing that sea from whose shore no voyager returns. Johnny's homecoming had become his homegoing. For the one-time kid from the Close it was the appointed time, the appointed place, the appointed season.

What many a preacher had said he would not mind happening to him, the fierier ones going so far as to will it to happen, had happened to Johnny. He had gone out like a light in the pulpit. Or rather he had stepped out of one room and into another; out of a dark one and into a lighted one. He had gone to meet his Maker, though not for the first time. For heaven, as Wullsie for one had never doubted, was in him before he was in heaven.

Even as the doctor certified that he had died of an enlarged heart – enlarged, the Reverend Fergus Boyd maintained, with the love of God – the public press, acknowledging that the world was in the late autumn of its moral decay, a time of falling fig-leaves, looked for his like in a certain cooper-preacher who, fragrant as a white rose, had walked in this same wilderness a hundred years before and turned it into a garden of glory. It was a judgement inspired not so much by Johnny's life as by what followed soon after that life ended. For, being dead, Johnny Halo, like Jeems

Turner a century before him, yet spoke. It happened as he lay in state at Mr Last's house.

An old man from Sandness, name of Hector Tarick, known to the multitude as Taricky and lately widowed, finding himself in town on the day of Johnny's funeral, and mindful of the hard time he had given the deceased forty years ago when he had scoffed at all attempts to save him from a life of unbridled looseness, went to the manse to pay his first and last respects and, lifting the white drape that covered the face, beheld such serenity that he broke down, fell upon his knees, and gave himself to the Lord.

'He slew more in his death than in his life,' Johnny's last and posthumous convert, thinking of Samson, was later to proclaim joyfully to the world.

To Wullsie, remembering the days when the world walked with a humbler step and life was more of a pilgrimage than it was nowadays, and aware of his old crew-mate's departure just when the last of the boats would have been setting out under a banner of hope for the herring grounds in the south, where in a few days the moon would be as full as the sea was when the *Bounteous* was landing a cran or two, it seemed a better memorial to the fire that had finally burnt itself out than a monument that scraped the sky.